PRAISE FOR *THE LOST CHILD*

'Phillips writes with acute insight...heart-breaking.' *Independent*

'Caryl Phillips is seen by many as the father of Afro-British fiction... At the heart of Phillips' book is the widespread (and continuing) abuse of women and children, and he writes sympathetically and powerfully about both.' *New York Times Book Review*

'Vividly re-created...fascinating. The atmosphere and language are intricately done, shifting with the decades and locales in a kind of linguistic odyssey.' *Herald*

'A highly original narrative that is both startling and strangely moving.' James Lasdun, author of *Seven Lies*

'The thematic links between the modern story and *Wuthering Heights* only become clear over time, and – even then – they're too rich and subtle to work as simple allegory. Empire and race are among Phillips' concerns, but he also offers heartbreaking depictions of alienation and the fragility of human relationships...Gorgeously crafted and emotionally shattering.' *Kirkus Reviews*

'Powerful...affecting.' *Spectator*

'Phillips explores the themes of displacement, not fitting in, and racism with subtlety and power...Yet unlike Brontë's tale of revenge, Phillips' book is suffused with forgiveness...[A] consummately literary, deeply human novel.' *Barnes & Noble Review*

'A literary gem...haunting.' *Woman's Way*

'A biting commentary on empire and the vulnerability of family life. This is a devastating novel from one of our best writers.' *BookPage*

'His riff on Emily Brontë's masterpiece is like a jazz improvisation: Phillips plucks the themes that resonate most deeply with him and transposes them into a polyphonic narrative…[He] employs his multilayered text as a counterpoint to *Wuthering Heights*, expanding the novel's horizons overseas and across centuries while honoring Brontë's vision of lives directed by ferocious internal imperatives as well as external conditions. His vision is less romantic, but just as sorrowful and moving.'   *Boston Globe*

'With uncanny intimacy, eloquence, and compassion, Caryl Phillips stitches together past and present, the world of classic English literature and of hardscrabble, contemporary English life more movingly than ever before, speaking through every one of his characters with humbling depth and understanding. The simple, startling result is that, after *The Lost Child*, English literature looks richer, more mysterious and more human.'   Pico Iyer, author of *Abandon*

ALSO BY CARYL PHILLIPS

FICTION

In the Falling Snow

Dancing in the Dark

A Distant Shore

The Nature of Blood

Crossing the River

Cambridge

Higher Ground

A State of Independence

The Final Passage

NONFICTION

Colour Me English

Foreigners

A New World Order

The Atlantic Sound

The European Tribe

THE
LOST CHILD

CARYL PHILLIPS

ONEWORLD

A Oneworld Book

First published in Great Britain and Australia by
Oneworld Publications, 2015
This paperback edition published by Oneworld Publications, 2015

ISBN 978-1-78074-798-9
ISBN 978-1-78074-700-2 (eBook)

Printed and bound in Great Britain by Clays Ltd, St Ives plc

Oneworld Publications
10 Bloomsbury Street
London WC1B 3SR
England

For Tatiana

CONTENTS

I

SEPARATION

S he likes to sit down by the docks in a place where sunlight can discover her face. Once there, she leans back and listens to the monotony of seawater lapping against the quayside, and she has no concept of the hour. She disturbs no one, but she hears footsteps passing in each direction. She is a woman in debt who can no longer find anyone willing to employ her at the loom; she is a diminished woman who, before her time, has yielded reluctantly to age and infirmity. They call her Crazy Woman, but she smiles and forgives them. It is spring, but winter is still in the air. She puts on a sad demeanour and fumbles at the hair buttons on her dark worn coat, and then she hears a penny drop into the box and she looks up and offers a toothless grin to the tall frock-coated man who is now walking away from her. She wants to tell the man that it hasn't always been like this, truly it hasn't. She wants to tell him, but to what purpose? The man wears a tight smirk of derision, which signals that he imagines himself more ingenious than anyone else, and who is she to argue? These are busy men. She hears the stiff wheels of a carriage turning laboriously against the cold flags and the noisy tattoo of horses clipping diligently towards their destinations. The incessant blasting of a ship's horn disturbs her reverie, but the sluggish rhythm of burbling water eventually begins to lull her into the receptive arms of slumber.

The seven-year-old boy stands over her and can see that she is asleep, but not at rest. The woman's body startles, then settles, and it is clear to the boy that pain has again established residence and has no desire to quit his mother's body. His has been a good day, and his box sings half full with a medley of coins, but he knows they must now leave, for soon it will be dark. He reaches down and takes her hand, which she snatches away from him. (I will kill you.) When she opens her eyes, the boy can see that she is suffering from an awkward upsurge of shame, for her harsh words have been misdirected, and her haul is woeful. The un-blinking child stares back at her in a manner that suggests that the requirement that he bear responsibility for her well-being sits surely on his young shoulders, for after all, neither of them has any other companionship. People continue to walk by in both directions, and unable to disguise their loathing for the skeletal woman who is slumped against the ground, they simply avert their gazes. The poor boy hovers protectively over his afflicted mother, for she looks now as though she might, at any moment, abandon this discouraging world and attempt to gain access to the next.

She remembers long days in the West Indian fields digging with a rod of pointed iron under the burning sky; she remembers restless nights as black as soot listening for the sound of footsteps approaching the door and wondering whether tonight it would be her turn to be covered. But Master never came to her. (A Congo woman, too dark.) In the morning a skillet of Indian corn, or yams seasoned with peppers, would be thrust into her hut, and together with the others, she would leap up and tussle for the food like a wild beast. Having eaten, they would commence the march (Quick! Quick!) out to the fields for more digging, and weeding of grass, and gathering of stones until one day she was hoisted onto the back of a wagon full of sickly property and carried to the town square. The least of the female litter, she mounted a wooden platform and waited until all the others had been taken. She stood alone now, but the ship's captain eventually nodded without enthusiasm, and her short time in the Indies reached an abrupt conclusion.

On her journey to the Indies it was the rats that had inspired the greatest fear, for they fed with conviction and grew huge and profited handsomely from their passage. The human cargo was chained and manacled in the hold, where they rolled to the left and then back to the right, their rotations determined by the undulating waves, but on each occasion that the vessel dipped, the cargo received the blessing of a libation of slime. Soon they were too nauseated to eat, and most were too grief-stricken to cry, and she lay surrounded by the doleful mourning of those who rotted in the darkness. They whispered in plaintive tongues that were beyond the comprehension of her half-chewed ears, and they composed themselves for their own private journeys. During the second voyage she remained anchored to the splintered floor of the captain's cabin unless he had business with her. A crude depravity marked this man's crumpled brow, and she soon perceived that her captor was fired with a lust for unconditional obedience. His brutish appetite rose and fell like the ship, and at the termination of his cowardly attacks he would reshackle her and then reach for his pipe and smoke the tobacco that appeared to offer him some vestige of peace in mind and body. Moving even a little caused the chains to bite urgently at her wrists and ankles, and so she would simply curl up in her corner and watch as he began to blow plumes of smoke. It troubled her that the lengthy crossing was making her dull, and so, trembling like a palm leaf, she tried hard to recall the simple dignity of a bowl from which one might eat or the long-forgotten pleasure of a few breaths of clean, pure air.

How many years have I? She unseals her eyes and sees the boy trying once more to pull her upright, and she smiles. It is true, there is no dignity in lying slumped among a sea of masts. But look, vessels at anchor! Still, like her, and she feels grateful that her child is helping her. Now she is startled by the warm water between her legs, but she welcomes the sudden flush of heat. She knows this pleasant feeling will soon pass and only the stench and irritation will remain. (I'm sorry, my child, but tribulation is upon me, and I must sleep some more before standing. Please sit with me and keep me company for one hour more, this is all I ask. Just one hour, and then we two shall leave together.) She deeply resents the fact that these people look pitifully upon her son, whom she has ruined by the example of her own indolent misery. Their foolish tongues used to ask: Can the boy speak English? Can he dress hair? Is he sober? Is he fit to wait upon a gentleman? But no, no, no. She has seen the other boys, ornately attired in silks, with silver collars and satin turbans, walking behind fair ladies so they might attend to their mistresses' trains, or quickly administer smelling salts, or take charge of their fans. But other boys, not her child. Her son will never walk behind a fair lady. He looks down at her, his wide eyes brimming with a concern that threatens to spill over into tears. She can, however, detect that a strong and tenacious heart beats in his tiny body. This being the case, all is not lost.

✦

As the pale sun sinks beneath the watery horizon, filth-encrusted sailors, ready to roister anew under the cover of darkness, appear from all directions. She never evokes any compassion from these men, who lurch confidently past her, their aura of superiority fed by excessive familiarity with rum and other strong liquors. The boy helps her to her feet, for they must leave before the quarter descends into violence. They stagger off, her feet clad in mismatched shoes that skid through fetid puddles of waste. (The sailors don't see me; they never see me.) Suddenly, the shoes are temporarily held captive in the unforgiving mud of an unpaved road, but she nevertheless struggles to remain womanly in her deportment. They press on and twist and turn through a tangled nest of cobbled streets, avoiding yawning doorways where slops may unexpectedly be thrown out, climbing laboriously up worn stone steps, ducking under low-hanging tavern signs, and averting their senses from the narrow entrances to cellars. The people who have buried themselves in these hovels will venture out only after nightfall to sit around a bonfire and drink and sing before retreating to their damp and crowded burrows, where body heat alone, sur-reptitiously stolen from a stranger, feeds the pulse of life.

Having reached their destination, she lies down on a handful of straw in a tiny room under the low roof. The broken windows are stuffed with brown paper and scraps of besmirched fabric, but the cacophony of noise still penetrates. She receives the drunken tidings of night, and she understands that the doglike howling and yelping from the Flying Horse Inn, which at all hours teems with degraded humanity, will persist until dawn. But what can she do? The wooden stairs that lead to this bleak attic room begin to creak, but she is not expecting anyone. (Is someone there?) Her son lifts a small finger to his lips and encourages her to be quiet. The dank wall is made visible by candlelight, and extended across its full breadth she can see the shadowy image of the boy's furtive gestures, but the intermittent rubbing of her irritated eyes now results in her closing them tight.

It hasn't always been this way. Before, having pushed back her wooden chair and swathed herself in a moth-eaten shawl, each evening she would set forth and leave behind the rattling and clacking of the looms. And each evening she would assume that this must be the day on which the lonely man has had to re-turn to his inconvenient wife and children, but for almost a week her suitor has confounded her expectations and waited patiently by the gates with a small bunch of freshly picked flowers, which he presents to her with more extravagance than is necessary in the hope of gaining her approval. He walks with her and talks, and he understands that she is not blessed with pretty features, and he suspects that she would most likely freely admit this, but he knows that she possesses elegance, although undoubtedly some men see only a harlot as common as the dirt under their feet, a lamentable object they might use for either commerce or humour. He has seen these men, the desire for entertainment gleaming in their faces as they greedily watch the commotion of her dress against her hips. She steps back out of range as a large carriage with heavy wheels carves its way through the busy street and awakens clouds of dust, and then she walks, and he walks with her, and again he tries to solicit conversation, and finally, after a five-day campaign, she reluctantly agrees to accompany him to the back room of the Queen's Head tavern for supper.

They sit. There is no linen upon the table, and a narrow bed stands in one corner, but mercifully no eyes are upon them. (You must dine heartily, and I promise you will soon reap the benefits of doing so.) She accepts oatcakes and a little boiled mutton, and the serving boy brings chicken pie, beans, and a glass of Burgundy for her host, before ceasing his capering and once again closing in the door. (I am a man of some influence who has not yet entered the evening of my mortal span, yet I confess to being bedevilled of late by unpredictable bouts of melancholy.) His breath is unsavoury, but this aside, there is an inoffensive fragrance to the man in whom she discerns goodness. He is endowed with courtesy and displays a great delicacy of manners, and he seeks to engage her with his wit and not tax her with wearisome tales relating to his own standing. He admits to being puzzled by her situation but essays an observation. (A third homeland in one lifetime, and now you are intoxicated with liberty and perhaps thirsting for enlightenment? Does this represent your predicament?) She smiles. Not entirely. She admits to having been discarded by a sea captain and living without daylight in a place where to draw breath is to risk ruination, and he immediately offers her money with which she might obtain decent lodgings, but she refuses. (But you reside among whores and ruffians in the vile courts of this sometimes pestilent town.) She sees the frustration rise in his body, but she continues to smile.

She opens her eyes, for she can hear the rasping voice of a drunken ballad singer competing with that of a deep-throated pie vendor, both of whom congregate below in the echo chamber that is the narrow courtyard. The boy has squeezed himself against the wall, and the wood groans as the landlord now lumbers across the crooked floor. A simple scrap of carpet would have assisted with the chill, but it is too late. She watches the animated glow from the man's swinging lantern as the light searches for her figure. (Have you heard from your gentleman?) The landlord's slovenly wig has slipped sideways, and his forehead wears a circumspect frown. Her child crawls to her side and holds her arm. He looks defiantly at the man with ill-disguised scorn lighting up his young eyes, but his mother reassures him. (It's alright.) Seven bitter winters have passed since her son shouldered his way into the world on these grimy, uneven boards. Her gentleman paid for the doctor, but she worried that her child's father might now uncouple his affection as a result of the taint in his offspring's breeding. The landlord moves his lamp to improve his view of her face, which is coated in sweat as thick as oil. This man once radiated understanding, but his disposition is now much altered. He asks her, How many weeks must I wait? She no longer possesses the strength to draw her tongue across the speckling of blood on her mouth; she no longer enjoys the ability to smile.

✦

The first time she saw the ghost quietly leaving her body she shook with fear, but he quickly reentered her. The ghost appears and disappears stealthily, like a halo of breath on a looking glass. She knows that soon the ghost will leave her frail body, and this time she will utter a series of long, shallow gasps and fall silent, and then follow him and begin her final voyage. But not yet. A single candle gutters in the draught, but its shimmer illuminates the obscurity allowing her to watch over her sleeping child, and again she feels her consciousness slipping away and the worrisome present subsiding into a peaceful dream. She lowers her heavy lids and abandons vigilance.

During their first apprehensive dinner her gentleman had been careful to admit to her that as far as ardent passions were concerned he was something of a novice. But by their second meal together she could observe it in his aspect that he felt emboldened.

A small fire was her gentleman's gift of comfort to her, and they both studied the tiny flames as the serving boy added fresh logs and then raked up the loose waste from under the grate. After the boy closed in the door, her gentleman friend stood and crossed the room and drew the bolt. She could see that he was nervous, and some crumbs clung stubbornly to his chin, but he had forsaken drinking while he still remained in full custody of his sensibilities. She looked favourably upon him, convinced that integrity and kindness were lodged in his bosom. He removed his satin vest and lace ruffles with impeccable dexterity, which helped to soothe her own nervous condition. Then he came to her with the honest ardour of youth, and she made an earnest attempt to return his interest.

Although the considerate man took his time and let his fingers gently explore the soft curves of her body and whispered to her throughout, she was unable to prevent her mind from collapsing under the stress of memory. She found herself back on the ship with the captain stirring himself to quick, frenzied spasms, after which she was confined to her corner, where she prayed that he might now leave her alone. A civil frigidity entered the captain's voice as he commanded her not to submit to sulkiness, and then one morning the exasperated man ushered her to the foot of a steep staircase and then to the upper level, where she experienced a change of air. He pressed a guinea into her palm and, the ship having docked in the night, he pointed to the great port that lay spread out before them and turned her loose to find an occupation and seek shelter. It was some while before she moved off from the docks, being unsure if she was at liberty to walk abroad, and after a few hours of edging her uncertain way along bustling streets, a forthright workingwoman, with a fine white cloud of hair, came to her aid and made it her objective to help this lost soul reclaim her grit and establish a new home in this clamorous town of ships and sailors.

It was later, after she had accommodated her gentleman's devotion on a half-dozen separate occasions, that she discovered herself with child and, thereafter, her circumstances declined. (We've no work in this place for a woman with child.) She felt bereft of mettle in her increasingly tattered clothes, and shame began to regularly flicker across her face. (No, miss, we've no work for you.) No longer a bewitching presence, her reduced self aged a year with each dismissive glance, and she wept bitterly at the thought that she would most likely never reestablish herself in employment. Occasionally he still came to her with tender warmth and a charitable heart, and he appeared to look upon the child with genuine regard, but she could see it in his eyes that despite her attempt to maintain some grace to her natural movements, his zeal for her had been extinguished. Mother and child were now little more than a burdensome secret, and although her benefactor continued to press money upon her, it was manifest that he was growing progressively detached. And then meetings with the gentleman ceased, and other assignations commenced as the curse of destitution began to pollute her life. (No, please, no! No!) These scowling men revelled in improper conduct and were prepared to pay to have brisk knowledge, and once their joyless noises were at an end they dropped a coin on the way out as they stepped over the pile of tatters that was her child. Her poor son, who lay with his body curled tightly and his desperate hands clasped over his ears. (My child what have I done to you in this place? Will you ever forgive me?)

At dawn he appears before her and can see she is enduring a resurgence of distress. He looks across at her sleeping child but knows that there is little to be gained by waking the boy. The stench of decay torments the room, but it is illness and misfortune, not idleness, that has enabled this malodorous atmosphere to flourish. Her cheeks radiate heat like tiny twin furnaces, and blood leaks steadily from her nose. He sees the yellow tarnish to her defeated eyes and listens to her breathing in low, labored gasps. It is clear that the conflict will soon be at an end, so he will not reenter her delicate body. The woman is powerless to rise and meet the day, and it is time for her to pass safely over the threshold and be on her way. The woman opens her eyes and looks lovingly in the direction of her peaceful child. She taught the boy how to walk, and now she must walk away from him. She must go. A skeleton hung with rags. Another journey, another crossing.

II

FIRST LOVE

T owards the end of her second year at university, Monica Johnson listened as her father told her that he had given the matter a great deal of thought, but sadly he couldn't be expected to tolerate her behaviour for a moment longer. He cleared his throat and wondered if he had soft-soaped things by using the word "sadly"; she was staring at him with those large, unblinking brown eyes of hers and waiting for him to continue. He had misjudged things, for he had anticipated tears, but instead of a torrent of emotion his twenty-year-old daughter continued to grimace and wait for him to explain himself. Being a schoolmaster in one of the most highly considered grammar schools in the north of England, he was, of course, used to making advanced concepts intelligible to young people. However, they both knew that this was a subject upon which there really was no need for him to expand any further. After all, standards were standards, and although it disappointed him to have to take such a stance, Monica knew full well that once he'd made his mind up that was it.

They sat together in her room at the top of a narrow nineteenth-century staircase in the back quad of one of Oxford's smaller and less prestigious women's colleges. Between them a fully laden tray sat atop a rickety wooden table, which rose little more than a foot above the threadbare rug. Two untouched pieces of Dundee cake decorated a white china plate, which was flanked on one side by a bright red teapot and on the other by two ill-matching cups stacked one on top of the other. She had thought long and hard about what to wear and had assumed that her father, who had fixed ideas about how women should present themselves, might even be expecting her to be decked out in her tutorial garb—a nice dark sensible skirt, black stockings, and a crisp white blouse. She had chosen instead to wear a sloppy grey pullover and tan slacks but further confused the issue by tying back her long, straight hair with an incongruously cheerful yellow ribbon. Although she knew full well that she wasn't much to look at, this year men had begun to notice her and even if she couldn't prove it scientifically, she was sure that the more she dressed like a *townie*, the more attention she received. But she certainly didn't want scrutiny from this warped man, who had already bullied his wife into near-mute submission. By the time Monica was a teenager she was fairly sure what type of person she was dealing with, and it was she who had decided to generate a distance between them, which she closely monitored, carefully widening the gap with each passing year.

Having ushered him into her room and hung his overcoat and hat on the back of the door, she directed him to a chair that offered a view, out of the sloping attic window onto the somewhat hideous modern red tiles that crowned the college annexe. The four-hour drive from Wakefield had provided him with the opportunity to reflect and choose precisely the right words, and once he was seated he came straight to the point, which he knew would leave them ample time for debate or, if his daughter so wished, time for debate *and* refreshment. But as she continued to stare at him with that particularly rebellious sneer she seemed to have cultivated in her sixth-form years, he began now to question his tactics and wondered if he should have taken a cup of tea and a piece of cake before easing his way into the assignment.

She looked at him, fully aware of the fact that to open her

mouth right now would only result in her coming out with angry and resentful words, so she bit down hard on her bottom lip. Monica wasn't in the habit of revealing emotional vulnerability to this man, for she knew that the end result of such stupidity was having your wings ripped off. As she tasted the first sting of blood, she reminded herself of her promise to keep things nice and steady.

"So that's it then? You're washing your hands of me?" She swallowed hard but didn't take her eyes from him. "Well?"

He raised a warning finger. "Now then, there's no need to take that tone with me." And then he realized how he must appear, with his finger dangling foolishly in midair, and so he quickly swivelled his wrist and opened his palm. "I could pussyfoot around, but to whose benefit would that be?"

"So that's it then?"

He looked at the pot and imagined that the tea must now be cold. Why did Monica always have to be so bloody wilful? No matter what he did she seemed set against him. She'd been stubborn as a girl, but nothing out of the ordinary—as far as he could tell—until she started budding. That's when his daughter went from diffident to downright disobedient. One day she was prepared to answer his admittedly tedious questions about what classes she liked best at school or if she'd be interested in coming with him to a musical concert at the Town Hall (the answer was always no), and then the next day it was as though all communication between the two of them had totally broken down. He knew that she liked Wordsworth, so he broached the idea of a walking holiday in the Lake District, just the two of them, but Monica rolled her eyes and said, "No thanks." And then after she'd been accepted at university, when he made it clear that he'd love to motor down and explore the place with her, she just laughed and carried on watching a programme on the newly purchased television set.

"Well," she said, breaking off a piece of Dundee cake with her fingers. "Is that all you've got to say to me?"

He wanted to smack the girl, but it was too late for this. As usual, her attitude was entirely regrettable, but he knew enough about young people to understand that he had to continue to exude assertiveness and control, and so he climbed to his feet.

"So it would appear, Monica. So it would appear. I've no desire to fight with you." He paused, and for a moment their eyes locked. "Listen, I'd best be off before the traffic starts building. And Monica, I'm sorry."

His daughter heard his bumbling apology, but she said nothing and simply unhooked his overcoat, then his hat, and handed them to him. He looked at his child, but for him to say anything further would involve stepping too far outside of himself, and so he simply offered her a weak smile. Then he caught a glimpse of himself in the small mirror on the wall to the side of the door and realized that this afternoon's effort had put five years on him. As she picked up a small bunch of keys, Monica broke off another portion of cake.

"I'll show you the way out of the college."

They crossed the quiet, shadowy quadrangle and then traipsed their way through a narrow archway and out into the sunlit brightness of the front quad, where two clusters of students shared the lawn, playing separate games of croquet in neighbourly proximity to each other. As they walked together, he felt a momentary surge of panic, knowing that this final act of his performance would be improvised. They stepped through the huge wooden door and out onto the street, and then he stopped and gently held Monica's arm through a handful of grey jumper.

"You will keep in touch, won't you?" His daughter looked at him but said nothing.

He let go of Monica's arm and fished in his jacket pocket for his car keys.

"I'm parked just down this road and around the corner. No need for you to trouble yourself. I can find my own way." Why, he asked himself, couldn't he add "love"? I can find my own way, love. But he knew that it wouldn't do to confuse her. Once he turned the corner and passed out of sight, he took a handkerchief from his pocket and discreetly blew his nose and then dabbed at his eyes. Mission accomplished.

✦

Soon after Monica's birth, his wife had dropped a few broad hints that she wouldn't mind having a second child, but Ronald Johnson had determined that one would suffice. After all, there was a war on, and it was incumbent on all English families to make sacrifices of some kind. Monica had arrived in 1937, when it looked as though Chamberlain, whom Ronald greatly admired, was well on the way to securing some semblance of peace. Three years later, any mention of his affection for the former prime minister caused him to go beetroot red, and so his wife knew full well to avoid this topic. By 1940 the whole country was hunkered down and silently preparing for the worst, so he thought it unnecessary to engage with Mrs. Johnson on the question of a second child, and the idea was quietly dropped.

A teenage bout of pneumonia had left him with a shadow on his chest, and so he was deemed unfit for active duty and therefore able to continue with his career teaching geography to boys, whose only real interest in their studies seemed to relate to troop movements in various corners of the globe. At a time when the duties and obligations of war were causing many families to temporarily break apart and accustom themselves to the novelty of female leadership, Ronald Johnson was able to continue to exercise a benevolent patriarchal authority over his household and therefore take a keen interest in the development of his daughter.

From the moment she was born he had tried to please Monica. During the day he often found himself ignoring the rows of pupils ranged before him, preferring instead to stare out the window and ponder what trinket or sweets he might bring back for her that evening. Even in the most austere of times there were shopkeepers who knew how to track down scarce commodities, and he had forged a good relationship with one or two of them who seemed to be able to get their grubby paws on chocolate or licorice. As soon as he reached home and pushed his way through the door, there she would be staring up at him and patiently waiting for her goody. When she was a little older, and her school held a VE Day pageant, it was Monica who wore the Union Jack robe and tinsel crown and proudly held aloft the placard proclaiming "Peace," and he almost burst with pride when he read the letter from Monica's headmistress that confirmed that his daughter was one of the three "specially talented" girls chosen for music lessons.

Ronald Johnson had carefully mapped out a postwar career path for himself that would accommodate only fee-paying or grammar schools, for he was sure that his spirit would wilt in the barren world of the new secondary modern schools that the local council, in keeping with government guidelines, was rapidly establishing to accommodate those who had failed the Eleven plus examination. However, despite his achieving some success and securing a junior master's position at the local Queen Elizabeth Grammar School, money remained tight. Nevertheless, when Monica was ten, he declared that this was the right time for the family to buy their first house, a small terraced affair in a better part of town, but he wasn't prepared to put Monica's future, to say nothing of her happiness, at stake. This being the case, he funded her piano lessons with extra money that he earned giving Saturday-morning instruction to the twin Shadwell boys, who he knew stood absolutely no chance of passing the Eleven plus. Monica, on the other hand, sailed through her examination, and she began to win certificates and the odd trophy at music festivals all over the north of England. The mantelpiece and sideboard in the new living room supported a sequence of expensively framed photographs of his daughter flowering into a beautiful girl, and late at night, after everyone had gone to bed, he liked to sit alone and marvel at the images that showed off her poise and self-belief to best advantage, although occasionally he did find himself irritated by the seemingly nonchalant path that his daughter seemed to be steering between his own indulgence and his wife's silent pride.

"Daddy," she had once asked him, "are you happy?" She was

barely twelve at the time and was balanced carefully on the arm of the settee with her legs dangling over the side. The question disturbed him, for he didn't know just what it was that his daughter was seeing that prompted her to ask such a thing, but he simply swirled the ice in his drink so the cubes tinkled together like the percussion section of a band. Then he leaned over and snaked his hand around her midriff and tried to tickle Monica, but she pulled away, and the unanswered question hung in the air between them.

His daughter seemed to take it in her stride that an Oxford college had accepted her without any stipulation that she achieve a particular set of grades. It had been her own idea that in addition to applying to redbrick universities she try both Oxford and Cambridge, but her headmistress had called him in and warned him that the school had no history with either university. She also reminded him that familial ties appeared to count at both places, and Monica would not be able to point to any relative who had attended either institution. Nevertheless, he let the headmistress know that he fully supported his single-minded daughter in her application, although he never mentioned anything to Monica about going into the school. On the morning she received the letter announcing her acceptance, Monica reluctantly shared the news with her parents over tea and toast and then trotted off to school as though this were just an ordinary day. Her father, on the other hand, drove to work with his briefcase deftly balanced across his knees, and he utilized the whole journey planning how he might break his news to the staff room in a casual manner so it wouldn't come over as though he'd joined up with the boastful brigade. However, by the time he began the long walk down the corridor towards the staff room he realized that it was going to be impossible to contain himself. When Miss Eccles, the French mistress, asked him if he would like a cup of instant coffee, he just blurted it out: "Our Monica's going to Oxford." He immediately felt his face colouring up, for after all, he spent most of his working day trying to exhort boys to speak grammatically correct English, and now listen to him. "Our Monica."

Miss Eccles beamed. "Well, Mr. Johnson, that's marvellous news. Just marvellous. Congratulations."

Given all her advantages and ability, it made absolutely no sense to him that Monica should be throwing everything away by getting involved with a graduate student in history nearly ten years her senior who originated in a part of the world where decent standards of behaviour and respect for people's families were obviously alien concepts. She never bothered to send letters or postcards home to them, and so once again he had been forced to write asking how she was, and by return of post Monica had given her parents the disturbing news, delivered, unsurprisingly, as a fait accompli. Naturally, he had little choice but to share the disconcerting information with his wife, and then he began to make plans to undertake the four-hour drive sometime in the next few days in order that he might lay down the law. When he eventually knocked at the door to Monica's college room, he discovered his daughter, far from giving out any impression that she might be pleased to see him, to be in a particularly truculent frame of mind.

He had stared out of the queerly shaped window that afternoon and listened to Monica's increasingly strident voice as she talked openly of being with this man. Quite unexpectedly, he realized that her flat vowels had, if anything, become more pronounced, as though she were now trying to flaunt her northern origins. In fact, were he to close his eyes he would no longer be able to swear that it was his own child speaking.

"Look, you haven't even met him. How can you judge somebody that you don't even know?"

"I want you to understand that your mother and I are concerned about *you*, not some Tom, Dick, or Harry. I haven't motored all this way to waste time talking about somebody else."

"Okay then, why *have* you come all this way? It's not like you to take a day off school."

And so there it was, she had put him on the spot before any tea could be poured or cake eaten, and it looked as though he was going to have to tell her that it was either this man or her parents. Monica was going to have to make up her mind. He drew himself upright and began by letting her know that he had given the matter a great deal of thought. Inwardly he was devastated, for this wasn't how he wanted it to go. He had hoped that there might be some preliminary discussion in her room, with perhaps a glass of sweet sherry, and then a walk around the college grounds or maybe down along the banks of the Cherwell. In his most optimistic moments, he pictured her excitedly begging him to hire a boat and smiling at his attempts to punt. That would be something, punting down the river with his daughter, the Oxford student. But now there would be none of this, for things had rapidly collapsed. When she once again insisted on introducing her friend's name into the proceedings, he had little choice but to deliver his prepared statement that contained the word "sadly," and thereafter they both had plunged into an abyss of silence. It had all happened too quickly. He wasn't naive: he knew that girls of her age went giddy over romance and probably talked extensively about the opposite sex; no doubt a small number of young women, finding themselves beyond the parental home, were quite possibly active and prepared to risk the ignominy of landing themselves in the family way. But nothing in Monica's upbringing had ever led him to imagine that his daughter might turn out to be loose.

Whenever he thought the blubbing was over, the tears would come again, each time with a greater vigour. He now found himself clinging to the steering wheel with his gloved hands in an attempt to stop shaking, but he realized that this was no good, and he would have to pull over into a lay-by. He sat perfectly still as a platoon of lorries thundered by and shook the Wolseley, and then he reached for his handkerchief and blew his nose with a loud, messy snarl. He would have to sort himself out, for he couldn't allow his wife to see him like this. Alone in the house, she would be eagerly anticipating some account of their child's situation, and it was his responsibility to report the events of the day with a sobriety tinged with an appropriate degree of sorrow. He dried his eyes and quickly checked in the rearview mirror to make sure they were not bloodshot. He adjusted his tie and then took one, two, three deep breaths, and each time he was careful to exhale slowly. Then he lowered his head onto the steering wheel and began once more to sob.

✦

After her father left her standing outside the oversize door to the college, Monica decided to go to Julius Wilson's basement flat and tell him what had happened. Having assumed that he would have the whole afternoon to revise the footnotes to his doctoral dissertation, he was clearly surprised to see her, and for a moment she couldn't tell if he was pleased or put out. He was wearing that enigmatic grin she couldn't always read, but he was not the type of man to play games, so she guessed that he would tell her if he needed some more time to himself, and she would happily read until he was ready. However, once she had kicked off her shoes and curled herself up in his cosily padded armchair, he began to relax and carefully placed his papers in a large grey box file and then turned off the desk lamp. He crossed the room and perched on the edge of the armchair before slowly unfastening the yellow bow so that her hair tumbled out across her upper back and shoulders.

"Would you like me to make you a cup of coffee? Or I could go out and get something stronger."

She looked up at him and offered a forced smile, but it was still too soon for her to talk.

Julius Wilson was a tall, gangly man who had spent the greater part of his short adult life cultivating a patina of gravitas that might belie the boyish smoothness of his face. In his private moments, when he felt safe, he was capable of a giggly skittishness that suggested one drink too many, but he would never let this aspect of his personality out in public, having invested too many years perfecting his air of studious severity. "I am not here to play; I am here to make the most of this opportunity" was his stock answer to his fellow students who pointed to the fact that, as secretary of the Overseas Student Association, he might wish to take advantage of his position and socialize a little more often. "Oh, for heaven's sake, I have no interest in chasing girls. I had plenty of girlfriends before I came to this country, and if I am lucky, I might have one or two more before it is time to renounce my bachelorhood." Julius would offer a brief chortle, yet deep down he would wonder why these people didn't understand that he had sought the position as secretary of the association as a way of making contacts that might aid him in years to come. But six months ago his world had been shaken when, at the association Christmas dance, a curious-looking undergraduate actually approached him and asked if he would care to take the dance floor. At first he thought there might be something wrong with the girl, for she had a lethargic, expressionless gaze that was a little off-putting, but he didn't want to be rude so he took her hand, knowing that she would soon discover she had chosen an uncoordinated man who didn't really dance. By the end of the number it was discernible that she too took no real pleasure in dancing, so he offered to buy her a drink and they found two seats at a table near the bar and she prevailed upon him to tell her all about how he had come to be in England as a scholarship student. Throughout Christmas and New Year he had found it impossible to banish strange Miss Johnson from his thoughts, and by the time students were once again rattling through the city's broad streets and narrow lanes on their clanking bicycles and readying themselves for the new term, he had made up his mind that this oddly intense northern girl had the right resources of strength and courage to make the journey with him.

During that first wintry night in his bed, he admitted to her that something about her quiet generosity and ability to listen made him feel safe and anchored in England. He whispered: "This is what you have given to me." As she once again enticed him to cuddle under the blanket, he didn't tell her that never before had he experienced what it felt like for a girl to be hungry for him and eager to please but equally keen to attain her own satisfaction. He had been in the country for seven years now, but possessing Monica Johnson signalled an arrival. They both wriggled out from beneath the blanket and listened to the sudden commotion of hectic, scurrying footsteps up above on street level, and then she pulled herself onto one elbow and simply looked down into his dark eyes.

"Monica Johnson," he said, "you are a remarkable young woman."

"Thank you, but I'm just being myself."

She pecked his lips before rolling back onto the pillow and staring up at the cracked plasterwork of the ceiling.

"And your other romances, Monica? Is it alright if I ask about them?"

She smiled to herself and remembered the one boy, a new student like her, whom she'd let go all the way. After he'd left her room to shin over the back wall of the college, she sat up in bed and could feel that her lips were swollen where he'd had a good go at the open pouch of her mouth. Is this what he wanted to know about? She continued to gaze at the ceiling but said nothing as she didn't want to talk about anything to do with her miserable, lonely first year as a student. Eventually he'd come to understand that her silences weren't always to do with him. He wasn't the only one with stuff going on in his head.

By the end of the second week of Hilary term, Monica had decided that scooting through the quad at dawn and then dashing up the narrow staircase to her room no longer held any appeal. Having carefully arranged things so that it might appear to the college servant that she had simply slipped out on some trifling errand, she packed a small suitcase and moved into Julius Wilson's basement flat. He couldn't have been happier, for this young Englishwoman seemed to take enthusiastic pleasure in cooking, cleaning, and studying, as though each activity flowed naturally into the next. Her simple rearrangement of the furniture created more space, and replacing the heavy curtains with cheap blinds brought light flooding into the flat. Not a day went by without his looking up from his desk and delighting in this alluring barefoot creature who moved silently through his world. Often, late at night, he would steal a glance at her as she slept and feel the urge to beg her not to leave him, but he knew these words must never cross his lips. Four years ago, during his divorce proceedings, his wife had made a statement through her solicitor claiming that it was his selfish insecurities—to his face she used the word "immaturity"—that had caused the breakdown of their marriage. "My husband," she said, "doesn't understand that I too have needs." But this Monica Johnson never agitated for more visibility in the relationship, and she appeared to be content to anticipate his desires and protect him from the world.

As he neared the completion of his dissertation, Julius began to evaluate the idea of marriage, for he felt that he ought to offer Monica some form of security in order to convince her to remain by his side. After all, she seemed to have made a complete break with her parents, and it was therefore his responsibility to provide this young woman with something solid and dependable in her life. The day her father drove down to deliver his ultimatum, she had come running to his flat and, having gathered herself, began to explain how wrong she felt her father was about Julius and what her father called "his kind." As soon as she opened up on the subject of her father, however, Julius detected anxiety beginning to rise inside her, and she retreated into a silence that quickly became strained and, for a moment, threatened to overwhelm them and poison the atmosphere in his flat.

Julius waited until the end of the academic year before taking her out to the pub for a drink and bringing up the question of marriage. Monica heard him out, and once he'd finished she couldn't think of any reason *not* to get wed to him, and so a few weeks later they were married by a visibly agitated registrar in a dull office that reminded her of a dentist's waiting room. Having already received worrying reports from two of Monica's tutors about her often flighty state of mind and proclivity to wander in her head, the principal of her college readily granted Monica's request to take a leave of absence from her studies. As a result, when Julius accepted a junior lectureship at a new polytechnic on the south coast of England, in a seaside town that appeared to cater to retirees, Monica was free to join him. The newly married couple rented a small flat on the first floor of a detached brick house near the campus, and to celebrate their move, they opened a bottle of red wine and tried to drink themselves into frivolity. The landlady, a small grey-haired widow, whose behaviour was informed by old-world Eastern European manners, lived downstairs, and once they had made the decision to take the place she made a grand to-do of announcing that she hoped they would be comfortable. Then she fixed the pair of them with her wearily bagged eyes, and offered them whispered reassurances that they must not worry, for should they be unable to produce a marriage certificate this would in no way jeopardize their rental arrangement.

While Julius settled in on campus and made a few cautious stabs at friendship with his new colleagues, Monica walked the blustery seafront and scoured secondhand furniture shops in search of small items, such as wooden stools or table lamps, that might signal the permanence of their shared adventure and put a personal stamp on the characterless flat. During the third week of term they invited a fellow junior lecturer and his mousy fiancée to a spaghetti and wine dinner at their now moderately homelike abode, and although the tipsy couple obviously enjoyed the evening and even stayed for a second cup of coffee, Julius found the stress of receiving visitors difficult to tolerate. He knew enough to understand that when hosting he mustn't always be the centre of attention, but he really couldn't bear to have these people in his place, who acted as though their trivial complaints regarding the weather or the town's lack of telephone boxes might be of some interest to him and his wife. Later that night, as Monica was completing the washing-up, he looked up from the table and told her he would prefer to keep his work and his everyday life separate, and although

Monica wasn't quite sure where this would leave her in terms of things to do, she said nothing.

Despite his misgivings about both the town and the polytechnic, Julius adjusted easily to the new business of lecturing. As he often practised in their cramped living room, Monica was able to observe him quickly mastering the art of the theatrical pause, the rhetorical question, and the self-deprecating humorous anecdote, all carefully calculated to enhance an already burgeoning reputation as a popular teacher. When he wasn't giving a lecture, most of Julius's energy was devoted to the founding and leadership of the Anti-Colonial Club, but by the end of the first term its success among lecturers and students alike was causing him to regret his involvement. Long nights in disagreeable pubs debating whether the struggles of Hungary and other countries under the jackboot of Moscow should also be on the agenda for discussion were, to his mind, torturous. Why not include them? he insisted. Oppression was oppression. But what was he to make of the argument that the Anti-Colonial Club should view the struggles of people trying to avoid being beaten up by English teddy boys as part of an ongoing problem whose roots lay in colonial exploitation? His tolerance for lacklustre, drawn-out evenings waned as rapidly as his interest in warm English beer, and all too frequently he found himself staggering back along a chilly, windswept promenade, listening to the powerful engine of the sea, and then tiptoeing up the ill-lit backstairs to their small flat before sliding into bed next to his young wife.

Sunday afternoons had a tendency to drag for both of them. Julius would often finish folding the pile of clothes and then slump down onto the settee and watch as Monica continued to iron the shirts and skirts that needed special attention. Playing the part of a husband was something that he had taken on in order to make Monica feel more secure, but after only a few months in this role he was already unsure if he truly possessed the stamina, or the desire, to continue with the drama. He had no idea what the secretive and inscrutable Monica did with her time while he was on campus and no clear understanding if she possessed any goals in life, either short or long term, for she appeared to be reluctant to speak of herself. Once again Monica asked him to get up from the settee. Julius accepted a large paper bag full of rubbish, while Monica grabbed a fistful of empty milk bottles, and together they tramped their way down the stairs. As they descended, Julius realized that even though he had no idea of what lay ahead for them both, he should perhaps at least try and talk to his wife about his uneasy feelings. He pitched the rubbish bag into the dustbin and replaced the lid with an earsplitting clatter. Monica shot him a disdainful look. "Sorry." He paused. "I've got a lot on my mind." When they returned upstairs, Julius poured a small finger of whisky and began to pace the room, while Monica carefully draped one freshly ironed shirt after another over wire hangers and hung them, one by one, in the small cupboard by the front door that served as their wardrobe. He could feel Monica watching him out of the corner of her eye, but as usual, neither of them said anything, and so once again he reached for the whisky bottle and took up a seat on the settee.

✦

Julius wrote to a young law student at Cambridge, a fellow countryman who was the latest recipient of the same island overseas scholarship that he had been awarded. He asked the young man if it was true that Lloyd Samuels, his former high school classmate, had formed an opposition party. The young man replied and confirmed that shortly before his own departure for England, the newly qualified Dr. Samuels had returned from his studies in Canada and opened a general practice in the poorest part of the capital. Apparently he had also formed the People's Action Party, among whose earliest recruits was the would-be lawyer, who was thoughtful enough to enclose the details of both Lloyd Samuels's place of business and his private residence.

Dr. Samuels was pleased to hear from Julius, and his first letter was notable for an excess of excitement, which reminded Julius of his friend's laughable attempts to make his stuttering, overly verbose points during classroom discussions. On more than one occasion, he remembered looking across at Lloyd and wondering just what would become of the jovial, plump boy who held his pencil like a spike, and who by the time he donned long trousers was astute enough to have given up any ambitions of the island scholarship. Young Lloyd's accent was already beginning to be seasoned with a slight American affectation, which suggested the direction in which his mind was starting to drift, but a medical school in a provincial Canadian university, as opposed to an East Coast Ivy League establishment, was probably the right level for his friend. Dr. Samuels's second letter encouraged Julius to meet with the chief party organizer in London, but after a day-long excursion to the capital, during which Julius spent much of a frustrating afternoon and early evening sitting in a noisy London Transport depot tea room, waiting for this busy bus driver to discover time between shifts to discuss the matter of their country's road to independence, he wrote to Lloyd and wished him well with his political endeavours. A week later, Julius received the telegram suggesting that he leave the south coast of England, move to London, and take over as chief party organizer in Britain, with a salary that would be drawn from whatever subscriptions he could raise and supplemented by sales of a projected monthly newspaper to be called *The People's Voice*, although Lloyd made it clear that Julius was free, within reason, to use whatever title he wished.

✦

"Eventually I'll have to give some talks and go out on the road, but not now, not during summer, for people are either away or just relaxing."

His wife was standing by the window and staring across the street at a café outside of which a few small metal tables, surrounded by a random assortment of chairs, were arranged on the pavement in a manner that blocked the flow of pedestrian traffic. It was

Monica who had organized their move to London and found this single bed-sitting-room in Ladbroke Grove, a down-at-heel but affordable location whose chief virtue was its proximity to the tube station. Travelling up to London by train and scanning cards in newsagents' windows had finally given her something to do, for although she had not let on to Julius, she was not sure how much more she could have endured of her aimless existence on the south coast. Once she had set up their flat and explored every nook and cranny of the drab seaside town, she had quickly come face-to-face with the dispiriting reality that beyond Julius, she had no community.

"Right now I have to identify nationals working or studying here so that when the time comes, we have a caucus of votes to draw upon."

"But you're not independent yet."

She said this without turning from the window to face him, and although he wanted to admonish her, he said nothing.

"When the cross-party delegation arrives in London, I figure I'll accompany them to Whitehall for the independence discussions. But all of this is in the future. Right now we need to know who we can count on for what comes afterwards."

He watched as Monica crossed the room to the bulky electricity meter by the door, pushed in sixpence, and then turned the key. They both heard the rattle of the coin as it dropped into the metal box, and then the lights flickered to life, but Monica turned them off and took up a seat at the crowded kitchen table and pushed the newspaper out of the way. The early-evening sunset was illuminating the small room, but she knew that this was just a momentary prelude to the gloom that would follow. While her husband was talking, it had finally become clear to Monica that the real problem with the room was that it had been painted an ill-chosen mauve. To further compound the issue, there was nothing on the walls, no pictures, not even an old calendar or a mirror, so tomorrow she would begin the now familiar project of going out to the shops and street markets to see what she might find to liven up the place. Secondhand prints, cheap posters, anything would do, so long as they could be tacked up on the horribly coloured wall and would stay up, then at least they would have something uplifting to look at. Down on the street she could hear the noisy scraping of the tables and chairs being dragged back into the café as the owner prepared to lock up for the night. It was so oppressively hot, and she had already learned that if she kept the single window open, there was noise and soot to contend with, but if she closed in the window the room would soon become stifling. Either way, she couldn't win.

✦

On the first Saturday morning of each month, Julius travelled by tube and then bus to an unsightly part of South London. Moving to the city had made this ghastly journey far easier in practical terms, but for some time now the ordeal of fulfilling his parental obligation to the child from his first marriage had been taxing his dwindling reserves of goodwill and optimism. The eight-year-old girl had been born shortly after he'd arrived in England and made her first appearance during a blizzard-ravaged winter that people seemed keen to continually inform him was "unusual." The girl was slow, and he feared she might have been affected by English weather, but whenever he raised these concerns with the girl's mother, she looked angrily at him, which served only to stoke his resentment towards the woman. Until the girl was three, he commuted to university from their South London council flat, but when he finally packed his bags and resolved to leave London and scout for his own place in Oxford, a part of him wanted to miss his daughter. Five years later, however, he still feels uneasy that he has never, not once, been touched by any sense of guilt or loss.

The child is always neatly presented, as though ready for church, but some kind of skin condition causes her to constantly twitch and scratch, and her glum disposition merely confirms his suspicion that she is in perpetual discomfort. What worries him most, though, is that when she deigns to smile, she does so with an openness that he feels sure some man will exploit before she is too far into her teenage years. For the first hour of each visit the girl's mother retreats to her bedroom and closes in the door behind her in order to give father and daughter time together. This suits him, for somewhere beneath her swollen face and bloated waistline he can still detect the woman he married, and he has no desire to look at her. Back home he rescued this woman from a life working as a shop assistant in a haberdashery on Liverpool Row that was run by the Lebanese Sahaley brothers. He offered her the choice of forty more years serving customers, with the fresh sea breeze cooling her through the open jalousies, or marriage and a trip to England and a new and exciting beginning. She had waited dutifully for him during the three long years he had dedicated himself to his coursework and earned a Bachelor of Arts at the University College on the larger island to the north, and when he returned, it was to claim the island scholarship and sweep her off her feet and onto a ship bound for England. But she had country values, and whereas most women would have considered the possibility of a life in England to be a lavish reward for simply waiting faithfully for a fiancé, he soon discovered that their arrival in England served only to stimulate the woman's materialistic cravings, about which he had hitherto been ignorant. After he had rejected her and found a basement flat in Oxford where he felt he could live and work for the four remaining years of his scholarship, she hired a lawyer and began to harass him. Mercifully, and with help and advice from the University Overseas Office, he was able to quickly secure a divorce and put this marriage behind him. He speculated that perhaps some years hence, when she had finally grown up a little, she might well make some man a loyal and decent spouse, but this would be in the future and would be none of his business.

As his former wife emerged from the bedroom, he looked from mother to daughter, and again he wondered how he could have miscalculated so disastrously. The place contained not a single book, and as the woman began to speak, he was once again reminded that her conversation never ascended above the banal: their daughter's life at school, her new job as a cleaner at a local hospital, her friend the nurse who minded the girl when she worked the night shift. He had read about such people, but it didn't seem fair that he should be connected to them. His former wife had, as always, prepared rice and peas and chicken for him, and he watched as she carefully spooned out his food onto a plate, and then she and the girl sat and stared as he ate, and he knew that this charade would end only when he handed over the slim brown envelope of money that they were expecting. Until then he forced himself to appear amicable, all the while stealing glances at the girl, who, when she opened her mouth, exposed teeth that had already been attacked by sugar.

Sometime later he sat on the tube and stared at his reflection in the smudged mirror that was the glass, and he knew it was essential that he empty his mind of the events of the day. He had made a mistake and he was paying for it and that was all there was to it. Once he got off the tube, instead of going straight home, he made his way into a noisy pub next to the underground station and stood by the bar and began to order drinks. Once the landlord called time, and the pub began to let out, he wandered into a small park and sat alone on a damp bench with a slat missing. Monica needed help, he knew this, and in fact he had begun to worry about her before they had even moved to the south coast. It was not just the blank stare that perturbed him, for the truth was she had always displayed a tendency to lapse into these trances; what alarmed him the most was her ability to withdraw completely from him yet continue to function as though nothing were happening. It was clear that at such moments she wasn't listening to him, and when she finally came back to herself, she seemed to have no understanding that she might have been behaving oddly. He knew that Monica couldn't be happy, but how was he supposed to know what to do about it if she wasn't prepared to talk to him? He sighed. Really, when all was said and done, this wasn't the ideal moment for him to be dealing with this. Not now.

By the time he was ready to stumble home he had no clue how late it was and no idea how his life could have taken such a depressing turn. He quietly pushed the key into the door of the bed-sitting-room, hoping that Monica would now be asleep. He eased the whining door shut until he heard the reassuring click of the Yale lock, and then he stepped on the back of first one shoe and then the other and silently slipped out of his jacket and trousers, leaving them pooled on the floor. He watched as his increasingly mutinous wife extended a thin arm out over the side of the bed. He stood half undressed in the doorway and continued to look across the bed-sitting-room at Monica, who stirred and then, with her exposed arm, lifted the blankets over herself and turned away from him and onto her side.

✦

When Monica understood that she was pregnant, she began to visit the local library and borrow poetry books and novels; apart from trips out to the shops, or to the odd matinee at the local cinema, these were about the only times she ever left the room. She spent long mornings and afternoons folded up on the settee, reading as she had done throughout her first perplexing year at university, when she had found everything vexing to cope with, be it making friends or simply handling the heavy silver knives and forks in the college dining hall. Now that she was expecting, however, she realized that reading aside, she seemed to be investing countless hours trying to anticipate the sensations that she suspected would soon be overpowering her. She had been alarmed by a few early-morning episodes of vomiting and nausea, and she continued to suffer from an ongoing inability to find a truly comfortable position in which to sleep at night, but beyond these inconveniences she soon came to the conclusion that, far from confounding her, the experience of being pregnant was fairly boring. As she began to show, Londoners nodded and made eye contact when they passed her in the street, and passengers on the bus actually stood up and offered her their seats. All of a sudden she was visible, and she wasn't sure how she felt about this. With the onset of winter the weather turned bitter, but it annoyed her that she could still feel herself blooming, a peculiar northern flower in an ominously arid southern landscape.

"You know," she said, looking up from the settee, "unlike other mammals, our babies spend far too little time in the womb. They come out helpless and unable to run from predators, and that's just not right."

Julius set down the cup of coffee that he was cradling in both hands.

"Really, I don't know what you are reading, but these days your mind is full of all sorts of craziness."

"I'm feeling fine, Julius." She patted her stomach somewhat forcefully. "And I wouldn't say no to an extra three or four months of this if it meant the kid might stand a chance of coming out walking."

They called their son Ben, a name that she convinced Julius suggested some substance. He quickly agreed, but they both knew that he did so in order to avoid causing a scene of any kind. As far as Monica was concerned, their one room was now impossibly small, and a basket of unwashed laundry seemed to be permanently calling out to her from its hiding place underneath the table. And then there were the exquisitely fusty smells that, to her husband's bemusement, spurred Monica to start walking around the room with a white handkerchief tied over her mouth and nose. However, when spring finally arrived, she was able to crack the window and release the accumulation of sour mustiness into the street, where the clattering noises from the café, like the bells of a village church, heralded the start and close of each day. Eventually her husband learned to touch her again, at first tentatively, and then with more confidence as he tried to reintroduce an intimate routine to their lives, but Monica was forced to acknowledge that, at some point during the late winter or early spring, they both appeared to have abandoned the ability, or desire, to converse with each other on any topic beyond the minutiae of daily coexistence, which, these days, generally related to the needs of their son.

Monica soon ran out of books that she wished to take out of the local library. She had methodically worked her way through the small poetry section, and she had also read most of the contemporary novels that she thought might interest her, but having moved on to short stories, which was a form she particularly loved, she had to admit that none of the collections aroused any elation in her, and more often than not, the volumes were returned unread. Monica knew what the problem was—discussion, somebody to talk with about the books—and once she had accepted that such exchanges were unlikely to occur she fell into the habit of going out into the world without her borrowing card. Sitting by the Serpentine watching the ducks seemed to amuse her young son, until she realized that it mattered little to the child whether he was looking at a duck or a double-decker bus, for all he saw was movement. She had discovered the free museums and tourist attractions of central London, but the hardship of navigating such a vast city with a child, and with precious little money, did nothing to increase her affection for the capital, whose thunderous indifference to her, now that she no longer looked like an expectant mother, was matched only by her progressively detached husband, who, with each passing month, seemed to be investing greater amounts of time attending to his efforts on behalf of Dr. Lloyd Samuels.

One afternoon, while sitting on a crowded Metropolitan Line train with her sleeping son in her arms, she abruptly opened her eyes and was shocked to discover that she had missed her stop. She quickly gathered her belongings, but when she tried to stand up in order to get off at the next station, she felt as though two hands were pushing down on her shoulders and pinning her and the child to the seat. She closed her eyes and counted slowly to five, then opened them, and as soon as she heard the unoiled grating of the doors, she shoved her way off the train and up the escalator and out into the daylight. The sun was blazing hot, but the thought of reentering the underground or getting on a bus made her head spin. She threaded her slow way through the seemingly endless maze of pedestrians, but the torment of drumming in her head receded only when she came to a junction and could momentarily feel space around her. The child began to cry with an initial whimper that soon grew into a wail, and by the time she turned into her street Ben's arms and legs were thrashing, which suggested he was in the throes of a fully fledged panic attack. Her eyes began to brim with frustration, and although she could clearly see the scruffy house that held the room in which they lived, with every step she took the building seemed to be receding farther.

The sweet-smelling man guided her gently into one of the café's metal chairs and placed a glass of water before her. She relinquished the squirmy child without protest and watched as her son looked into the foreigner's face and stopped kicking.

"I think it is too hot to be carrying a child."

"I'm sorry."

She tried to guess the man's accent, but she immediately gave up. No doubt he hailed from some exotic location, but having never travelled abroad she couldn't pretend to know more than this. He was staring directly at her with an overly kind smile that she knew was meant to reassure her that there was no need to say anything further. She imagined that perhaps the man already understood that she was pregnant again. If so, maybe he wanted her to come and live with him in his country, and if he did, why didn't he just ask her?

Monica was lying full length on the settee, and letting the hot air and noises of London wash over her through the open window, when Julius ambled through the door. He had long ago given up insisting that she listen to his boring talks about the future of his nonsensical stupid country, but as he sat down, she found herself once again dismayed by the gaudy African shirt and leather sandals he had taken to wearing. Why on earth had he not sought her advice before adopting this costume? His once trim and neat hair was now wide and ludicrous, and when it first began to assume this unshapely form, he had quizzed her as to whether she thought it suited him. Not really believing that he could be asking this of her, she simply laughed and then asked him why he had started to wear sunglasses when there was no sun in the sky? In fact, why did he sometimes wear them inside of the house?

As Julius slipped his feet out of his sandals, she understood that her husband didn't actually care what she thought of his hair, or his attire, or anything, for it was all part of a larger transformation that was taking place that neither required nor depended on her approval. Julius appeared to be casting aside his studious aspect and making some clownish attempt to entertain worldliness. Last week she had found some rumpled notepaper in the wastepaper basket and could see he had been trying out a new name. The evidence pointed to two preferred options: Dr. J. Livingstone T. Wilson or Dr. Julius L. Terrance Wilson. Of course, she didn't know either man. She watched him bend over and begin to ransack the canvas bag that he had deposited on the floor. He finally discovered what he was searching for and plucked an LP out of the bag, which he then nudged unceremoniously out of his path with the outside of one foot. He took two short steps to the record player and, as he slipped the disc out of its inner sleeve, handed her the LP cover and urged her to read the notes on the back. His laughter seemed to bubble up from deep inside, and it was punctuated with his constant repetition of "Oh, man, you've got to hear this." Jazz was a new passion of Julius's, although he had balked when she called it a passion.

"Monica, jazz is the only category of music that you can really study. It has a theoretical intent."

She had looked at him but didn't want to argue. Perhaps he had forgotten, but once upon a time she had been regarded as musically proficient. However, as her father's pride in her achievements increased, her interest in playing the piano had fallen away to the point where it had now been many years since she had perched herself on a piano stool.

"Anyhow, just because you can theorize about the music doesn't mean that you can't also be passionate about it."

"And miss seventy-five per cent of what's going on?"

Julius had looked at her with palpable contempt, and Monica couldn't help herself as she began to laugh. These days the ponderous weight of self-regard seemed to infuse Julius's whole body; it affected how he stood, how he walked, and how he held himself when he was getting ready to make an announcement.

He took the LP cover from Monica without giving her a chance to read the notes, and then he closed his eyes as the shrill saxophone opening began to blare out. "Oh, man." Monica stood up and went to the fridge for a bottle of beer, which she handed to him, hoping he might understand that small gestures like this were about all she had left to offer in the way of a deposit on some kind of continued future together. But it was beginning to feel futile. As he took the beer, she picked his bag up off the floor and stared at her ridiculous husband. She had been waiting a long time for them to perhaps turn a corner in their relationship, but she now realized that they both were navigating a long, hopelessly unforgiving bend, and she was tired.

"I bought this LP at a new secondhand place on Baker Street."

"Can I have some too?"

He looked puzzled, and so she pointed at the bottle of beer, which he then handed to her.

"Well, do you like it?" he asked. "Are you digging it?"

"Julius, please give Ben a kiss."

"Jesus, you act as if I've forgotten my own son." He looked at her as though she disgusted him. "Just let me finish listening to the music, okay?"

"And could you please turn it down? You'll wake him up."

✦

One early winter's afternoon they both returned in silence from their unscheduled visit to the doctor's surgery. The man confirmed that despite Monica's slipping on a patch of black ice outside the tube station, everything seemed to be alright with the baby that she was carrying, and he dismissed them without making any further comment. While Monica implored Ben to take an afternoon nap in the cot to the side of their bed, Julius poured a tumbler of whisky and slumped onto the settee in a manner that let her know he would not be going out and speaking at a meeting tonight. Ben appeared to be settled now, so she edged her way to the sink and started to fill the kettle with water while making as little noise as possible. Having turned on the stove, she looked down at Julius.

"Don't you sometimes think a television set would be nice?"

"I don't think so."

Of course, a friend would be a better alternative to a television set, and a part-time job would be a godsend, but she knew that with this erratic man she should tread carefully around the word "lonely." She would find some other time to raise the idea of her perhaps going back to university, for clearly this was not going to be an easy conversation.

"I don't mean now, Julius. Look at us, we've got to get out of this room first and get ourselves a bigger place. I just mean later on. In time."

"Later on when?" He slammed the whisky down on the coffee table and woke up Ben, who began to cry. "I'm doing the best I can."

He stood now, the toes of his bare feet curling into the mangy rug and his face radiating anger, the source of which was not understandable to her. She picked up her son and tried her best to comfort him in her arms, but she continued to stare directly at Julius. After a minute or so her agitated husband began to finally relax, and he reached behind himself in order that he might master his balance as he sank back down onto the settee.

"For Christ's sake, Monica, why do you insist on provoking me in this way?"

She continued to rock Ben in her arms and waited for him to finish.

"You know I couldn't give a fig about the television set, don't you?"

"I know." She paused. "I know."

"We don't have the money for another child, you know that, don't you?"

"I know."

When their second son was born, Monica considered asking Julius if he minded if they named him William, after her favourite poet. However, they left the understaffed local hospital and returned to their disheartening bed-sitting-room with their new child still nameless.

✦

Outside, the snow continued to fall gently, while two men sat in the window seats of the café nursing cups of tea that had long ago gone cold. She looked down on them and could see that one man had on a khaki jacket that looked like part of an army uniform, but nothing else about him brought to mind the notion that he might have any familiarity with military discipline. His short hair was uncombed, his shoulders were hunched, and occasionally he would slap his gloved hands together and then tuck them back into his armpits. His friend was swaddled in an overcoat that was clearly two or three sizes too big, and his face was half hidden beneath a trilby hat that was set at an improbably jaunty angle. An overstuffed shopping bag occupied the third chair, but it wasn't immediately apparent to which man it belonged. The ashtray was full and looked as if it hadn't been emptied all day, but it was pushed to one side, for neither man showed any inclination to smoke. Without warning, as though receiving a prompt from the wings, the man in the overcoat produced a folded newspaper from inside his coat and with a pencil began to circle various items before tossing the newspaper down in front of his friend, who displayed no interest in the offering. The gesture seemed designed to goad his companion to please look for a job—or perhaps a room—but the colder man hugged himself and stared out of the window, where a light drizzle had begun to fall and was already making an icy grey soup of the thin layer of snow that had settled overnight. The more generous man stood and slowly buttoned up his overcoat. As he left the café, it became clear that the shopping bag belonged to the military man, whose head didn't move, but whose cold, rheumy eyes followed the tall man out onto the street and then tracked him as he flicked up his collar and began to trudge away from the café.

Standing by the bedroom window and looking down at the two men in the café had kept Monica busy for most of the past hour while her two boys slept peacefully on the bed behind her. Last year, after three problematic years in the cramped bed-sitting-room, she and Julius had finally scrambled together enough money to move one floor up into a one-bedroom flat that offered the same view over the café, but this time from both a bedroom window and a window in the living room. At night the two boys slept head to toe on the settee in the living room, but during the day, if they needed a nap, she let them lie out on the double bed. She sometimes worried that the acrid fumes from the paraffin heater might be harmful, but she assumed not or somebody would have written an article in one of the posh Sunday papers, which was most likely how she would know. She moved across to the bed and looked down at the boys, but they both seemed alright. She re-mained unconvinced that she would ever grow comfortably into the role of a mother, for the speed and ease with which her body had dealt with pregnancy suggested a lack of any real engage-ment with the process. And of course, part of defining herself as a mother involved watching and appreciating the role of the father, but not only did Julius continue to behave indifferently towards his wife, these days he appeared to be also increasingly removed from his two children.

Monica passed quietly into the living room and felt sure that the two men seated on the settee would have some understanding of the scene in the café, but she also knew they would have nothing to say to her on the matter. Were she to try and describe the situation, Julius might glare to let her know that she should be quiet, but the other man would most likely be insulted that a relatively young Englishwoman was addressing him, and of course, offending this man might make life difficult for them all. Their talks were not going well, this much she knew, but Lloyd Samuels seemed unconcerned. There was an air of quiet arrogance about him that didn't match up with what Julius had told her when he returned from the trip he had made back home. His supposedly charming and charismatic school friend had funded Julius to fly out and deliver a full report on the situation in England, but the conceited man sitting in their living room was definitely smaller and more rotund than the man Julius had described. Furthermore, Julius never mentioned Lloyd Samuels's insecurities, but from the moment she had opened the door and welcomed him into their flat she could see vulnerability in his darting eyes.

Once again the snow was falling, but this time it was not settling. The café was closing up, but the semiuniformed man was still sitting at the table with the two discarded cups in front of him. He must have picked up the newspaper, for it was now jutting out of the top of the shopping bag like a chimney pot that was about to topple over. Julius stood up and snapped on the lights, which made it challenging to see out, and she realized that the few hardy souls wandering the snowy streets could now look up and enjoy the theatre of their lives. As she pushed back the sleeves of her cardigan, her full attention returned to the window, where she found herself longing to see a flower or a tree. Gardens were the missing factor, and she thought of her childhood friend Hester Greenwell, whose family had a large spread of a garden behind their detached stone house, but her father was the local doctor, so such extravagance was to be expected. Her own father always seemed uncomfortable whenever she went around to play at Hester's, making it clear that she couldn't stay for tea because Hester's mother insisted on calling it supper. "Invite her over to our place," he said. "After all, we've got a garden too." And so Hester started to visit Monica's house, and more often than not she would stay for tea.

Monica sat down at the table and tried to busy herself so the men wouldn't think she was eavesdropping. Thanks to Julius, there was now enough light to read the newspaper she had bought last weekend when she took the children to the park. If there was a match on, she would go to the top of the hill and look down into the distant football ground and try to convince Ben to remember the names of the players and take a general interest in the game. She knew it was the kind of thing that a dad should be doing, but there was no point bargaining on this from Julius. However, because there was no match, she had sat apart from everybody else by the playground and watched Ben enjoying himself on the slide, while she let Tommy hurdle over her knees and pass from one side of the bench to the other. Her attention was suddenly seized by the wind combing through the trees, and then she looked up to the heavens and watched an aeroplane drawing a desperately slow line against the sky. Almost imperceptibly, she could feel herself striking out on one of her puzzling journeys into make-believe, and she knew she had to get a grip on herself. As Ben left the playground and began to run towards her, she saw he was in danger of being swallowed up by a group of Japanese tourists who were chatting incessantly and taking photographs. They parted abruptly and opened up like a river flowing around a protruding rock, and once they had passed on their way they left behind her bemused son all fresh and clean and standing before her.

"Of course, I understand." She listened to Julius trying gently to press his own case. Now that the island appeared to be moving closer to independence her husband wanted the promise of a government position, or a title of some description, but this was beginning to seem unlikely. As Monica stood and moved back to the window, a quick glance revealed that the men were now angled towards each other on the settee, but she once again gave them her back.

She heard Julius laugh unconvincingly. This was the second time that Lloyd Samuels had visited their flat, but unlike earlier in the week, when he had scarcely crossed the doorstep, this time it was clear that he intended to stay awhile, and Julius had asked Monica if she would make coffee for them both. She thought that the men might talk for an hour or two before moving on to the pub and then go on from there to their evening meeting, but she now found herself wondering if their meeting had been cancelled because of the weather. It was perfectly possible for her to make more coffee, but she concluded she should wait until asked, for these were men who didn't like to be interrupted.

"If the two parties merge, and you take the deputy seat, will you be in a position to offer me a role?"

She could hear unease in Julius's voice.

"My friend, these people are better funded, they have resources, and there is no need for the opposition to be split like this. We must seek and greet consensus."

It was typical of Julius to be so caught up with himself that he was ignorant of what was going on. She already had a powerful intimation of her husband's fate, for she felt sure that his vain, overweight friend was the type of man who would happily go to the grave in his own embrace. A third visit would be unlikely.

As Monica continued to stare down into the street, she thought again about the upsetting truth that Julius had never once offered to take her and the children across the road to the café as a treat. In fact, since she'd had the boys, he had never exercised himself to take her anywhere, and she suspected that it embarrassed him to be seen in public with her. The poor man had probably exaggerated his knowledge of women, and while she couldn't claim to have a great deal of experience with men, she knew enough to be aware that his colleague Lloyd Samuels was once again stealing clumsy glances at her. Her legs were bare, and her slender feet encased in tight pumps that were neither slippers nor shoes, but she fancied they made her movements appear graceful. When she bent over to look down out of the window, her cardigan rode up and exposed a thin band of flesh that drew the man's eyes in. She could feel the inelegant weight of his gaze, but as long as he respected the fact that she was not available to him, and never would be, there was really nothing for her to do except adjust her cardigan, which she did.

"After Notting Hill," said Julius, "it's just one problem after another."

"And the police?"

"The police and the teddy boys are as bad as each other."

Her husband was chased once, but he would never speak with her about what had happened. It exasperated her now that she could hear him talking about the incident to this man. She had held his head over the sink and dabbed at the cut on his cheek and stopped the blood, but he wouldn't even make eye contact with her. That night a morose and wounded Julius had had the same abject look on his face as the poor man who had spent the greater part of the afternoon sitting alone in the café with only the shopping bag for company.

She turns, having decided that she should once again go and check on the children. As she steps towards the bedroom, she sees that their guest has begun now to use his hands as he speaks, but he has modified his voice, which suggests that they have moved on to some new issue that makes them both feel a little more at ease. However, this new sense of comfort with each other will be only temporary, for Julius has told her that this evening he will ask for more money to help with the children. He will tell Dr. Samuels that it is no longer possible for him to manage in the absence of a proper wage and without guarantees of some sort. She closes in the door to the bedroom behind her and can see that her two children are still sleeping peacefully. Then she turns off the lights and goes and stands by the bedroom window and looks down at the now shuttered facade of the café and waits for the snow to stop falling.

✦

Shortly after the talks between the British government and the delegation from his country collapsed, Julius applied for a job as a lecturer at the institution that had awarded him his bachelor's degree. There was no need for him to inform Dr. Lloyd Samuels, for relations between the two of them had finally broken down one wet Monday night in the lounge bar of London's Grosvenor Hotel. That night, despite his obvious distress at Samuels's duplicity, Julius remained in the hotel bar long after his former friend had cleared off and downed one drink after the other. He knew there was no way he could share the news of their falling-out with his wife and give her the satisfaction of being proved right. If it had just been he and Monica alone, he felt sure that they would have put an end to their misery a long time ago, but the presence of the sullen-looking boys seemed to elicit some unspoken guilt in them both, so they had lingered on across months and years in their cramped flat with little money, and without any coherent idea of where life was taking them. But that night, alone in the bar of the Grosvenor Hotel, Julius looked around, and it finally dawned on him that he had no real interest in giving anything to this country that had now been his home for over a dozen years. After all, what had he received in return from these people? A late-night beating from some hooligans, and the problem of an increasingly sloppy wife who insisted that the children call her Mam as opposed to Mommy, or even Mama, and who long ago seemed to have relinquished any appetite for improvement or accomplishment.

To begin with, Monica *had* given him security and purpose as he struggled to finish his dissertation, but she had never really shown full appreciation for his reciprocal gift of marriage. For some reason, she seemed to have grown to resent him, and over the years she had made no effort to claim a role and had simply deposited herself as a burden at the centre of his life. Whenever he tried to talk to her about what she might do, she stared abstractedly at a point somewhere over his head. Of course, what really infuriated him of late was her new habit of using the children as a shield behind which she hid from any real discussion with him. "Please, Julius, keep it down. You'll wake the children." The one time he proposed that she seek help, and even consider some kind of a reconciliation with her parents, Monica snapped at him that he didn't know what he was talking about—which was true, but at least he was trying. As he paid for his drinks at the hotel bar and reached for his coat, he knew full well that things between them could no longer go on in this fashion. If she and her boys wanted to begin a new adventure with him, then he was willing to continue to make an effort, but only if she assured him she would start to pull herself together.

✦

Julius had received a short, enthusiastic telegram in response to his application for the lecturer's job, and he now held in his hand the official letter confirming his appointment. It was an early spring day, and he and Monica were sitting together at the living room table. The opportunity to go home and make a contribution, and perhaps try again to revise his dissertation and turn it into a book—this, he told her, was his true future.

"You still have faith in the book, don't you?" He moistened his dry lips with a quick circle of his tongue.

"Julius, it's some time since I read the manuscript."

"Well, what are you saying? Do you feel I should write a new book?"

"Who knows what you should do?" Monica began to laugh and ran both hands back through her stringy hair. "In fact, who knows what you *will* do from one moment to the next."

He watched her closely as she poured some milk from the bottle into a teacup and then lifted the chipped vessel to her lips. Having drained the cup, she fumbled at her blouse and undid the top button, for the weather was unseasonably warm. Monica had started to buy presliced white bread, and so she thought about toast, but almost at once the idea seemed too complicated. She put her feet up onto a chair and proudly exhibited her unpolished toenails. Julius seemed confused.

"Can I have some milk?"

Monica poured some milk into the same teacup and passed it to him.

"Back home we drink Carnation milk, but I know you'll soon get used to it."

"No, we won't." Again Monica laughed, and she began to push up her sleeves, first one arm and then the other. "You'll be going by yourself, Julius. I'm moving back north."

"To do what?"

"Is that all you have to say?"

Monica stared at this sad dreamer of a man she had married, and shook her head. Did he truly imagine she was going to just sit around for the rest of her life waiting for him to make all the decisions? Really, just who did he think he was? After the break with his friend, he started to have a go at England, which she knew was just another way of getting at her, but that was it. She knew that she had to take the boys away and make a fresh start. Wake up, you spaz, I'm not going to follow you around. We don't have much money, only what I've been able to save up from the housekeeping, but I've got myself a job, and we're off, okay? I came to you, Julius, because I thought you might be a better kind of man than my father, but you were never really interested, were you? I've made a bit of a twat of myself, haven't I?

"Listen, Julius, tomorrow morning I'll be taking the boys and leaving, okay?"

"No, it's not okay. Leaving to go where?" He looked angrily into her face. "Why are you doing this to me? To us?"

She pointed to the open window. "Please keep your voice down."

"For crying out loud, you cannot tell me what to do."

She watched as he threw himself back into the chair and kicked one leg over the other in what she guessed he probably thought was a study of calm repose. She looked closely at him and wanted to giggle, but she knew this would be mean. After all, she didn't dislike him; she just felt sorry for him. Seriously, did he think she was barmy enough to pack up her life and her two kiddies and follow him halfway across the world? *Julius, Julius, Julius, I've already taken charge of the situation and made my own plans.*

"Let me ask you, Monica, do you know what love is? You have made a commitment."

"You need somebody else, Julius." She wanted to add: *perhaps you should buy a dog.*

He sprang to his full, lanky height so that he now hovered over her. She could see that he wanted to shout, but as she stared up into his knotted face, a slow ripening into resignation began to smooth out his features.

"For Christ's sake, Monica. Really, where the hell do you think you're going? What on earth is the matter with you?"

What's the matter with me? Nothing, Julius, except I'm tired, poor, and worried that because I don't know how to be myself, I don't know how to be a mother to these two boys, who deserve a damn sight more than we've been able to give them. I've lost myself, you buffoon, which is pathetic, given how much effort I put into looking out for myself before I met you. You didn't come banging and knocking and demanding; it was me, I came to you, and I now reckon that I shouldn't have: that's what's the matter with me, Julius.

He moved across the room to the settee and sat down heavily.

"So, we've come to this. You've got nothing to say? No discussion, no nothing, and you've made up your mind, and tomorrow morning everybody will know that we're a failure, is that what you want?"

"I made a mistake, Julius." She paused. "Sometimes it occurs to me that maybe I'm not worth loving. I know I've not got the looks, and I'm hardly the outgoing, vivacious type." Again she paused. "Anyhow, I've got to try and do what's right for these children."

"But I love you, Monica. Don't you remember?"

Monica began to smile. "I'm sorry, Julius, but you never really loved me."

"And you think running away with the children is going to help you? You know you've already run away once. You think you're strong enough to do it again, this time with two children?"

✦

The success of being promoted to deputy headmaster had encouraged Ronald Johnson to buy a brand-new semidetached home on an estate on the northernmost extremity of the town, out past the dejected jumble of half-empty warehouses and run-down factories. Once you'd gone through the last roundabout, and just before the start of the Outwood Road, you made a sharp left into a country lane that quickly opened up and revealed a maze of modern houses. They all were laid out like a child's model playground, with neatly trimmed lawns and freshly planted trees that still needed to be supported by upright sticks and bits of tented string. Ronald Johnson's house was situated at the end of the first cul-de-sac, and through the window he could see an ever-changing cast of birds flitting about the wooden feeder that he had struggled to assemble one Sunday morning. Spread out before him on the desk in the corner of his bedroom were various pieces of paper whose contents he was trying to collate and then précis into a short, but comprehensive, report of the school's achievements, both educational and sporting, during the past academic year. Part of his increased responsibilities included making a short annual presentation to the board of governors and then passing around a copy of his report to each person present.

His wife knocked and opened the door at the same time, a habit that irritated him no end as the abrupt rudeness of the second gesture rendered the first pointless.

"I'm sorry to bother you, but I expect we ought to be making our way to the station."

Ronald Johnson slowly replaced the cap on his fountain pen and carefully laid it down on top of the foolscap notepad.

He stood before the bathroom mirror and meticulously dusted the dandruff from the lapels of his jacket. He didn't feel as though he had aged, but when she looked into his face, what would she see? A greying man who was still moving upwards in his chosen career, and with whom she would now agree that discipline and effort are the twin paths to success. Or would she see a stubborn man, with a solemn expression, who continued to refuse to accommodate her waywardness?

That afternoon, when he arrived home from school, he was surprised to see his wife sitting at the dining table with a letter open and visible next to a carefully slitted envelope. She looked up, as though in possession of news that might disturb him.

"Monica's got a job in Leeds, and she's coming back."

He sat down and picked up the letter and briskly read it through for any references to him, but there were none. He had assumed that his wife and daughter maintained some pattern of contact, and while he didn't necessarily approve, it at least afforded him the opportunity to conjecture that they both still enjoyed a relationship of sorts with their only child. But out of the blue, in his hands, there was the possibility of a potential reconciliation, and he immediately convinced himself that he ought to make an effort for the sake of his wife. But Monica's timing was awful, for the governors' report would be his first real test, and now his wife was rushing him before the pair of them had even had the opportunity to discuss the dilemma of where to put the two boys. He turned away from the bathroom mirror and decided that at some point on the drive to the city centre he would raise the problem, although he took it somewhat for granted that Ruth would have already anticipated the quandary and prepared the back bedroom to accommodate all three of them.

He saw them huddled together on the platform like evacuees, and all that was missing were their name tags. Monica looked like a big sister who had been placed in charge of a large suitcase and her two little brothers, but as he and his wife walked towards them, he could see the exhaustion on his daughter's harried face. Ruth stood to one side while he quickly kissed Monica's bloodless cheek and then attempted to muss the hair of the older child, before self-consciously touching the nose of the younger one with his forefinger in the manner of a drill sergeant inspecting for dust. His daughter looked tense, as though she had arrived for a prearranged Christmas holiday already burdened with a resigned sense of obligation. He could see that his wife was holding back the tears, and he prayed that she'd continue to do so; the last thing they needed was waterworks.

He sat alone in the bedroom hunched over his desk and continued to work on his governors' report while giving mother and daughter time to reacquaint themselves. The drive home was stressful, and if it hadn't been for his own valiant efforts to make small talk and try to fill in some of the events of the past six years, Monica, it seemed, would have been happy to pass the time in silence. Clearly she wasn't ready to take any responsibility for her reckless choices, and her chippy behaviour implied that she still believed that there were no consequences for the decisions you made in your life. Why did the girl always seem so intent on making him feel uneasy by steadfastly refusing to share any thoughts? He put his pen to one side and remembered that it was only after his wife had assured him that she had spoken with Monica about the birds and the bees, and that he would therefore face no ticklish questions on this front, that he tried in earnest to engage with his daughter on a wide range of subjects, including music, but she was impossible to reach. And then, sometime after her sixteenth birthday, it became apparent to him that beneath her fierce intelligence and studious determination Monica possessed a wayward, slightly ethereal streak, and he started to fear for his child and wondered if he should put her down for counselling.

As they started for home, he began to steal furtive glances at her in the rearview mirror, and he wondered if he was being hasty. Perhaps her recent experiences *had* finally chastened her into a new appreciation of his way of thinking, and the evidence of the transformation would become tangible only after she had recovered from the journey. However, every time he glanced up Monica was staring moodily out of the window, seemingly lost in her own dreamworld and giving away nothing. As for the two children, he had difficulty seeing who would be kind to them now that their father had completely failed to value his daughter's affections and disowned them all and run off back to wherever it was he came from. He felt sure that at some point somebody would have to plead with his obstinate daughter to accept the introduction of the word "adoption" into her vocabulary.

Monica returned from the bathroom and took up her seat at the dining table, and he could tell she had washed her face. It even looked as though she had applied a bit of makeup, but he couldn't be sure about this, for his wife had never stooped to cosmetics, and tarting oneself up was not sanctioned for the female teaching staff. But, painted or not, a little blush had certainly returned to his daughter's cheeks.

"I suppose it will be different for you living back up here after all that time in the south. It might take a bit of getting used to."

"I don't see why. I'm from here."

"No, well, you're right there," he said, eager to agree with her and avoid any guise of confrontation, although he wanted to remind Monica that it didn't cost anything to be affable. Her letter to her mother had explained that having been successful in her application for a job as a junior librarian in a small branch library in Leeds, she had made the decision to break off with London and leave her so-called husband.

"But you've never worked in a library, have you?"

He saw what he assessed to be a frown starting to crease his daughter's face, but as it grew, it revealed itself to be a look of bewilderment.

"You mean for money?"

"Well, yes."

"No, I haven't." She paused. "Have you?"

"Well, not as such."

He would have liked to have offered to help financially, but he already knew what her response would be. He also wanted to ask about this man Wilson and ascertain if he'd made any provision to send her some kind of an allowance, and suggest that if it would help her in any way, then he would happily set his solicitor on the bugger, but he elected not to trespass. Having had some smattering of conversation with her and successfully avoided the use of the phrase "begin again"—as in "so you'll be beginning again"—he knew that he shouldn't push his luck.

Ruth backed her way through the door with a tray laden with crockery, a teapot snug in a colourful cosy, and two packets of ginger biscuits. Monica stood up to help, and he wondered whether he ought to offer to wake up the two children, or if this was something that his daughter, or his wife, would prefer to do, so he erred on the side of caution and said nothing. As Ruth poured, he tried to determine what he would have made of this Julius Wilson now that he felt free to think about him in the past tense. But the man had never made any attempt to write and advocate for a meeting at which he might explain himself to his senior, perhaps fearing that having already walked out on one marriage, he might well find it testing to justify why he considered himself a fit and proper person to start another. And now look what the fool had gone and done: he'd abandoned his only child with this permanent stain on her reputation.

His wife began to admit how much she missed the old terraced house and her few friends, while careful to point out all the modern conveniences of the new semi and stress the fact that there were plans afoot for a whole row of shops to be built on an undeveloped parcel of land to the back of them.

"Eventually the number twenty-four and twenty-six routes will be extended so that we're the terminus, but they've not said when."

She could feel her husband closely scrutinizing her, and she began to feel oafish in herself. However, Ruth knew that there was still plenty of time before she would be collecting her pension, although she had to admit that she sometimes looked, and even acted, like a lady whose Tuesday mornings were spent lining up at the post office to get her book stamped. Her hair had turned prematurely grey a decade ago, but rather than colour it, or at the very least have it cut into a borrowed style that might change the shape of her face, she had begun instead to bunch it on top of her head and hold the hysterical tangle in place with an assemblage of carefully placed hairpins. She imagined it was her ever-ripening plumpness that was causing both a little arthritic slowness and shooting pains in her feet and ankles, so much so that these days she wore only carpet slippers, and had even bought a pair for outdoor use, but her husband had drawn the line at this vulgarity. She didn't argue, but that was pretty much how she had managed to maintain what she assumed was a tolerable marriage, by not arguing and locking away all her talk inside of herself.

Thirty years ago Miss Patterson had been a vivacious, buxom young shopgirl who, from the time she left school at fourteen, had taken the eyes of the local lads, all of whom fell over themselves trying to get her to agree to go out with them. He'd known that if he was going to stand a chance, he'd have to somehow conquer his ineptitude and give over yanking at doors marked PUSH, or forgetting which pocket he'd put his bus ticket in when the inspector got on. Once he had acquired enough discipline to stop betraying himself, he started to woo her, and as he hoped might be the case, it was she who began to ask questions of him when he stopped in for his *Yorkshire Post* and ten Woodbines on his way to his very first teaching job. He imagined that the briefcase and suit helped rouse her curiosity, plus the fact that he eschewed a cap and chose to go about bareheaded, but whatever it was, it was soon obvious that the curvaceous Patterson girl in the shop was going to be his bride even though people, including his own parents, might well be surprised to see him stooping down to the bottom drawer and marrying a girl without his advantages.

She peeled off her apron and carefully draped it over the back of a chair as she spoke. "When I was younger, I'd have killed for the kind of kitchen facilities you lot have at your fingertips. I mean, you don't know you're born really, do you?" It was with some surprise, and alarm, that she found herself jabbering away to her daughter, for whom she had once happily baked and even encouraged to lick the cake mix from the bowl. However, one day teenage Monica suddenly turned her nose up in the air at such foolishness, and she did so with a flash of meanness that convulsed their relationship into a premature formality that made her mother want to weep for her loss. And now, she wondered, what does our Monica see beyond a pudgy woman whose poor neck is little more than a wide set of stairs descending from her ears down to her shoulders, and whose bust contains the secret of a growth that her doctor claims is "well under control"? "But remember," insisted Dr. Owen, "it's only a fool, Ruth, who tries to push open the door to the future." She looked closely at Monica, and wanted to clutch her daughter to her bosom and confess to her the source of her fretting, but she was shaken out of her abstraction by a sudden storm of footsteps up above, which could mean only one thing.

"I'm sorry, love, but I should have said. You will be stopping here tonight, won't you?"

"I can't. I've made arrangements for lodgings." Her mother looked dumbfounded, so Monica continued. "We can stay for another hour."

"But surely you don't have to go up to Leeds today? It's Saturday. And the kiddies should nap some more. They need their rest."

Ronald Johnson sat upstairs in the bedroom at his desk, but he was finding it impossible to concentrate, for he could hear the pair of them in the kitchen. He threw down his fountain pen with more force than he had intended and watched as the gushing ink described a near-perfect semicircle, which began boldly at one end and tapered to a thin italic whisper at the other. He made a gavel of his hand and noiselessly pounded the desktop and demanded silence, for he needed to concentrate. For Christ's sake, what's with all this ruddy carrying on? He didn't like to consider it too deeply, but in nearly thirty years of marriage his wife had completely failed to introduce a single topic into their table talk that had either surprised or even interested him. Was that too much to ask for, a question that he might research, or an issue that it was possible for them to exchange ideas about? And now what was she trying to do to their daughter, whose education should have placed her beyond Ruth's influence? Was this to be his legacy, two gossiping women and two misfit children? He stared at the defaced fair copy of his report and silently shook his head. It troubled him to admit that at some point he had made a decision to marry a shopgirl who wouldn't even be able to take charge should an emergency be forced upon them. As he opened the desk drawer to search for some blotting paper, the unfairness of the situation continued to darken his humour.

At just before seven, he dropped Monica and her two children at the train station. He removed her hefty suitcase from the boot of the car, and then he and his wife followed their daughter, whose boys clung to her, one to each hand, down the full length of the platform. Monica was hurrying, like somebody who'd heard the five o'clock whistle, and he could see that her slip was showing, but he knew that it wouldn't do to say anything. For a moment it crossed his mind that perhaps there was some mystery man with whom she would be rendezvousing when she stepped down from the train in thirty-two minutes' time? Or maybe she really did have an unnamed coworker who had agreed to meet her and the children and take them to their new flat. Monica temporarily released the two boys, and she gave her father an unenthusiastic hug, which made him feel foolish. She then kissed her silent mother on the cheek and moved away before her mother could grab her arm.

"Take care," he said as he hoisted the suitcase up and onto the train after her and the children. She looked down at him with a puzzled expression. "Of yourself, I mean."

"And you take care too," she said. "Of yourself."

III

GOING OUT

S he wiped Tommy's mouth with her hand and then shoved the remains of the food into a bag that she slung up onto her shoulder. She had saved a salad cream sandwich in case her older boy was hungry, but when she looked around, she still couldn't see him. The sun had gone behind a cloud, and it looked like it might rain, so she knew that it was time to leave this sorry excuse for a park that was littered with dog mess and empty beer cans and pop bottles. Having straightened Tommy's shirt, she looked again and spotted Ben playing on the swings with a group of Pakistani children, but when she called to him, he ignored her and kicked his feet up in an attempt to climb even higher. "Don't you make me have to come and fetch you." She could feel the intrusive stares from the foreign men and women, who sat on the grass in a circular group around a seemingly endless supply of food that the wives had no doubt slaved over. They behaved like it was their park, which in a way it was now.

When Ben saw her striding towards him, he jumped from the swing and ran and hid behind a tree. "Ben!" Ten years old now, she thought, and still playing the fool. "You stop right where you are or I'll give you what for." He darted out into the open and then hid behind another thick oak, but he knew it was no use.

"Okay, I give up," he said as he walked towards her. She twisted her grip on his wrist and accidentally gave him a Chinese burn.

"Oi, leave me alone!"

Then, with her free hand, she slapped the back of his head, which served only to make her palm sting. The Pakistani kids began to laugh out loud and point, irritating her no end. However, she didn't want to say anything to the little buggers in front of their parents, so she just glared at them as she frog-marched Ben back in the direction of his temporarily abandoned brother. Ben turned up his nose at the salad cream sandwich, so she asked him again just to make sure. "So you're not hungry then?" He shook his head, but he still wouldn't meet her eyes. "Right then, it's staying in the bag, and don't bother me with any nonsense on the way home. Come on, we didn't bring a brolly, so we'll have to be lively."

The wide entrance to the park bespoke a civic ambition that had never truly come to fruition. To the left of the iron gates stood an immodestly large statue of a former lord mayor that was now speckled in bird droppings, while the ceremonial urns on top of each gatepost sprouted thriving weeds. As she passed out of the park and turned right into Stanhope Lane, she silently reattached Ben's hand to that of his brother and looked at the older boy in a manner that let him know that he should not let go. The roots of the trees had cracked and displaced the flagstones on this stretch of pavement, so it was treacherous for an adult, let alone two kids to try and walk here. They wandered by dismal-looking pubs and corner shops with paint peeling from their facades and windows that were securely grilled, but she understood that these places had no need to attract clients, for the faces that appeared each day, and the words they uttered, were as depressingly predictable as the cast and script of a long-running soap opera. After four years as a librarian in this run-down city that, despite the evidence of increased poverty, recently had the temerity to make a bid to host the Commonwealth Games, she was quietly desperate to escape back to Oxford, or even back to London, where she thought she might make a better fist of it given a second chance. Stamping out books five days a week, and rearranging shelves, and keeping the periodical subscriptions up to date, and shooing tramps, before spending her weekends at the park with the kids, was doing her no good at all. But what choice did she have? When she finally worked up enough courage to contact the admissions office at her old college, they wrote back and told her that she would be most welcome to return and complete the final year of her degree, but only after she had "established a domestic situation that would be compatible with study." She scrutinized the piece of yellowish notepaper embossed with the college's crest, and she read and re-read the offending words.

Monica kept this news, and all her other business, from her boss at work. Denise wouldn't shut up about how smart the city was getting, especially down by the river, where a cake shop and a place that sold flowers had recently opened up. Some of the greasy-looking blokes who liked to come into the library with the express purpose of trying to chat her up, they too wouldn't give over about the virtues of the newly revitalized city centre. However, she felt that if you've never been anywhere, then you don't know, do you? And what's more, it was all well and good talking big about a place if you didn't have children to bring up. She assumed that anywhere, even this dump, could look acceptable to you if you didn't have kids.

Ben kept hold of Tommy's hand as instructed, but he tugged at her skirt with his free hand.

"I'm hungry, Mam."

"Well, we can't stop now, understand? I don't want to get wet, and your brother's tired."

They waited by the side of the dual carriageway, which ran like a scar through this part of town. On one side were the older terraced houses and run-down factories, including the town brewery, which they were now standing beside, but the sharp, sweet smell of malt and hops turned her stomach, and so she was always anxious for the traffic lights to change. A brand-new footbridge spanned the road at this point, but hardly anybody used it as you had to climb up two dozen steps to reach the bridge proper, and in her own case how were you supposed to do so with two kiddies who treated it like something you'd find in a playground? The cars and lorries thundered by in both directions, but once the lights turned green they hastened over to the far side, where the houses had been knocked down and replaced with a warrenlike collection of grey low-rise flats that the council had named after battles in the Second World War. On this far side of the road the only evidence of the past was the decrepit redbrick swimming baths building, which stood out like a rotten tooth all by itself. If you looked at the estate from a distance, you might easily imagine the swimming baths to be some weird architectural reminder of the Edwardian past, but despite the fact that it was falling to pieces, most mornings of the week school kids still used the place. When they first moved in there used to be a grassy picnic area and a place for kids to kick a ball outside of their range of flats—Arnhem Croft—but the council had decided to gravel it over and make a stab at a play zone. Of late, teenagers had claimed the area, and from dawn till dusk they colonised the place and exchanged their cigarettes and swigged cider, and occasionally a boy and a girl would slip into the tunnels of the concrete castle for a snog, but the adults just watched and left them alone as long as they didn't bother anybody.

It was always hit or miss as to whether the lifts would work. Monica pushed a button, and as she waited, she heard the thunderous clamour of debris tumbling down the central rubbish chute.

"Mam, I'm really hungry."

The lift doors opened, and she looked at Ben and nudged him forward. Truthfully, she was too tired to scold him, so she jokingly pinched his mouth shut and gave him a fatigued smile. A few moments later they all stepped out of the lift, and she looked down over the balcony to the gravel pit of a play area three stories below, where she could now see one of the teenagers urinating behind the slide. She had spent her first month in Leeds in a mournfully stark one-bedroom flat that Denise had arranged for her, but the council then informed her that because she was one of their employees, and a single mother, they could relocate her to this award-winning estate without her having to spend any time on the waiting list. The woman at the council office told her this in a manner that made it clear that Monica was to regard this as a great privilege, but from the moment she pulled up in Denise's Mini and squinted out of the window at the bleak, characterless landscape of this new community, she instantly knew she would never be happy in such a place.

But she was stuck, for Julius never sent her any money, and she couldn't afford to move out into private accommodation, so she reckoned she'd just have to make the best of things. The elderly man next door, who said he'd retired from the merchant navy, but who had no stories to tell—real or invented—of adventures he had experienced, or far-flung places he had seen, was forever taking the heel of his shoe and banging on the wall and complaining that the kiddies were making too much bleeding noise. At first she took it personally, imagining it to be a vendetta that was aimed at her, until she met flashy Pamela at the rubbish chute and discovered that she lived on the other side of the retired seaman, and being a single mother with a nine-year-old daughter, she too was receiving the same treatment with, no doubt, the heel of the same shoe.

By the time she had manhandled the boys into the flat and closed in the door behind her, Ben was once again moaning about how hungry he was, and so she reached into her bag and pulled out the sandwich, which she thrust into his grateful hands. It wasn't until she had got Tommy out of his coat that she realized the flat was cold and the pilot light to the boiler must have gone out again. For the past fortnight she had arrived at work each morning and immediately called the council office and asked them to send somebody to fix the boiler, but their excuses were becoming increasingly abrupt, and she had now accepted that she would just have to wait until they were ready. A box of matches lay on the kitchen countertop for exactly this situation, and as she removed the glass panel and struck the match, she wished, above everything else, for somebody to help her out, for she knew that things couldn't go on like this for much longer.

On the third match she managed to light the damn thing, but by then something had broken inside of her, and she stopped and stared into midair.

"Mam, what's the matter?"

She looked down at Ben and smiled.

"Is something the matter again, Mam? Are you alright?"

"Your mother's just tired, that's all. You just go and squeeze up next to your little brother and give him a warm, there's a good lad. I'll put the kettle on."

She heard the impatient clatter of the letter box, and as she moved to answer the door, she pointed Ben in the direction of Tommy.

"Go on, give him a quick rub."

"Alright, Monica," said Pamela, in her overly familiar way as she pushed her daughter forward and into the flat. The walkway was covered, but it had started to pour now, and the wind was sweeping the rain in towards the flats so that it made a light tapping noise as it struck the walls and windows. Monica closed in the door and then turned to face her neighbour, whom she might normally avoid, but on this wretched late Saturday afternoon she was glad for the company.

"The kettle's just on. Do you fancy a cup of tea?"

"Well, I'm not stopping, but if you're having one. It's been a bugger of a day." Pamela cast a quick glance at Lucy, whose mouth was smeared with chocolate. "Now," she said, "I don't want to hear you using any rude words."

"I don't know any rude words."

"No, you don't, and let's keep it like that. Go and play with Ben and Tommy."

But Tommy immediately bent over and picked up the toy

train that he had inherited from his brother and clutched it to his chest, clearly aware of what might happen next.

"Well, Ringo Starr's been giving it with the drumming on the walls again, so I went round and gave him a gobful, but you'll never guess what he tells me. The cheeky bleeder says he's reporting me to the council because I have too many visitors late at night. Like who? I said, not that it's any of his business, but he just kept insisting that we understood each other, gormless sod. I was steaming, but I couldn't just sit in the flat, so I went to the bingo with Lucy, and we were dead jammy and we won. Two quid. Amazing, isn't it? I keep telling you, you should come with me. Perhaps we'd get lucky and win some money, and then maybe we could go on holiday together."

She handed Pamela a cup of tea with a saucer, and then sat opposite her at the kitchen table.

"So where have you been all afternoon?"

"I took the boys down to the park by Stanhope Lane."

"But it's always so crowded down there, and it sometimes smells funny, don't you think? Bloody thousands of them. But you know I don't mean anything by it, don't you?"

Pamela's idea of a conversation was to occasionally draw breath and ask if Monica agreed with her before continuing to talk.

"Look, I've got an idea. I'm famished, so why don't we all have tea together? I'll go down the chippy and get us some fish-and-chips with the winnings, and then we can sit here and cheer each other up."

"Are you sure?" Monica tried to remember where she'd left her bag. "But we don't need to spend your winnings. We can pay for our own."

"I know you can, but you won't. It's on me." Pamela finished her tea and stood up. "Just excuse me a minute, will you?"

When Pamela came back from the bathroom, it was apparent that her neighbour had touched up her eyes and tidied up her "Autumn Sunset" hair, and she knew immediately that Pamela must have used her makeup and comb without asking. She didn't understand why Pamela had to dress the way she did in a narrow miniskirt, with nylons that tended to rasp when she moved, and a tight cream blouse that showed the bones of her bra. She was always dolled up like she was about to go out somewhere, and Monica knew that it was only a matter of time before she would discover Ben staring at Pamela, and maybe then she would be forced to say something to her friend.

Ben had his ear glued to his tiny transistor, but Tommy was sitting on the living room floor with a restless Lucy, who, much to Tommy's evident disapproval, was jumping up and down and switching the television set from one channel to the other and then back again.

"Now then, Tommy, don't you be a maungy tyke. Lucy's just trying to settle on something you'll both enjoy." But Tommy said nothing to his auntie Pamela, who turned instead to Monica. "He's a good lad, isn't he?"

Monica wished she could say the same about Lucy, but Pamela's daughter was a mean-faced little sprite with pursed lips who took no notice of anything her mother ever said. Then again, Pamela always made a big show of talking to her daughter in a loud, firm voice when out in public, but she suspected that behind doors Pamela dispensed with the talking and knocked the lass about with the flat of her hand. Which, of course, is why Lucy played up so much when she was out, for she knew she wasn't going to get hit.

"The boys will share a portion, right?" As ever, Pamela's question was delivered as a statement. Monica wanted to ask her to bring the boys a portion each, and if they couldn't finish theirs, then she would eat any leftovers, but she smiled gratefully and nodded.

"A portion between them will be fine."

She knew that Pamela would get Lucy a full portion and eat whatever her daughter couldn't manage, but that's just how Pamela was. Outside, they both heard a rumble of thunder, and then the rain began to sizzle against the balcony.

"Oh, Jesus, I'd best be making tracks before all hell breaks loose."

Pamela was drenched when she returned from the chip shop, but it would have been really grim if she hadn't borrowed Monica's belted raincoat and her flimsy umbrella, whose fretwork was admittedly a little buckled out of shape but had still managed to keep most of the downpour off her friend's head. It turned out that Pamela had ordered extra scraps for the boys, so their one portion was more than enough, but Lucy could eat only half of her fish. Much to Monica's surprise, Pamela offered to share the other half with her and quickly broke off a piece and passed it over without further comment. When everybody had finished, Monica balled up all the paper and pushed it in the dustbin, and then rinsed out the empty bottle of dandelion and burdock and placed it on the side so that it was ready to go back for the deposit. Then she set about putting the worn-out boys to bed. Once they were safely tucked up, she piled some blankets on the floor between them and made a makeshift bed for Lucy, and kissed the girl on the cheek before closing in the door to the bedroom.

Pamela was sitting at the kitchen table and had already helped herself to a small glass of brandy from the bottle that Monica kept in the cupboard to the side of the stove in case she ever needed some for cooking.

"Like a glass?"

Her friend poured Monica some brandy without waiting for a reply. There were no windows in the cramped kitchen, but they both knew that if they went through to the living room, they would risk waking up the children with their conversation. In any case, the view through the open curtains of the living room was depressing, with the dual carriageway down below and traffic streaking by in both directions, and then beyond the road the belching emissions of factories that struggled to operate around the clock.

Pamela lit a cigarette and slowly blew out the smoke. "Only a few weeks to go now till the kids' summer holidays. I can't wait, can you?" But of course, Monica could wait, for the summer holidays meant putting the kids in the day care centre, and paying for them to be looked after until she finished work at the library. Pamela packed Lucy off to her parents, and so she was totally free, but this option wasn't open to Monica, who, aside from the odd letter from her persistent mother, had pretty much cut off contact with home. Last year Pamela had come around to the flat with some brochures for Majorca that she'd picked up at the travel agents, but Monica knew full well that the closest that Pamela had ever got to Spain was a weekend in Blackpool with an insurance man called Steve whose name, she had made clear, she never wanted to hear again.

"Perhaps this year the two of us can go off to Scarborough?" suggested Monica. "Or maybe somewhere else, just for the day."

Even as the words came out of her mouth, she was aware of how impractical this was, for getting somebody to watch the kids at the weekend would mean finding extra money she simply didn't have. Mind you, the more she thought about it, the more she asked herself if there might be somebody at the day care centre who would be willing to do her a favour and take them on for a Saturday or a Sunday?

"Really? You'd come with me to Scarborough?"

She watched a visibly surprised Pamela pour herself another brandy.

"That's great, Monica. I've always said that you need to get out more. It will do you good, and you'll be in a better mood for the kids. In fact, how about tonight? Why don't we just pop out for a quick one, the two of us?"

"Tonight?"

"Maybe we could go to the Mecca Ballroom and have a dance? I went once, and lots of women our age go by themselves. It's not just young lasses, and it's not a pickup place if that's what's making you go all dithery; it's just somewhere that people have a good time and talk. You've never been, have you?"

Of course, she hadn't been, and she wasn't even sure if she knew how to dance properly. She tried to redirect the conversation.

"We can't just leave the children."

"Yes, we can, they're asleep. Our Lucy's out for the count, and there's no way she'll get up till eight in the morning. You don't mind if she spends the night here, do you?"

She wondered if this had been Pamela's intention all along, to leave Lucy with her and go off gallivanting.

"Look, there's no harm in the two of us going out. It doesn't make us tarty if that's what you're thinking."

Which was exactly what Monica was thinking. She stared at her friend, who drained the brandy from her glass in one gulp.

"Are you sure you wouldn't rather stop in and talk?"

"Well, it's up to you. If you're frightened of what folks might say, then let's stop in, but you know you can't live your life like that."

Pamela tossed her hair back and lit another cigarette. In this half-light she looked beautiful, but Monica knew that the real source of her friend's attractiveness to men would be her confidence, for she never gave out the impression that anybody could knock her off her tracks.

Monica put on her only dress, the blue one that her mother had bought for her before she went off to university. She had last worn it to the library on her first day at work, but it became clear, simply by the way that Denise was looking her up and down, that she was overdoing it, so unsure if she'd ever have an occasion to take it out again, she'd put the dress away. It was made of blue satin, with a bow on the front by the bust, and it was all she had to dress up properly for a night on the town. She felt funny using her own comb after Pamela had used it, but because she'd recently snipped her hair short, these days it needed only a few rapid strokes. Monica gave her face a hasty towelling and then took a deep breath. It was evident that she wasn't that pretty, and she had long accepted this reality as a bearable fact of life, but when she was set against Pamela, the full extent of her plainness was all the more noticeable. She carefully hung the towel over the side of the bath and realized that at the moment her main source of worry was not her looks but her raincoat, which, having had fish and chips pocketed inside it, would stink, as, in no time, would her dress.

"Well, how do I look?"

She heard Pamela lie and say "marvellous," but she knew that at thirty-one she looked ten years older, and most days she felt it. A trip to the hairdresser's was top of the list of things to be done, for having had a good go at her hair with the kitchen scissors, she desperately needed the ends trimmed and the whole mess straightened out. And of course, her nails were a disaster, but it was too late now.

"I'll have a quick check on the kids?"

Monica stepped quietly inside of the boys' bedroom and gently moved Tommy's hand from his face. Then she looked down at a peaceful Ben and Lucy before closing in the door behind her.

"Well, Mary Poppins?"

"The kids are asleep."

"Good, we won't be long."

Pamela insisted that since it sounded like it was only spitting now, they needn't bother with coats, which was something of a relief. Monica quickly hung the smelly raincoat back up on the hook by the door.

✦

Pamela had made the Mecca Ballroom seem like a quiet and civilised little place, but Monica had never seen anything like it. From the outside it could easily be mistaken for a cinema, but once they stepped inside the foyer and out of the sprinkling rain, she could feel the combined energy of noise, music, and lights just beyond the double doors. In front of them a shabbily suited man sat behind a desk, tearing tickets off a roll and dropping the money into an oversize metal cash box. He sat up straight when he saw her friend and greeted her by name ("Hey, Pam!") in what he clearly hoped might pass for a gangster movie accent, but Pamela ignored him and snatched the tickets and then pushed her way through the double doors without turning back to make sure that Monica was following behind.

The dance floor was before them, but Pamela started to climb the circular staircase to their left, and once they reached the balcony she claimed a small table near the railings from whose vantage point they were able to survey the antics below. While Pamela went to the bar for two rum and Cokes, Monica looked all about and could see that the balcony encircled three sides of the dance floor, and was decorated with tables and chairs and the occasional settee where people could relax and drink until they were ready to once again take the plunge. Downstairs, girls were dancing in groups around their handbags, while blokes dawdled against the walls, smoking their cigarettes and trying to muster enough courage to make an approach. She could see that the downstairs girls were all sturdy curves and improbable inclines, and compared with them, she wasn't much. Up here on the balcony she was marooned with the less glamorous set and the drunken men who, too shy to approach any lasses, had decided instead to drink the night away. She was older than most of the people, and as she saw Pamela teetering back towards her with their two drinks, it struck her how ridiculously formal her own dress must look, and she began to ache with embarrassment.

The two men at the next table kept looking at her and Pamela and smiling, but her friend didn't seem to notice. Monica knew they were being talked about, and she had a sense that these men were not being kind. She held her glass of rum and Coke in both hands and tried not to look over in their direction, while a preoccupied Pamela propped herself up against the balcony and conducted a running commentary on who was here, and who was with whom, oblivious of her friend's discomfort.

"Have you seen Angela Marsden's top? She's barely in it. Always queening it, she is."

Monica was fully aware that she had lost the years in which you were supposed to learn what to do in a situation like this. While she was still living under her parents' roof and studying for her exams, she had no interest in going out to places like the Mecca Ballroom. Other girls went, but they were the types she wasn't keen on mixing with, and even if she had wanted to go out with them, they would almost certainly have shunned her. During her first year at university she made a conscious effort to attend the Christmas Ball, but the young men there affected to take delight in both her accent and her blue dress without showing any real interest in her beyond the obvious. For Monica this was the final indignity, and she thereafter retreated to her room, where she buried herself in reading for the rest of the year. At the start of her second year, fearful that she might completely lose sight of herself, she decided to seek friendships and alliances outside of her college and eventually discovered the Overseas Student Association, whose members seemed better able to recognize her. And now, all these years later, she found it ironic to think that finally here she was, in the Mecca Ballroom, but suffering from all the same insecurities that as a teenager she had intuited would plague her were she ever to set foot in a nightclub. As she continued to gape at the gyrating dancers, she knew that she ought to get a grip and make the best of the situation, and at least try and enjoy herself.

"I beg your pardon." She suddenly heard Pamela, who was now leaning back in her seat, addressing somebody. She turned quickly as her friend continued. "Are you talking to us?"

The two men from the next table were idling over them, drinks in hand and with what they believed to be winning smiles on their faces.

"Well, we reckoned we'd come over before we go blind with staring. Can we join you?"

The taller, handsome one was doing all the chatting, while his less impressive friend lagged a little behind him, anxiously sipping at his pint of beer and quickly wiping away his frothy moustache. There was something about the friend's combination of cocky assurance and nervousness that made her immediately like him.

"Well," said the taller one, "we didn't know that we had a model agency in the town?"

Pamela rolled her eyes. "Does that usually work for you?"

The man grinned and shrugged his shoulders.

"Well, come on then, help us out. Are you local, because we've not seen you around. I'm Victor, and this is Derek."

"Victor. Derek." Pamela threw her friend a quick glance as though checking if it was alright for these two to join them at their table.

"Can we sit down? You know we're not going to bite."

"Alright, go on then."

Monica moved her chair closer to Pamela's, and while Victor sat on Pamela's right, Derek pulled up a chair opposite her so the two women wouldn't be hemmed in on both sides.

It was only after the men had settled into their seats that Derek held out his hand for Monica to shake.

"Derek Evans. I'm sorry if we've interrupted your evening."

He was a reasonably handsome, clean-shaven man, and his collar and tie were still firmly fastened, unlike his friend, whose dangling tie was complemented by the evidence of stubble. Derek Evans offered her a cigarette, and when she declined, he put the pack back into his jacket pocket rather than smoke alone.

"I don't mind if you smoke."

Derek smiled gently and shook his head. She guessed that he was probably about thirty and maybe a civil servant of some kind. He really didn't seem the type to be out trying to pull birds on a Saturday night.

"It's alright, I don't have to smoke. But I was thinking, if you're from around here, then I'm surprised I've not seen you before."

She explained to him that she was really from Wakefield, but she lived here and worked at a local branch library. She paused and then added the missing information:

"I live with my children. I've got two boys, Ben and Tommy."

When he asked if she had any snaps of them, she immediately felt bad, and worried that he'd think she was a failure of a mother. In the absence of any photographs she decided to describe the boys to him, and she said a bit about what they liked to do, how they both liked football and how Ben seemed to be taken with pop music. Derek Evans listened to her without once taking his eyes from her face. When she finished, Monica reached for her drink, and then from his wallet Derek Evans produced a glossy snapshot of his nephew and niece, regretting the fact that their mother, his sister, was emigrating to Canada next week because his brother-in-law wanted to make a fresh start out there in the building trade. He wasn't sure when he'd see them again, but he had a feeling that the kids would be all grown up by then, and he'd particularly miss the lad, whom he'd introduced to the junior football team that he helped out with on weekends.

"You can always make pen pals of the children and keep in touch that way."

"I suppose I can." He was quiet for a minute, then tucked the picture back into his wallet. "I hadn't thought of that. I like to do a bit of writing, and I'm always reading, but I typically use the main library in town, which is probably why I've not seen you. I'm partial to taking out books on rambling and bird-watching, as I'm a bit of a nature buff."

She watched as he took a quick sip of beer, as though eager not to lose the momentum.

"So do you like it then, at the library?"

For all his kindness and good manners, she knew that this was not the time to be sharing her ambitions of going back to university. After all, she hadn't told anybody, including Pamela.

"I suppose it's like any job. It can have its frustrations, but it's a job, isn't it?"

"I see. Maybe I'll drop by and visit one day, if that's alright with you?"

"Well"—she smiled—"it's a public library, so I can't rightly stop you."

Victor tapped the table with the bottom of his beer glass.

"Right then, Derek, it's about time you offered these ladies another drink, don't you think? Your round, lad, and look lively."

By the time Derek returned to the table with the pints of beer and two rum and Cokes balanced precariously in his hands, Pamela and Victor had decided to go downstairs to the dance floor. Monica craned her neck over the edge, but she couldn't make them out in the swell of heaving bodies, and for a moment she wondered if Pamela had deliberately abandoned her with this Derek. But at least he was a gentleman, so she didn't feel too worried.

He explained that he and Victor worked on the *Post*, and while nowadays he'd moved on to the management side, Victor was still a reporter. As she listened to him patiently explaining both his job and his prospects, she speculated as to what would become of her two boys when it was time for them to enter the world of the opposite sex. Would they frequent places such as this and try and pick up lasses? Would they be brash and know-it-all like Victor, or more gentle, caring souls like this Derek?

"Would you like to dance?" When she heard his voice, she snapped back to attention and realized that the music had changed. The dance floor was now speckled in shards of turning light as couples held on to each other.

"I hate to admit it, Monica, but I'm not a very good dancer. That said, it seems a shame to come here and not give it a go, don't you think?"

She was too nervous to answer him directly, but she knew that it would be rude to ignore his question, especially as she could feel his eyes upon her.

"Will it be alright to leave these drinks on the table?" She coughed nervously. "I mean, nobody will take them, will they?"

The first touch was difficult, as it had been so long, but once she got used to his hand on her waist she started to breathe again as they both attempted to shuffle purposefully in the cloying mist of cheap eau de cologne. She looked over his shoulder for Pamela, but she still couldn't see either her friend or Victor, so she closed her eyes and didn't resist when he made a move to pull her closer to him. The music was a mystery to her as one slow song blended with the next, and she assumed that he might expect her to know the names of the groups that were singing, though quite honestly she hadn't a clue. Sometimes she'd put on a pop music station to liven things up as she made tea for the kids, but while Ben seemed to like the music, she soon grew bored with the noise, and much to her son's disappointment, she would turn off the wireless and encourage him to go and watch the television instead.

As Derek escorted her to the top of the stairs and began to usher her back in the direction of their table, she noticed that Victor's hand was resting on Pamela's leg in the space between the hem of her skirt and her knee. Her friend appeared to be either unaware of this act of trespass or comfortable with his hand, but either way Monica found it unnerving. There was also a second drink standing beside the still-untouched round that Derek had brought from the bar. She took up her seat and spoke to nobody in particular.

"You'll have to excuse me, but I don't know if I can drink that much."

Victor immediately made a grab for one of his pints and raised it in a toast.

"Of course you can. Drink up, Monica. To us."

She lifted up her glass, but as she did, she noticed how Victor was looking at her, and she now had a good idea of what he thought of the two women that he and his pal were drinking with, but it was too late to say anything to Pamela.

Monica couldn't really remember what happened next, for everything began to go fuzzy and she felt a headache setting in. Victor insisted that Derek go to the bar for yet more drinks, although she remembered Derek's suggesting that they finish what they had in front of them first, but Victor teased him and called him tight, and so Derek reluctantly stood up from the table. Once he'd gone she had nobody to talk with, for Pamela had scrunched herself into Victor so completely that her skirt was riding up near the top of her nylons and Monica wanted to throw a blanket or something over her. When Derek came back, he pretended not to notice her friend's performance, but the awkwardness didn't last, for Pamela soon came up for air and started talking thirteen to the dozen. Then Victor sent Derek back to the bar for another round, and then another. At some point all four of them were on the dance floor, that much she was sure of, and they were dancing as individuals, not as couples, but Derek never took his eyes off her, which made her feel anchored and grateful. At some point, Monica remembered, the room started to spin, and Derek offered his arm, which she took, but the stairs back to the balcony were definitely steeper than earlier in the evening, and it seemed like there were more of them. Derek sat her down at the table while he went to the bar for a glass of water, and it was only now that she picked up on the fact that the place was starting to empty out, and for the first time all evening she felt truly unsure of what she was doing.

It was Victor who suggested that they go for a drive in his Ford Cortina and look at the moonlight on the river. Pamela jumped in the front passenger seat while Monica slid into the back next to Derek, who kept both hands on his knees and gazed out of the window. She was adamant that she didn't want to do this, but nobody would listen to her when she muttered that she ought to be getting back. Before the car engine even started, Victor grabbed hold of Pamela and they began to engage in a bout of quick, open-lipped palaver that was only interrupted by Derek's half-pleading, half-laughing "Hey, come on." Pamela collapsed in a fit of giggles, and Monica closed her eyes and listened to the laboured cranking of the car engine as Victor tried to start it up. When they got to the river, Victor peeled Pamela from around his neck ("Chuffing heck, pack it in for a minute will you, Pam?"), and the two men excused themselves and began to stumble towards the water. In his haste Victor had left the driver's door wide open, so Pamela reached over and pulled it shut and then hoisted herself around so that she was facing the back seat.

"They're alright these two, aren't they? And they've got brass." Monica shifted her head so that she was now looking in the direction of the two men, who stood on the bank of the river clearly competing to see which one of them could pee the farthest. Pamela began to shriek. "I mean look at them, pair of daft clots. What are they like?"

This was a question that a confused Monica was beginning to ask herself, for in her presence Derek seemed reserved and almost timid, but with Victor he appeared to willingly take on the role of comic sidekick as though the pair of them were some out-of-date music hall act. As far as Monica was concerned, Victor just didn't come up to scratch. She opened the back door and stepped out of the car, and careful to make sure that she wasn't facing the river, she began to gulp the warm night air. She looked up at the stars in the black sky, and then she asked Pamela if she could see the clouds moving. Monica began to turn in a circle, and again she asked Pamela the same question, and then she asked it again, but Pamela wouldn't answer, and then she felt Derek drape his arm around her neck like a warm scarf, and then he moved it down across her moist, sweaty back and lifted her into the rear seat of the Cortina. She heard him tell his friend that they'd best be going as it was getting late.

Victor searched through the cupboards in her kitchen, noisily pushing cups and saucers to one side until he found four ill-matched glasses, which he placed on the small table.

"You don't mind, do you, Monica?" Pamela was smiling at her. "I told Victor about the brandy, for I'm not sure what I've got at my place."

Victor paused before pouring, as though he had suddenly re-membered something. Then he reached over to the stove and hauled himself up and onto his feet.

"What happens at the end of the picture before you go out?"

Victor didn't wait for an answer. "National anthem. Let's have a good rousing singsong to show some respect."

Victor began singing, but Derek lunged across the table and pulled him back down and into his seat.

"The children, Victor. We'll have to keep it down, alright?"

An annoyed Victor smiled sarcastically and began to pour, but Monica took this as her cue to stand up.

"I'm sorry, but I've got to go and make sure they're still asleep."

Derek also stood up. "Shall I come too?"

"No, please. I won't be a minute."

Pamela giggled. "Our Lucy can sleep through a thunderstorm and not twitch a muscle, isn't that right, Monica?"

Monica stopped and, looking at her friend, noticed that she could now see the black roots of Pamela's "Autumn Sunset" hair beginning to emerge like blighted crops.

She quietly cracked the door and peeped through the darkness at the two boys, whose breathing was shallow but regular. Some days it felt as though the two kids were drawing the stamina right out of her body, for she was forever chasing them, or picking up after them, or placating one or the other, or simply begging them, but for better or for worse they were all she had, and not a single day passed when she didn't remind one or the other of them that they had a responsibility to look out for each other. Ben's arms were splayed above his head as though he was waving to a friend with both hands, while Tommy was curled into a tight ball with one half of his face entirely buried in the pillow. Between them, on the makeshift bed on the floor, Lucy slept on her back with her thin lips parted so a discordant nasal whistle sang out with every breath. Jesus Christ, what was Pamela thinking of? When they pulled up at Arnhem Croft, her friend didn't say a word, and she just led the way until they all were standing on the walkway outside of Monica's flat.

"Well," said Victor, "are we stopping out here all night waiting for the tooth fairy?"

For some reason Pamela found this side-splittingly funny, and because she began to roar loud enough to wake all of the neighbours, Monica decided that she had no choice but to quickly find her keys and open up the door, feeling, not for the first time, that Pamela had let her down.

When she walked back into the kitchen, only Derek was there. He was sitting at the table and quietly drumming his fingers against the side of the half-empty bottle.

"Where did those two go?"

Derek half stood as she took up a seat, which struck her as an oddly polite way of going about things. However, she had to admit that she quite liked it.

"They went to your friend's flat to see if she can find anything else to drink. Victor's not much of a brandy drinker."

She eyed the bottle and arched her eyebrows. "Really? You could have fooled me."

She wanted to ask him why he went along with playing second fiddle to his obviously more idiotic friend, but this wasn't the time.

"What about you?" he asked. "Are you partial?"

What kind of an antiquated phrase was that? It was like this Derek Evans was talking to somebody twenty years older. She guessed that he probably spent a lot of time with his father, or grandfather, down the allotments or going to dog races, or engaged in some other manly pursuit where the vocabulary of one generation could be casually absorbed by the next without any regard for its relevance to the present time.

"I'm not much of a drinker as I don't get out that often."

"I see." He pushed the bottle away from them a little; then he looked at her and smiled. "I meant to say, back there at the Mecca, that I thought your dress was smashing. But seeing it now, in the light, so to speak, it's even better."

"I bought it when I went to university. Or more accurately, my mother bought it for me, but I felt a bit out of place in it tonight."

"No, you weren't." He stopped suddenly, as though aware that his response might be interpreted as being overenthusiastic. "You looked grand, but I didn't know that you went to university. It's just that you don't meet many lasses, or lads for that matter, who've been to university. Well, at least I don't, although we're beginning to get some applications now from students who want to begin on a regional newspaper and then work their way down to London."

"Is that what you're hoping to do? Work your way down to London?"

He laughed nervously, but Monica could see she had put him in a bit of a bind, for his eyes made it clear that he was trying to work out what it was that she wanted to hear. Either he wanted to go to London, and he therefore viewed the north as inferior, a kind of stepping-stone, or he was happy to stay put, which might give her the idea that he was a bloke without any kind of ambition. She regretted putting him in this predicament, and wished that she could take back the question.

"London's a big place, isn't it? I've been, but just the once to visit the Imperial War Museum. I used to be into history, particularly anything about the last war, but I've not got much time these days. But it was a great day out, riding on those red buses, and I even got on the tube a couple of times." He paused and lowered his voice. "Listen, I know it's none of my business, but I was just curious if there's a dad in the frame. For the boys."

Now it was her turn to laugh. "Well, if there is, I think you'd best be making your exit before he gets back." She paused and watched his alarmed face. "I'm only joking. Would you laugh if I told you that I've hardly ever been out with anybody? I once wore this dress on a date with a chap at university. He took me to see a film called *Giant*, a western, and all I remember thinking was, Is this picture ever going to end because I'm ravenous? And when it did end, he never asked me out again."

"Is that so?"

Now that she was able to get a good look at Derek she could

see that he really wasn't anything exceptional. Average height, sandy-coloured hair that was prematurely thinning, and a nice face, if a bit podgy; however, his charm was his best feature.

"Well, *I'd* have asked you out again, that's for sure. I think I told you, I'm a bit of a nature buff. I'm fond of rambling."

Monica smiled to herself. She had nothing against nature, but it wasn't really her thing. In fact, she didn't even like plants in the flat, for they grew so slowly you could never tell what they were up to.

"I'd like to kiss you, but I'm not one to force myself upon people. But would I be right in thinking that there'd be nothing wrong with a kiss?"

Monica reached over and took a tiny sip from her hitherto untouched glass of brandy, and then she put it down and braced herself, for she knew that she wasn't going to be able to stop it from happening. She wished that this man could have found the courage to kiss her on the dance floor in the darkness while he'd had his hands on her waist, and while nobody could have possibly seen them, but he had been too busy playing the gentleman. Now he was getting her involved in the process, which she instinctively knew was the wrong way to go about these things. He reached over and placed a slightly clammy hand to the side of her face.

"I'll stop whenever you say."

"No, Derek, they'll be back."

His collar and tie were now unfastened, and as he listed towards her, she could smell the alcohol on his breath.

"I'm pretty sure they'll not be coming back, Monica. Not if I know Victor."

She suddenly remembered how messy and noisy kissing could be. It was nothing like in the films, and as she felt her mouth drawing tight in anticipation, she closed her eyes and promised herself that she wouldn't resist.

Monica lay back on the bed and looked up as the man reached clumsily for a cigarette and lit one. She watched the tiny orange circle glow into life as he took a deep pull. "I hope you don't mind," he said. She touched his cheek with a finger as though making sure that he was for real; then she noticed his surprisingly weak chin. She tried not to think of the chaotic trail of clothes that she imagined lay on the floor between the kitchen and her cupboard-like bedroom, but she realized that at this very moment she should be factoring in the consequences of one of the children's waking up and walking in on her.

Derek was concentrating hard, and then he blew a perfectly formed smoke ring, which gave him another reason to be pleased with himself.

"Do you have anybody special, Derek? I should have asked."

He carefully laid the cigarette down on the pack in such a way that the lit end was hanging over the edge of the box and would burn itself out at the filter. Then he rolled over next to her and pulled her close.

"I do now."

He moved in and kissed her quickly on the mouth.

"I'm not like Victor, with birds everywhere. As I said, I'd be keen to see you again."

"Go steady, you mean?"

"Well, one step at a time, but something like that. My situation's a bit complicated as I've got a wife, and so has Victor, but unlike him, I'm kind of separated."

She watched him disengage himself from her, and then he hauled himself out of the confusion of bedding and propped himself up on a supporting arm.

"We were really young when we wed, so things haven't been that straightforward."

She felt as though she'd been slammed up against a wall.

"Look, I'd best be going before your boys wake up."

"They're fast asleep, but I should probably go and check."

"No, you're alright." He clasped a gentle hand to her shoulder. "You look great just like that."

When exactly, she wondered, had he worked the wedding ring off his finger? She could see him looking closely at her, as though somewhere inside of himself he was celebrating a kind of muddled triumph.

"I'm sorry, Monica, but I've really got to get back."

She watched him spin slowly out of bed and begin to step into his underpants. Then he lit another cigarette and picked up the now-empty pack and went in search of the rest of his clothes. She heard water running in the bathroom, then the toilet flush, and then he was back standing over her and raking back his straw-like hair with one hand while carrying his shoes in the other. She guessed that he must have flushed both the old and the new cigarettes down the loo. He gestured to the shoes.

"I don't want to wake up the young ones, so I'll put these on outside."

She pulled the sheet around herself and swung her legs around so that her feet were now touching the floor. Doubling his chin, he looked down at her.

"I'll come and see you at the library," he said. "Really, I will."

"It's the Ladyhills branch," she said. "Not the main one."

Monica wanted to add, the one with stained carpet and old volumes that smell of dirt and dust; the branch where men wait for me to climb the ladder before they sneak a look up from their books.

"I know which library." He stooped slightly and kissed her on the forehead; then he tousled her short hair and smiled. "And I've left my work number on top of the telly with my extension and everything, so they'll put you right through."

"Thanks."

"Maybe we can go for a drink after work one night this week? Just me and you, not Victor or your friend. Would you like that?"

It didn't make any sense to suddenly start feeling bashful, but she nodded and looked down at her crooked toes. When she raised her head, he was gone, and a moment later she heard the painful screech of the front door closing and then the click of the lock as it jumped into place.

Monica was alone, but she could feel herself hovering on a

precipice and in danger of being swept away by a torrent of emotions, among which guilt and shame featured with some prominence. She left the bedroom and quickly picked up her clothes from the kitchen floor. She puzzled as to why he had rescued his own but left hers lying there. Then she put the chain across the front door and hurried back to the bedroom and flung her wrinkled dress and knickers and bra on top of the dishevelled bedclothes and pulled on her dressing gown, but she couldn't afford to linger. Her task in the kitchen was clear. She washed out the glasses and put away the now depleted brandy bottle and continued to try to hide any sign that her flat had been visited by these people. Once she was satisfied, she checked on the children and discovered Lucy staring up at her with eyes wide open, although the girl's body remained rigid with fatigue. "Go back to sleep, love." She looked at Ben and Tommy and remembered their afternoon in the park, and what a slog it had been to get them back to the flat as the rain began to fall. But they were good kids, all of them, even Lucy, and it wasn't their fault. None of it was.

In the living room she leaned up against the window, where drops of rain were shivering to life and then transforming themselves into thin, hesitant lines as they descended the pane. Down below she saw a man crossing the new bridge over the dual carriageway, and then scuttling down the stairs on the far side by the brewery. It was him, Derek Evans. Maybe she would write to him at the *Post* and simply say thanks, and tell him that she'd had a good time. She already knew that calling him on the telephone would be too much for her. If somebody else picked up the phone, she'd only get flummoxed, and how was she to describe herself? Jesus, Monica, what have you done? She could see that up in the sky there were no clouds to obscure the thin pendant of moon and speckling of stars, and down on the ground no evidence of the late-afternoon storm, aside from the odd puddle that cars continued to splash through. Despite the light drizzle, the world seemed quiet, peaceful almost, and then she noticed that he'd left his empty pack of cigarettes on top of the television set, and a dog-eared business card and a ten-shilling note were tucked underneath it. She picked up the discarded box and moved it to one side. He'd left money for her, which meant that either he'd got the wrong idea about her or he really cared, but as she turned and watched him disappear down the street that ran parallel to the brewery, she didn't know what to think.

IV

THE FAMILY

The creaking of the door announces the late-morning arrival of her dear sister, who she knows will be bearing a discreetly lacquered tray upon which a bowl of broth will be carefully balanced. A full submission to nourishment will be demanded of her before she is left alone to linger through another feverish day. She opens her eyes and attempts to lift her head from the damp pillow, but the weight is too much. She unseals her lips and moistens them with the tip of her tongue, and then moves her mouth in an attempt to form words, but no words emerge. Through the slender window she can see the naked branches of the oak tree beating frantically in the keen morning wind. The funereal December light illuminates this macabre dance. Heavy limbs, like her own, but she never danced. *I never danced.* Not once, although Papa never forbade it. *Five girls and not one of us a dancer.* Branwell frequently danced in the streets of the village when befuddled with drink. The rascal son who danced, but not the girls.

She watches attentively as Charlotte sets down the tray on the chair next to the narrow bed. Her clothes make a tremendous noise. Silk on cotton. Cotton on silk. Once again her sister is occupying too much space in the room. *Dear, dear Charlotte. Please, no more of this.* But she must be considerate to her sister, for she understands that it was her own guilty preoccupation with the worlds of the

Grange and the Heights that occasioned a distance to grow between them. *Please, Charlotte. Forgive my selfishness.* An arm begins gently to burrow beneath one shoulder and tunnel its way across her back. A free hand cradles her head, and in one unhurried motion her bones are levered up and forward. She can feel Charlotte calmly stuffing a dry pillow behind her, and then her sister releases her, and—lo and behold—she is balanced upright. Charlotte's are affectionate brown eyes, although around their perimeter they are now decorated with the furrows of age. When her sister smiles, pages of the calendar turn. Poor Charlotte: her one true love released her, and no one was there to catch her as she fell.

Her sister places the tray in her lap and then waits, silently willing her to eat but unsure if the invalid will be able to manoeuvre the delicate spoon to her own lips. Dear Charlotte. How long ago was it? A year? Two years? Walking quietly into the Black Bull to rescue Branwell and overhearing her brother and his quarrelsome friends speaking uncharitably of "the plump one." Her brother's wolfish smile and mocking laughter continued even as his vulgar friends fell speechless. Poor gin-soaked Branwell, seemingly determined to ride at speed towards ruin, who later that night leaned heavily against her, merriment spilling unhinged from meaning, as she led him by the arm up a moonlit Church Lane and back in the direction of the Parsonage.

Charlotte guides the spoon into her sister's mouth. At the foot of the bed the maid is unfolding an extra blanket to assist against the day's raw chill. The busy woman works swiftly, aware that her presence in the room is an intrusion best kept to a minimum. The door is partially ajar, and as Charlotte redips the spoon into the broth, they both can hear Papa preparing tomorrow's sermon in his study. She is her tall, gangling father's child, unlike Charlotte, who takes after the mother whom neither sister can fully recall. The numbness of loss followed them out of childhood and pursued them into adulthood. Again Charlotte proffers the spoon, but she now turns away and looks at the wall. Anne will be in the kitchen either sewing or reading her Bible by the hearth, and waiting for her eldest sister to return and report on the condition of their poor Emily. And then perhaps later one of them will convey to Papa the news that there has been no restoration of health, but only after he has finished committing his sermon to memory. Only then may Papa be disturbed.

Again she turns her head and rejects the spoon and its watery contents. The maid removes the tray from her lap while Charlotte takes a lace napkin and dabs prudently at the corners of her mouth. A deft expression of caring. She can now see that the morning light is already fading and the afternoon is preparing to set in misty and cold. Beyond the swaying tree, beyond the church, are the wild moors that call to her to rise from this confinement and race purposefully into the December wind and observe the landscape in its winter colours. *I must go. Let me go.* But the blundering sound of the maid edging her way out of the room breaks the spell. She is now released from the moors and delivered back to a place where a shadow cavorts on the wall as the tree continues to sway.

Charlotte speaks soothingly, but with a tone of fearful imploration elegantly threading its way through her sentences. Her sister wishes to know if her constitution remains obstinately weak, or does she detect any renewal of strength? *I am stricken and sinking fast. My hands tremble, and there is little feeling in my lower limbs. Would it help to make complaint and declare with resignation that I am permanently out of health?* Charlotte persists. Perhaps she might welcome a visit from tenderhearted Anne? *Surely only the most desperate would interpret the spectre of my pale, thin figure as being suggestive of a return to natural exuberance.* Emily stares at her somewhat overdressed sister, who is now perched solicitously on the edge of the chair with a familiar gloom in her aspect. The plump one. *No, that will not do, Branwell. Drunkenness is one vice, cruelty another.* Her brother stopped abruptly by the tall wall, leant his head against the cold stone, and emptied his stomach down towards his boots. *Please, Branwell. Papa keeps a respectable house.* He stood straight and gracelessly wiped his mouth with the tail of his coat, and then moved off boldly as though resolved to prove that he was now able to walk without assistance.

She followed, watchfully maintaining a dignified distance, enough to create the illusion of independence. However, she remained close enough that she might intervene with haste should her stumbling brother scuff his freshly stained boots against a protruding cobble and lose his footing.

Charlotte repeats the question. *Anne? Graceful Anne, forever suffering from a troublesome cough or a malady beyond known remedies. Wise Anne.* She has no memory of denying Anne access to her room. The full grip of the sickness has occasioned days and nights to swim away from her and be lost, but she would never agitate to keep dear Anne at a distance. Perhaps Charlotte has misinterpreted some half sentence mumbled in the depths of delirium and relayed this careless utterance below? She stares at Charlotte's round, tired face and then closes her eyes and lets her brother's name form on her lips and tumble out into the world. Her sister takes her hand and almost inaudibly reminds her that he has gone, but where she refuses to say. To Leeds or to Halifax perhaps? To London again? This unkind paucity of information is now Charlotte's way, and a small surge of despondency begins to crest within her. Surely, after all these years, Charlotte cannot still be holding bitterness in her heart because she refused to return with her to the Continent. Or is it simpler than this? Perhaps the evidence of this emaciated object has frightened her sister and made a leaden weight of her tongue? *Where is Anne? Is she basking in the warmth of a lively fire by the hearth?* She feels Charlotte squeeze her hand with an unexpected urgency and then release it. And now her suddenly voiceless sister sits back in the plain wooden chair and anxiously knits her own hands together. Her sister seized her with some violence, and the perplexing memory of Charlotte's impulsive gesture can still be felt as a warm imprint.

✦

Really, had they ever delighted in a close intimacy? Truly close? Six years ago they left Yorkshire and journeyed south to London before continuing on to Belgium. Two moderately impetuous maiden sisters travelling together, submitting themselves to a heroic adventure in the hope of acquiring an improved proficiency in the French language. They fully understood they were neither attractive nor fashionable, but they had been raised to eschew the approval of others. Papa had reluctantly given his blessing, and he hoped that they would watch over each other and safely deliver themselves back to his doorstep. After all, what could he do? Perhaps journeying was in the girls' blood? His own pilgrimage had taken him from the Ireland of his birth to Cambridge, where he had studied with anxious intensity as a shy and stammering commoner. His transformation from Patrick Brunty to Patrick Brontë fooled no one, and his attempts to scour the Irish brogue from his tongue and his halfhearted endeavour to dress above his station provoked ill-suppressed laughter. His priggish mien grew more intense and silent as he became aware that to his contemporaries he was an object of entertainment, and the handful of undergraduates he regarded as potential intimates soon began to avoid the ignominy of being seen in his orbit. The final stage of his own adventure saw him migrate north to Yorkshire, where he felt no inclination to impress any among his flock, and where he maintained an aloof and zealously gauged distance from the people of Haworth.

She peered into the churning waters of the tempest-tossed English Channel and realized that with this moonlit voyage she was now roaming beyond her dear father's imagination. The waves lashed the sturdy vessel, and she clung with wet hands to the rail and reeled back and forth, allowing herself to be baptized by the haze of briny spray. Charlotte was held securely in the clench of seasickness, and lay below deck, turning restlessly on her bunk, but she understood there was little she could do to alleviate her sister's turmoil. Charlotte had dropped and declined hurriedly, but Emily knew that this affliction would soon be resolved after a short, hard conflict that, at this stage, would benefit little from the consolation of human empathy. Above her the black sky was choked with stars, the same glorious constellation that jolted her sensibility on her late-night walks behind the Parsonage. She greeted her familiar heavenly companions and ignored the cry of yet another crew member who urged the long-legged woman to leave the deck. Ma'am, please. It will be safer for a lady down below. No doubt, no doubt. She offered the terrified young man an upwardly tilted chin and the faintest trace of a smile, before familiarizing him with her willowy back. She was travelling home tonight in the company of a forbidding wind. *Young man, if it will bring you peace, then you must take shelter.* Again she lifted her head to the skies. *Let those who need shelter seek it out.* She whispered, *Go, seek it out.*

Through the bleary windows of the carriage the sisters could see little but flat, ill-manicured land swimming out in all directions, and only the occasional scruffy village disrupted the monotony. After some time the villages began to embrace one another and form a town, and suddenly the town began to grow into a city. Brussels revealed itself without the fanfare of London's vociferous certitude. A continental city, melancholic in appearance, apologetic in tone, it remorsefully busied itself as though afraid to be discovered slacking. Her sister retained a pallid countenance from the exertions of the crossing, and once again she closed her heavily lidded eyes and allowed her head to loll sideways against the glass. Then Charlotte blinked furiously, as though embarrassed to have been caught in a moment of weakness, and she watched as her debilitated sister adjusted her slumped posture and readdressed her attention to the spectacle of the somewhat overcast city they had now entered.

Like a prison, she wrote. *Dear Anne, Monsieur Heger's school is like a prison with its high stone walls and heavy press of silence. I feel an iron weight constantly anchoring me to the earth. He simply wishes me to imitate the style of others, thus obscuring my own vision. I am twenty-four years of age and see no reason to stoop before the tyranny of this senseless man. In this school of learning I learn nothing except how to retreat into myself and survey the world about me with apathy. I am stimulated by little except the unwelcome aroma of one tedious day exhaling into the next, and time carries me forward against my will*. She informed her fragile sister that her French had improved considerably, so much so that she was able to think and even dream in the language, but Monsieur Heger was almost certainly not the cause of her advancement. She characterized him as a young man who exuded an elaborate sincerity that was ruined by his determination to grin and display his polished teeth. She read constantly, and having made a selection from the books in the small library at the back of the single classroom, she would bustle back to the tiny quarters that she shared with her travelling companion and once again indulge herself. A freshly rejuvenated Charlotte regularly volunteered for extra lessons with the master, and Emily therefore often enjoyed sole occupation of their room and was able to fully embrace her moody solitude. Occasionally she would venture forth and stroll in the gardens, where she risked encountering her captivated sister listening attentively to whatever it was her master was saying to her, the pair of them oblivious to her ghostly presence. At such moments, she made it her business to seek out the shadow of a broad tree that might enable her to linger unobserved. Poor Charlotte, who gazed upon the professor with ill-disguised ardour, was abandoning the modest dignity of an inner life for the farce of a fluttering heartbeat. In Brussels.

On Sundays they travelled out into the city and visited with a family with whom their father had connections, the origins of which were buried beneath any clear understanding on the part of either sister. However, after a half-dozen Sundays, the visits began to corrode into an obligation, which Charlotte tried desperately to make light of by taking control of the conversational territory. While riding the carriage towards their destination, her sister regularly compiled a list of topics to be discussed, and she rehearsed the order in which the subjects were to be raised. On encountering this insipid continental family, whose cakes and teas they both found unspeakable, it was Charlotte alone who made the effort to rescue the afternoon from catastrophe, while Emily retreated into an implacable silence that hinted at shyness, although her lustreless eyes invariably betrayed boredom, and her general demeanour indicated that she cared little for anyone else's opinions.

Late on Sunday night, the two sisters would prop themselves up in their uncomfortable beds and read their grammars. She oftentimes stole a look at Charlotte and silently apologized for her behaviour. She understood that her well-practised hostility made it impossible for Charlotte to engage in elegant repartee with their hosts, and the deathly quiet return journey in the lumbering carriage would be interrupted only by Charlotte gathering herself and then meekly scolding her headstrong sister. As daylight began to fade and their passage home continued, she would glance briefly at a discomfited Charlotte but say nothing, which seemed to temporarily satisfy her older sister, who, for some reason, always appeared to be transfixed by the cheerless views of the streets of Brussels through the begrimed windows of their carriage.

She stood in the cooling shadow of a spreading beech tree, her back to the pitted bark, her toes steadfastly gripping the soles of her shoes, which, in turn, marked the grass. The master was once again displaying himself in an immaculately tailored suit of clothes, and encouraging the overly studious gazing of the young woman who sat obediently next to him. It was unmistakable, to all but the besotted, that his allure was undermined by his inability to move beyond his charm. He stood and took his leave, playfully lacing his way through a line of trunks and ambling towards the elegantly carved door. He threw a quick, final glance in the direction of the bench, a look calculated to cast himself in a kindly light, before nimbly mounting the three steps and disappearing into the house where his wife would no doubt be waiting patiently for him. She watched Charlotte lift the plain envelope to her face with both hands and then smell its scent. This man was operating upon her with a fully conscious determination. Once again her sister drew the perfumed air to her and allowed it to overwhelm her senses. A fragrance meaning what exactly? From her concealed location, she witnessed poor Charlotte drift.

It was the week before Christmas, and they were squeezed

together in the back of a post-chaise that haltingly picked its way across the solemn moors in the direction of Haworth. This was the season when the desolate light of day simply expired and was quickly swallowed up by a sudden tide of blackness. It had been a tiresome journey, and her troubled sister had travelled with a sorrowful, closed heart that she knew would refuse any sentiments of sympathy. To offer solace would be to irritate, and so she had resigned herself to watching the dispiriting drama of Charlotte's further relinquishing governance over her emotions. Driving rain began to lash down and beat an impatient cadence on the roof of the flimsy box, but mercifully it was now possible to see the beacon light of a solitary candle sputtering in an upstairs window of a far-off inn, and the horses begin to trip with renewed verve. Charlotte, however, remained consumed by her deep melancholy. Her sister's petals had closed in upon themselves. She was returning to Papa as less than that which she had been.

The girls were back home, and on their first afternoon Papa extended an invitation for them to take tea with him. The house was empty, for according to Papa, Anne's teaching duties would delay her return until Christmas Eve. She assumed that Branwell was out frolicking with his friends, but they would not speak of the brother and the son, for the strain of doing so would cause Papa pain and embarrassment in equal measure. The son had become an object of scorn in the village; he was no longer a carefree young man with an untidy mop of red hair and a convivial face that radiated optimistic goodwill to all. Papa's son was a drunk who appeared intent on punishing himself for having squandered his talents and abandoned any ambition, and Anne's letters had been charged with an anxiety that Branwell might soon be found residing beneath the church flagstones. Apparently, when their brother was not swilling gin or begging threepenny packets of opium pills, he had taken to charging about the countryside in a filthy cart pulled by a wild horse in a manner that implied he knew of no other world beside that of the farm.

But they would not speak of the son. The maid had spent the

afternoon baking, and she generously laid out the cakes and poured the tea. Emily could hear an excited Keeper barking and agitating for her company, for according to Papa, he had truly languished during her absence. However, the dog need worry no more, for she had no intention of returning to Brussels after this Christmas break, and Keeper would once again have her by his side. She glanced at her sister, who had no experience with the art of dissembling, and whose brown eyes brimmed constantly with tears. Regretfully, she accepted that the blame for this pitiful display could not be entirely borne by Monsieur Heger, for she had come to believe that, prior to their departure, her sister's condition was such that her poor heart was ready to be cleaved by any man wielding interest. A bewildered Papa smiled at his daughters, and took his tea in silence.

Her bed felt strangely uneven, and the room was cold, but after the frustrations of the Continent she was relieved to have returned to the Parsonage. The rigours of travel had incited her hair to curl uncooperatively into an unruly, tangled ball, and the whole knotted mess nested uncomfortably on her head as though unfamiliar with the scrutiny of a comb. A sideways glance in any looking glass simply confirmed her irregular features; the sharply angled nose and the unappealing protrusion of her mouth were distinctions she had learned to live with, but she would always quickly avert her eyes. Through the slither of window, she stared at the brooding black sky and promised herself that never again would she range beyond this world. Her confidence had been much improved by exposure to the mediocre abilities of the dull girls at Monsieur Heger's school, but now she was home and able to issue out for a walk on the moors whenever she wished. Her poor sister would shortly discover that she must make her return journey alone, and risk having her heart truly shattered by the triumph of her own foolish urgings over the reality of her mentor's situation. Emily drew a strand of corkscrewed hair away from her eyes and continued to stare into the darkness, knowing that she would not sleep until she heard dear Branwell staggering up Church

Lane. However, while she waited, she once again climbed the short, steep staircase of her imagination, and again she found herself dreaming of the boy who came from the moors, and she listened to the sound of pebble-dashed soil drumming hard against the lid of a plain coffin, and she turned over and curled up in her mind and began to search for her boy.

✦

And now she hears her sister quietly rise to her feet and begin to sidle her way out of the room. Poor Charlotte. Her second year in Brussels poisoned her fortitude, and she returned home with eyes that flashed in all directions without ever alighting upon a single object, and an agitated disposition that refused to be drawn into any conversation on the wretched subject of her professor. She wrote increasingly imploring letters, but the master's wife eventually answered, and then there were no more letters and Charlotte finally released this man whom she had foolishly captured in her thoughts. Indeed, her sister did allow herself to grow plump, but time eventually took her in hand and by degrees soothed the pain of her loss. However, while Charlotte gradually recovered her equilibrium, Emily continued to wander in her mind out onto the moors, where she pulled the landscape gloriously tight around her like a worn green blanket and hid herself away. When she returned to this world, she took charge of the maintenance of the Parsonage, while her eldest sister looked on in puzzled amusement that Emily might find contentment in cooking and cleaning. Once she had finished performing the household obligations of a servant, however, she would again balance her portable desk upon her knees and exchange the sterile pleasure of this life for the soaring joy of her heather-clad world.

She hears Charlotte cautiously close in the door behind her and then begin to walk softly back in the direction of the kitchen, where she will report to Anne on their sister's unchanged situation. Oh, Anne, poor Emily remains unreachable, and to question her is to risk introducing great uneasiness in her pale, thin body. Anne will nod uneasily as Charlotte continues. At regular intervals her obstinate cough becomes trapped in her throat and causes her breath to rattle, but our dear invalid claims the situation is entirely tolerable and wishes to be a burden to none. Knowing that they have little choice but to pray and wait, Anne will put down her sewing and begin to replenish the smouldering embers.

Charlotte will not report to Papa, who has shown no desire to present himself at the bedside of his ailing daughter. Half the family gone, but still, he refuses to bestir himself and offer his fading Emily the comfort of his company. His stern demeanour and distant sentiments appear to be entirely unaffected by the predicament of his poor child. They used to be close, especially after Charlotte's return to Belgium in search of love, for this departure left father and daughter alone in the Parsonage. Each morning he would set a mark at the end of the garden in the direction of the church spire, and then give his lanky girl instruction in how to shoot a pistol. Keeper cowered in fear, and Emily brandished the weapon with a presumption that almost made her father forget the accident of one son. Standing tall, his whiskers brushed back scrupulously against his cheeks, his eyes bright and glassy behind his thin wire spectacles, Papa would warily move her elbow into the correct position, and she would concentrate hard and then scatter the crows. Of course, she always hit the mark. How well you have done, my dear Emily. She would smile, and then momentarily retreat to the kitchen and continue baking bread or ironing clothes, and simply wait until Papa had reset the mark, and reloaded, and was once again ready for her to resume practise. As she bounded from the kitchen in her unalluring clothes, she would cry out, *Papa, are you prepared? Are you?* It is now wrong of him to hide away and edge furtively into her room at the dead of night when he imagines that she is asleep. Or has she been dreaming this? Tonight she will lie awake with her head snug in the clammy nest of the pillow and wait for the whispering of Papa's stocking feet. She used to listen for the sound of Branwell's drunken braying, which heralded the pageant of his disorderly arrival, but now she waits for stealthy

Papa with her eyes open, and she dreams of a swift recuperation to accustomed vigour, and she hopes that Papa might revive her like a sudden burst of moorland air.

✦

And again she remembers: between father and son a gap widened by expectation and disappointment. The one feeding the other. Papa had sent Branwell to London to study art with the finest instructors in the kingdom, but the reports filtering back intimated that his heir was wasting his gifts and gratifying himself in the taverns of the capital. When Branwell finally returned, the two proud men looked upon each other and knew instantly that the time for conversation had passed them by somewhere on the road between Haworth and London. In truth, the experiment had been doomed from the beginning, for even as he silently packed his trunk in the simple room at the back of the Parsonage, the stubborn son understood that his disinterest in the rigours of study meant that he might soon be introducing failure into the world of his father. Poor Branwell, who chose now to make a sanctuary of the Black Bull. When the terse letter from the man in the next village arrived on Papa's desk, claiming that his son was carrying on an adulterous affair with the man's wife, Papa made it clear to Branwell that there would be no further sympathy or help, which served only to further stoke the fires of resentment between them.

The daily evidence of their brother's decline caused both Charlotte and Anne to grow increasingly ill at ease. The young man's beard was bedraggled, his clothes were unkempt, and Keeper growled each time Branwell slipped in and out of the kitchen door on his way to or from his tavern. Eventually an exasperated Charlotte and Anne abandoned their brother to Emily, who seemed unembarrassed by the task of caring for the failed artist, and each evening she was content to escort him upstairs and in the direction of his room before easing him out of his boots and making sure that his head was properly supported by a stout cushion. She knew full well that Branwell would have wasted hours in the public bar, inflaming his spirit with alcohol, advocating on the least popular side of all debates, and making a raucous pact with dissension whenever his fatigued colleagues proposed an honourable resolution to his illogical stances. Of course, his maddening obstinacy was informed by his knowledge that no matter how preposterous a position he adopted, irrespective of how brutally detached from reason he became, at the end of the evening, a gentle and compassionate hand would always appear by his side to conduct him to safety. *Sleep, sweet Prince. Put aside your torment.* And then, when she returned to her room, she would whisper, *Papa, grant him some air.* But in the morning, once again, there would be two men under a single roof and only enough oxygen for one man.

Even the roughest stone wears smooth and eventually offers no resistance. Branwell's final illness was swift, and he lingered only a week, during which time he became a smaller, frailer version of himself; suddenly he was a man who was too tired to dress or even leave his bed. His entourage from the Black Bull deserted him, and each sister took turn to sit vigil on his final journey around the face of the grandfather clock that stood on the staircase of the Parsonage. Papa turned the key in the lock on the door to his study. On the Sunday that he lost his thirty-one-year-old son, Papa managed to preach a long sermon without making any reference to his bereavement. His three daughters, their rigid and disconsolate bodies enveloped in black, occupied the family pew, and they could clearly see Papa's trembling hands as he clung to his text. The early-morning tolling of the bells had already alerted the village to the news that the fleeting conflict was at an end, but a stranger entering the church would never have suspected that the man with such disciplined posture, whose confident words rolled forth and filled every available corner of the stone edifice, had suffered a loss. A stranger would never have guessed the clergyman's plight unless, of course, he noticed the quivering hands.

And then it was time to conceal the red-haired son. She watched a now-impoverished Papa mumble his words and strive to hold down the pages of his leather-bound Bible. The sky continued to weep its drops of ice, and she could feel them in her palpitating chest. It occurred to her that her dear brother was perhaps attempting to wrest her with him. Papa fell silent and took the rainfall in the face, and then he decided not to wait. He turned and walked the short distance to the Parsonage door and closed it shut behind him. The three bareheaded sisters linked arms, her haggard figure in the middle, and they waited for the men to complete their work and repair the unsettled earth. Soon after, the sisters found themselves alone under the low, bruised sky, and Charlotte and Anne now realized that they were holding Emily upright.

✦

The truth is, since she took to her bed, she has lost sight of Papa. All that remains is the image of a sodden crestfallen man of God struggling to wrestle his Bible from the clutches of the wind before abruptly disappearing into the Parsonage. Poor Papa, over the years his losses have steadily multiplied. A wife, then two daughters, and now a son. Three surviving children occupy the house while he hides in his room. Once upon a time he would slip an arm around her waist and with the gentlest of touches raise her chin so that she was looking directly down the barrel of the pistol. Take aim. Now squeeze. Now rock with the blast, my dear. Don't fight it. The cold metal in her hands and Papa's warm arm laced tightly around her cumbersome, free-hanging skirt. She would take dead aim and scatter the crows. And then, after an hour of skipping between her duties in the kitchen and taking instruction, Papa would bestow upon her the briefest of smiles before reclaiming his weapon. But what was she supposed to do with this knowledge? *You have a son. I cannot be your son.*

Another day. The feeble morning sun spills through the window. Her austere, frost-kissed world is coming to life without her, but a calm of increased grace begins to console her mind. She closes her eyes and dreams of the boy who came from the moors, but she cannot see him. The boy who went back to the moors. She sees herself bounding tirelessly across the dry bracken and wispy grass in search of him, and she now enters a valley and finds herself running alongside a fast-flowing stream with long, unladylike strides and shouting to Keeper to concentrate and stay close. *Keeper!* She looks up at the sky, longing to vault from one cloud to the next; then she whistles loudly to attract the attention of her loyal wild creature. *Keeper!* She turns and stumbles, and now she sinks clumsily to one knee, her thin body racked with a seizure of coughing. Keeper nuzzles up to her side and continues to bark, but the boy has gone. She reassures her disquieted dog that all is well, for she knows that she will find the boy. A life reduced to one small window. This one view. The noise of her sister knocking gently on the door shakes her from her daydream. Again Papa has failed to visit. *But dear Papa, it would be so much easier if you would just come to me and allow me to uncouple myself from you and go in peace.* She listens as Charlotte pushes open the door and calmly closes it behind her. In a moment she will open her eyes and attempt to raise her head from the pillow. *Please, Papa.*

Dear Charlotte, do you remember when Papa deserted us for Liverpool and returned with the boy? The strange boy with blazing eyes who had lost his place in the world. Papa wrapped him in his cloak and brought him to us, do you remember? She feels her sister smoothing her brow and petitioning her to submit to the sombre inhospitality of the wintry day and attempt to rest. She knows that her sister has long ago forgiven her for abandoning her to heartache. *The poor wild child was standing before us.* When dear Charlotte returned from Brussels, she grew to accept that her younger sister was now dwelling in another place, and she asked Emily, Who are these unfathomable people with whom you spend your waking hours? But Emily would only smile distractedly, as she smiles now. She looks up into Charlotte's worried face. *Papa has little time for us, you do know this, don't you? As far as Papa is concerned, there was only the boy, and now he is gone, so what is Papa to do? Retreat to his room and mourn? He unwrapped the boy from his cloak like a gift he wished to share, and now the boy is gone.* Her sister lowers her voice. Please, Emily, you are confused. Your Mr. Earnshaw is another man. He is not Papa. Do you remember? *Like a gift he wished to share.* Her eldest sister continues to caress her brow, and Emily turns slightly and gazes at her and wishes that somehow she had been able to arrest poor Charlotte's descent into despondency, but she was too busy pursuing the boy on the moors, and her passion rendered her incapable of offering comfort to anyone. Even reticent Anne scolded her for her indifference, but surely her sisters understood that she could never behave with wilful disdain towards either one of them. *But dear Charlotte, Papa's boy lived with a ferocity that frightened the gods themselves, you know this, don't you? He deserved to be loved and protected, but it was the wickedness of the world that corrupted him. Papa's boy was too beautiful for this world, you do know this, don't you? You believe me, don't you?*

✦

It is early afternoon, and her eyes remain closed. Her dear sister has shared with her the hushed news that she reclines now on the black horsehair sofa in the more agreeable dining room. She can sense the presence of a quietly sobbing Charlotte continuing to sit vigil by her side, and she is obliged. Sadly, the eagerly anticipated gift of warmth has failed to materialize, and an icy draught pierces the room, for in her distress Charlotte has neglected to summon the maid to lay a new fire in the grate. However, it is too late, for she is overwhelmed and can fight no more. *Charlotte, I have waited for Papa, but now I must leave.* Too tired to raise her head, in her mind she whispers, like smoke, out through the window and onto her cherished moors. In the distance she is able to discern the silhouetted figures of three men on the horizon who appear to have just completed the digging of a hole in the earth. But for what or for whom? A dog, perhaps? She stands a safe distance off and clasps her bonnet to her head before the gust can strip it from her face. The fresh, dry air is healthier at this level and a pleasing substitute for the absent rustle of leaves. She was once forced to beat obedience into her dog, who loved her, but it was so, so exhausting, both the beating and the love. Now the three men lean against their tools and stare down into the chasm they have rent, and they wait. Having turned on her heels, she moves off slowly to the small stone farmhouse that is Top Withens and sits exhausted on a crumbling wall. What better place than this to commit a soul into the bosom of eternity? A beautifully bleak aspect and the steady flow of a beck, trickling unseen, in the valley below. Supported by stone and earth, she is ready now. She stands and pulls the hair from her eyes and begins to move down in the direction of home. She passes a craggy pillar with moss creeping up its foot; it marks the place where the pathway branches off to the right and back in the direction of the moors, which are now shrouded behind a thin veil of mist. She watchfully steps over the bare outcrops of rock that at this point litter the shallow earth that is too ravaged to nourish even the most stunted of trees. *Wait, I'm coming.* As the chapel bells begin to peal in the distance, she is blessed by the steady weeping of rain, which occasions a momentary smile to decorate her thin lips. She raises her eyes and sees Papa and Charlotte and Anne walking towards her at a lugubrious pace, the sisters flanked on either side of Papa as though ready to help him maintain his balance should he falter. She watches their leaden approach, and then she raises a hand in greeting. *May I join you?* They refuse to lift up their bereaved heads as they trudge past, leaving her rooted to the earth. She turns and follows them with her eyes as they walk towards the three men, who wait in silence. The rain begins to surge and swirl, and it saturates her bonnet. The first man moves urgently as he notices the approach of the father and his daughters, and he digs into a mound of freshly turned soil and carefully balances the stony dirt on the face of his shovel, before jettisoning it into the breach. She hears the noise of the debris thundering against the wooden box. She lifts her weak, gloved hands and covers her ears. She lives now in two worlds. She understands.

V

BROTHERS

3rd person/
memory Jones

The school secretary stops him as he is leaving the staff room and tells Mr. Hedges that a new boy will be joining his class, but he doesn't loiter to hear what else the woman might have to say, for her reputation as a gossip has been long established, and he doesn't like to get involved. A simple life uncluttered by marital obligations at home or any entanglement in petty disputes at school has served him well for nearly forty years, and he isn't about to lower his guard this morning. And now here is the boy, in the third row to the left, seated quietly behind a desk and looking pathetically out of place. She had shouted after him that the ten-year-old boy was in the care of the council, or a foster home, he couldn't remember which, but plainly something had happened to the lad, for it was highly unusual to be asked to try to assimilate a new face into the scheme of things once the term had started.

That morning Mrs. Swinson had made it her business to ensure that Tommy got to school in plenty of time to be introduced to the headmaster, who looked at them with a vacant squint and eventually remembered that it was this boy's older brother, Ben, who began school yesterday. Having delivered his long-winded speech about the new premises' being only two years old and the pride of the local education authority, and how in this school they'd given up the Eleven plus and brought juniors and seniors together (although, for administrative purposes, they liked them to start on separate days), he formally welcomed the new pupil and then pressed a dismissive button and let them know that his secretary in the outer office was ready now to receive them. An irritated Mrs. Swinson levered herself out of the chair, feeling put out by this man's rude button pushing, but Tommy, fascinated by the bald head behind the desk, bided his time for a few moments.

"Come on then," she hissed, glaring impatiently at Tommy.

Her stage whisper brought him back to reality, and he followed her into the outer office, where they were greeted by the jolly face of the school secretary. A humiliated Mrs. Swinson couldn't bring herself to speak to the woman, so she made a pantomime of buttoning up her coat and tying on a headscarf over her bun of grey hair.

"I'll see you after school."

She didn't wait for a response, and simply abandoned him to the care of the nice fidgety lady, who looked as if she would be better served working behind a shop counter and dishing out sweets.

"Are you ready to meet your new friends?"

He nodded and half walked, half ran after her down the full length of a long corridor and followed the secretary as she turned and entered an empty classroom.

"Just take this seat, love. The other boys will soon be coming in from the playground, but meanwhile I'll go and find your form teacher, Mr. Hedges. I'll let him know that you're here."

He sat with his arms folded and resting on top of the desk, but he was careful to pull himself upright so he wasn't slouching. Eventually, after what seemed like an age, the other pupils began to drift noisily into the classroom and look at him with curiosity before thumping themselves down behind their desks. Nobody sat beside him, which made him wonder if the desk was always free or if their hesitation was something to do with him.

"Quiet everybody." Mr. Hedges is looking directly at him. A round-shouldered, white-haired man with a chiseled face that appeared to have been manufactured in a quarry, he seems out of place in this modern school whose desktops remain unscarred by graffiti. "Well, stand up, young man, and tell us your name and where you're from."

Every head in the classroom turns, and thirty pairs of eyes are suddenly trained upon him. He pushes himself back from the desk and climbs to his feet, aware of how bizarre he must look in his oversize school uniform.

"My name's Tommy Wilson."

"And where are you from, Thomas?"

"I'm from England."

His fellow pupils release a volley of scornful cackling that threatens to swell into hysteria.

"Alright, alright, I'm not sure what you all find so amusing." Mr. Hedges scans the room before once again turning his attention to the new boy. "Well, Thomas, we were hoping for something a little more specific, but for now 'England' will suffice."

But every one of the thirty boys, who continue to stifle their laughter, feels sure that the queer apparition standing behind the desk has nothing whatsoever to do with their world, where despite the evidence of their brand-new modern school, people continue to live in back-to-back houses and washing is strung out across cobbled streets to dry on the breeze. They all know that the church is at the top of the hill, and the butcher, the baker, and the post office are at the foot of the hill, and the pub is somewhere in between, and it's blatantly obvious to each of them that this Tommy Wilson is most definitely a stranger.

"Well, sit down then, Wilson. I assume that everyone will introduce themselves in time, but for now you'll just have to muck in like the rest."

Again he hears sniggering.

"Are you asleep, Wilson? I said you can sit down, lad. This isn't the army, you know."

Mr. Hedges achieves the anticipated roar of laughter, and

a self-satisfied smile creases his lips. He has some sympathy for the stray, but he doesn't play favourites, and he isn't about to start now.

"You had better buck your ideas up, Wilson. You'll have to be on your toes to survive in these parts."

At noon the bell rings out, and as soon as Mr. Hedges picks up his books and papers and leaves the classroom, desk lids are opened and slammed shut, and the mad rush commences. Tommy follows the other boys, feeling the double humiliation of not having anybody to talk to and understanding that he will most likely have to ask somebody where the line is for those who have free school dinners. Once they reach the cafeteria he discovers it to be a raucous cavern of clanging confusion and raised voices, and he anxiously scans the room for his brother, but he can't see him. Perhaps the older boys eat in a different location? Despite the tight knot of hunger in his belly, he knows that this is neither the time nor the place to make a mistake, and so he turns and gently shoves his way back towards the door.

The gymnasium is in its own building behind the main school block, but between the two structures is a narrow gap into which neither sunlight nor noise from the playground can penetrate. He slumps down onto the shingles and leans his back against the brick wall of the school block. By pulling his knees up tight under his chin, he can make a ball of himself and therefore consider himself potentially useful. At the far end of the gymnasium building he hears a door smash open, and two boys in football kit, with shirts flapping out of their shorts, rush into view and head towards the playing fields. Intrigued, he stands and tiptoes his way along the loose stones until he reaches the gymnasium door, which remains invitingly ajar. Once inside he discovers himself to be in a changing room with its collection of shirts, jackets, and trousers hanging in seemingly random formation from various pegs, and he sees both white and black plimsolls and duffel bags scattered haphazardly on long benches and across the floor. He looks around and knows that he probably shouldn't linger, but this is the first time he has felt any sense of familiarity and comfort since his mother dropped him off at Mrs. Swinson's house on Saturday morning.

Mr. Hedges stands beneath the archway of the main entrance to the school with a whistle in his hand. The new lad is loafing by himself in the far corner of the playground, carefully watching two hastily assembled teams of boys playing an eleven-a-side match with a dirty tennis ball. The moment he saw the boy he knew it was an impossible situation. Thomas Wilson is not part of the group, nor does it look as if he'll be invited to join in. In fact, he suspects that timidity has most likely been introduced into the lad's soul by a neglectful upbringing. He sees it all the time—like whipped puppies, some of them—but there's nothing to be done, for on top of everything else, they can't be expected to minister to the welfare of the disadvantaged. They're teachers, not social workers, and it's an important distinction that some of his younger colleagues would do well to remember. That said, the curly-haired Wilson boy is clearly a special case. The lad has got his hands pushed deep into his trouser pockets, and occasionally he lurches and kicks out at the same time as somebody shoots, but then young Wilson remembers himself and quickly looks around to make sure that nobody has noticed. Mr. Hedges shakes his head. He blows his whistle and brings dinnertime to an end.

Tommy surreptitiously lifts himself off the chair and quickly hikes up his trousers so that none of the other boys notice what he is doing. He folds the waistband over and runs his hands to the sides to make sure that everything is even all the way around; then he plonks himself back down and slides forward so he is almost wedged under the desk. Their tired mother had left them with Mrs. Swinson on Saturday morning, but shortly after she went off back home, Mrs. Swinson took one disappointing look at their clothes and announced that she had no choice but to take them shopping that same afternoon.

"I've been doing this for a long time, and during the war I even had evacuees—Cockneys from London—dirty beggars all of them, and I couldn't understand a word they were saying, but at least their mothers knew to send them with some proper clothes. I mean, really. I'll wager she thinks she can use her depression as an excuse, but those plucked eyebrows give her away."

Tommy and his brother were each kitted out with a new blazer, a white shirt, and a pair of school trousers, but everything was at least two sizes too big. Mrs. Swinson made a big show of handing over the council vouchers, as though she wanted all and sundry to know that these two boys were in her charge and she was going out of her way to provide them with a roof and bring them up to scratch. But her mood changed when the man failed to produce the two school ties that she was anticipating, informing her that she would have to pay for them. Tommy was relieved, for at least there would be one item of clothing that they would not be required to grow into.

The four o'clock bell signals the end of the day, and a glassy-eyed Mr. Hedges looks up from his desk. He slowly draws his hunched body to its full height and surveys the room, the weight of his judgmental gaze falling on each boy in turn. Tommy is the new boy in the class, but he already understands that being assigned to this form means that he has probably drawn the short straw.

The boys push back from their desks, and as they file past Hedges, they hand him their exercise books, which contain the answers to the history questions that are still chalked up on the board.

"Good night, sir."

"Good night, Matthews."

"Good night, sir."

"Good night, Appleby."

He wonders if "Privet"—for Tommy has heard the other boys secretly referring to the teacher by this nickname—will remember who he is.

"Good night, sir."

"Good night, Wilson."

He worries about his answers, but this being his first day perhaps he will be forgiven for getting most of them wrong.

"Wilson." He stops but is afraid to immediately turn around. When he does so, he can see that Hedges has a biro in his hand and is gesturing with it towards his almost totally shrouded shoes. "I recommend a good-quality belt, if you get my drift?"

He hears some boys chuckling, but a quick swivel of Hedges's owl-like head restores order.

"Yes, sir."

He moves now with his eyes down, sure that everybody is laughing at him, and wishing that just one person—that would have been enough—could have made the effort to be his friend. He feels sure that when they see him play football, they will want to know him, but as he threads his way through the jostling crowds in the narrow corridor, he can't remember whether the games period is tomorrow or the next day. He does, however, remember where the toilets are. Once he has finished, he looks around and is surprised to see that the pristine walls are unblemished by either hastily scribbled girls' names or rumours and, increasingly implausible, counterrumours. He holds his hands under the cold water tap and quickly rubs them together, pretending that they're lathered in soap, and he begins now to focus his mind on the task of meeting up with his brother.

Tommy stands by the school gates and waits until the deluge of excited boys reclaiming their freedom becomes a dribble. He screws up his eyes, hoping to see Ben emerging out of the glow of the fading sun, but the rush of pumping arms and legs appears to have dried up entirely. And then he sees Ben standing nonchalantly at the bus stop across the street with a group of twelve-year-old boys all of whom are greatly amused by whatever it is his brother is saying. Tommy looks both ways and begins to cross towards him, but when he sees the embarrassment on Ben's face, he decides to keep walking. Behind him he hears his brother's raised voice ("See you tomorrow"), the chorus of voices that confirm the appointment

("Yeah, tomorrow"), and then the pitterpatter of a short, unenthusiastic jog that concludes when Ben reaches level with him.

"Hey, what's the matter with your trousers?"

Tommy stops now and turns and looks at Ben's grinning face.

"Pull 'em up, our kid. Simon Longbottom says you look like a dick."

"Who's Simon Longbottom? And what does he know about it?"

"He's my new best mate."

Ben pauses and points to a thin pipe cleaner of a boy who lingers by the bus stop as though waiting for Ben to disappear from view. Simon Longbottom's circular wire-frame glasses are recognizable as health service handouts.

"Him and some of the others have invited me to a boys' club on Thursday night."

"To do what?"

"I don't know, do I? Nesting in the woods. Maybe some footie."

Ben walks on, and it's now Tommy's turn to chase after his brother, who seems to have found a way to make Mrs. Swinson's baggy clothes fit his gawky body. He's noticed that whenever Ben walks in a group, even if he's lagging behind, it always looks as though everybody's following him.

"You know she'll not let you go."

"Well, I won't know that till I've asked, will I?" His brother loosens his school tie as he walks. "Our teacher, Mr. Rothstein, he sometimes calls us by our first names. And you know what else, it turns out that Simon Longbottom's dad is in the army, and he's got a skull and crossbones tattooed on his forearm. Apparently he's based in Germany, and before that he was in Gibraltar."

"Has he been?"

"Has who been where?"

"Simon Longbottom. To Gibraltar. And Germany."

"I don't know. I suppose so."

They continue to walk, but Tommy feels hopelessly inadequate given the evidence of his brother's second day at school. He puts his hand in his blazer pocket and gently cups his fist around the watch.

"You'll never guess what I found at dinnertime."

"Where did you get that? It's a beaut."

"I found it on the floor of the changing rooms. It was lying under a bench, and there was no teacher to ask or anything. It's one of those that you can wear underwater. Do you like it?"

"What were you doing in the changing rooms?"

"It was just somewhere to go, and the door was open. Do you like it?"

His brother shakes his head.

"You're mental, you know that, don't you? You're not supposed to just go into the changing rooms."

Ben begins to walk faster, and Tommy scurries after him and catches up with his openly frustrated brother as they turn into Mrs. Swinson's street.

"What's the matter with you?"

"Look, Tommy all you ever do is think about football."

"You're just copying what Mam says."

"Well, it's true. And I'll tell you what, when Simon Longbottom asked me if I had any brothers or sisters, I said no."

"Why did you say that?"

"Why do you reckon?"

Tommy pushes the watch back into his blazer pocket and tugs at Ben's arm.

"You're not going to squeal on me, are you? About the watch."

"Why should I care? You got yourself into this mess."

Tommy had hoped that the watch might be something that the two of them could share and take turns wearing, something that might make them forget Mrs. Swinson and her house. As he'd picked it up off the changing room floor, he was thinking only of his brother and trying to imagine the look on Ben's face when he showed him the watch. His brother has now stopped by Mrs. Swinson's front gate and is gesturing at him.

"Well, are you coming in, or what?"

Mrs. Swinson opens the door and looks down at them. She has unclipped her bun so that two strands of plaited grey hair now frame either side of her face, making her look like an old lady version of a doll.

"You're late. I was expecting you both ten minutes ago, so I called the vicar to see what I ought to do." They remain poised on the doorstep and look up at her. "Well, what are you waiting for? Let's be having you into the kitchen so I can take a good look."

They stand before her as she perches now on a stool by the Aga and pats Simla, the youngest of her three husky dogs. It occurs to both boys that they will most likely be inspected like this at the end of each day. Tommy looks over at the dogs, but he keeps his distance, for he doesn't much care for Simla and the other two. Mrs. Swinson blinks furiously as she speaks, but not in time to the words so everything appears to be frantic and out of control.

"Well, I explained to the vicar that you weren't quite ready this week, but he's looking forward to meeting the pair of you on Sunday. You have been baptized, haven't you?" She doesn't wait for an answer. "I don't know why I bother." She points at Ben. "And I don't want to see you with your tie like that."

"Sorry, Mrs. Swinson."

"And look at the state of the both of you. What am I supposed to do with this hair of yours? Can you run a comb through it?" Ben opens his mouth to speak, but she continues. "Well?" She points now at Tommy. "How was your first day at school? And you"—she jabs her finger in Ben's direction—"how was your second day?"

"It was grand." Ben immediately senses that he's said the wrong thing, but it's too late.

"Grand, was it? Well, be off with you upstairs and get changed; then I'll see you back down here for your tea, and for heaven's sake, no noise, for my head's splitting as it is, and Simla's feeling a bit under the weather."

Tommy puts on the clothes that he is used to wearing, and even though he's now back in short trousers, he feels a little better about everything. Ben has on long trousers as he's been allowed to stop wearing short ones, but Tommy can see that his brother seems disheartened to be taking off his school uniform. He watches Ben fold everything carefully and then open up the wardrobe and place his neat pile of clothes on the top shelf. The watch is lying on the bed, and Tommy picks it up and begins to strap it to his wrist.

"What are you doing?" Ben makes a grab for the watch. "Take it off, you prat. You don't want her to catch you with that, do you?"

Mrs. Swinson hasn't moved from the stool near the Aga, but she is now smoking a cigarette and making a big show of knocking off the ash into a saucer that she cradles in her lap. In the corner, the three dogs are curled up in their respective baskets and appear to be dropping off to sleep, but Tommy is never sure if they're just pretending.

"Well, the thing is, Ben, we'll need to know more about who these boys are and what it is they get up to at this club before we can allow you to go off with them just like that."

They eat their beans on toast and sip at their glasses of fizzy pop, but they keep glancing at Mrs. Swinson so she understands they are paying full attention. Ben has told her about Simon Longbottom, and how he usually comes in the top three in the class, and all about his dad's being stationed in Germany, and Mrs. Swinson has nodded sagely, interrupting Ben only to remind him that he shouldn't gobble his food.

Tommy's baked beans keep falling off the back of his fork, but he knows that this is the proper way to eat them, for their mother has drummed it into their heads that turning the fork the other way and shovelling them up is common. Tommy likes to think that she's looking at them both all the time, even though he knows that in reality she can't see them. However, whenever he tries to talk about her with his brother, Ben changes the subject or just gets annoyed and snaps at him, for it's clear that his brother is angry that their mother has sent them away like this.

Mrs. Swinson stubs out her cigarette and immediately fumbles around in the box and takes out another one. She pokes it in his direction, so there can be no doubt whom she's talking about.

"You ought to be more like your big brother and think on about joining the Cubs or maybe a church group."

"I don't want to join anything."

"I don't want to join anything." She mimics Tommy, and smiles at Ben, who chuckles approvingly. "Young man, you need to get your ideas straight. You'll soon learn that the secret to life is getting to grips with the fact that you can't always have what you want."

Tommy looks down at his plate and carefully cuts the last piece of toast into two, and then pushes some beans onto each bit. He's still confused and a little bit upset: Why would Ben tell Simon Longbottom that he didn't have a brother?

"You do know that when we go nesting, we don't keep the eggs." Ben carefully places his knife and fork together, and then looks up again at Mrs. Swinson. "We just like to count them, and then we put them right back in the nests."

"But you shouldn't even be touching the eggs. The mother bird's got them all nice and warm, and then you lot come along with your mucky hands and it's all back to square one."

"But is it alright to just look?"

Mrs. Swinson sighs deeply, and then once again gestures with the unlit cigarette.

"Your best bet is to just leave nature be, that's what I think."

It is now Tommy's turn to put his knife and fork together at attention and push the plate slightly away from himself.

"Well, what do you say?"

They both chorus, "Thank you, Mrs. Swinson."

"That's right. I hope I'll not have to ask in future. Now then, we've heard all about Ben's day at school, what about you? Before you go down to the basement to watch telly, I'd like to know what you've *both* been up to."

"Tell her about the watch."

He glares at Ben, who smiles weakly and then turns away and won't meet his eyes. Mrs. Swinson pauses before striking a match on the box.

"Well, what watch is this?"

"Tommy was telling me about a watch, but I reckon I must have heard wrong."

He suddenly feels angry, but he keeps his focus on the now-empty plate as Ben begins to stammer.

"I don't think I can have heard him right."

His brother is making it worse. Mrs. Swinson slips the cigarette back into the box, and then leans to one side so that she can place the saucer that she was using as an ashtray on top of the Aga.

"Well, Ben, either there is a watch or there's not a watch. Which is it?"

"I don't know," mutters his brother, which is the daftest thing he could have said, for now Mrs. Swinson has the bit between her teeth.

"Have you seen the watch, Ben?"

"Yes, Mrs. Swinson."

"Then you've told a lie, for you know full well there's a watch. Telling lies is a sin, but, as the vicar will tell you when he hears about this, we'll not be the ones judging you. We're all of us accountable to higher powers." She pauses. "Well? I, for one, would like to see the watch."

His brother's world is collapsing. The club on Thursday. Nesting. Simon Longbottom's dad and the army. Clearly nothing matters anymore because Mrs. Swinson now thinks his brother is a liar. He stares at Ben and wonders why on earth he decided to squeal.

Tommy puts his hand in his pocket and passes the watch to Mrs. Swinson, who is clearly surprised by this elaborate underwater model with an adjustable dial on the front.

"Now then, Sonny Jim, I want you to reason carefully before you answer me. Where did you get it, and don't be like your brother and think you're going to get away with any yarns, for I'm not fresh off the boat."

Tommy wishes that he'd just left it where he saw it and hurried out of the changing rooms, for Ben now looks as if he's ready to burst into tears.

"Well, I'm waiting. Come on, I don't have all day to be sopping up your dumb insolence."

"I found it, Mrs. Swinson."

"So, you're sticking to that cack-handed story, are you?"

"It's the truth. I found it in the changing rooms."

Ben coughs and puts his hand to his mouth to stifle the sound. "It's true." His brother has a scratchy throat, so he coughs again. "Tommy found it at dinnertime, and he was going to report it to his teacher."

"And how exactly do you know this? Were you in the changing room with him?"

"Yes."

Mrs. Swinson laughs scornfully. "And if I ask you again, are you going to continue to try and bamboozle me with more of your lies? Always the brightest kid in the year, your mother said, but you don't seem that clever to me."

Ben lowers his eyes, and the room gives way to a devastating silence, made all the more painful by the triumphant smile on Mrs. Swinson's face.

"You know, for a moment there I thought I might have got you two wrong, or at least one of you." Her eyes bore directly into Ben. "But you, Mr. So-called Brainbox, you're nothing more than a barefaced liar." She looks now at Tommy. "And you're a thief. In a fix, aren't we?"

Tommy watches Ben wipe away his silent tears with the sleeve of his pullover, and he feels nothing but intense hatred for this miserable woman, who is not their mother and never will be.

"Away to bed with the both of you. Tomorrow morning we'll return the watch to its rightful owner, by which time I expect to hear the whole truth. Am I making myself clear?"

Tommy can hear her downstairs locking up the house. When they came upstairs, Ben wouldn't talk to him, and he simply got into bed and turned his back. He knows that Ben has nicked a lot of stuff: sweets from corner shops, packets of biscuits from the new supermarket, stacks of comics and records. Ben has even taken money from the pockets of clothes hanging up in the cubicles at the swimming baths. (Ben told him that the teacher lined them all up and gave them a piece of paper and asked everyone to write down who they thought did it, and they all wrote down his name, while Ben wrote down "Colin Green.") But unlike his brother, Tommy has never nicked anything in his life, and he didn't nick this watch, he found it, and no matter what Mrs. Swinson says, he's not going to say anything different in the morning. He hears her plodding slowly up the stairs, and he looks again at his sleeping brother. He and Ben used to talk about everything, but all that seems to have changed. Mrs. Swinson opens the door to their bedroom and pokes her head in. He keeps his eyes squeezed shut until he hears her pull the door to, and then he listens for the snap of the switch as she turns off the lights in the hallway. Maybe things will be different tomorrow, but if they're not, he's still not going to change his story. She can call him whatever she wants to, but he didn't nick the watch.

They stand together by the front door and wait for Mrs. Swinson. It's obvious that Ben has been crying, for his eyes are all bloodshot, but Tommy doesn't say anything to him. Today his brother's school uniform hangs sloppily, and Ben looks as though he needs more sleep. Mrs. Swinson, however, has put on her powdered face as she tries to look bright and breezy, but as far as Tommy is concerned, she resembles a clown, and she smells of dog. She retrieves the black umbrella that's leaning up to the side of the door and looks daggers at them both.

"Well, have you anything to say before we set off?"

Tommy defiantly gives her the eye and watches her crabby face curdle into contempt.

"I didn't think so."

It has rained overnight, and as they attempt to match Mrs. Swinson's brisk pace, they keep an eye out for the slack water in the gutter, which sprays up every time a car or bus races by. When they reach the school, Tommy sees two older boys in the playground who stand together, bags abandoned on the rain-drenched ground between them, quietly arguing as though their lives depended upon whatever point they were trying to make. As Tommy passes by the boys, he catches sight of their prefect badges, and he assumes they have to get to school early to carry out some duty or other to which they've been assigned. To the side of the gymnasium, a mopey boy of about his own age is kicking a football up against the wall with a hypnotically monotonous rhythm, and Tommy notices that the boy's school shoes have already been scratched so badly that no amount of polishing is going to help. Only a few vehicles are parked in the staff car park, and being a new boy, he's not sure which car belongs to which teacher. Mrs. Swinson leads them inside the main school doors and pads her way down the long corridor and knocks loudly on the staff room door.

A grim-faced Mr. Hedges carries his mug of coffee with him from the staff room. When he and his party reach the classroom, he tells the two boys to sit at the two desks in the middle of the front row. Mr. Hedges takes a sip of his coffee as he crosses the room and shuts the classroom door, and then he moves back to Mrs. Swinson's side, and the two adults look down at them both. Mr. Hedges takes another sip and then rests the mug on his desk; he takes the watch from the woman and fingers it as though he has been asked to place a value upon the timepiece.

"Well, I'm not aware of any boy reporting a missing watch."

Tommy stares at him, daring him to ask a question. Mr. Hedges turns to the woman with the umbrella.

"And did Thomas tell you where he got the watch?"

"He took a watch that isn't his. In my books that's stealing."

"He found it," Ben shouts. "She said Tommy took it, but he never did. She's a liar."

Mr. Hedges holds up his hand with the watch in it. "Now steady on a minute. There's no need for that sort of thing."

"She called me a liar and our Tommy a thief, but it's her who's lying. He found it on the changing room floor, and he was going to give it back. Our Tommy just wanted to show it to me."

"Is that right, Thomas?"

He nods, but he can't take his eyes from his impassioned brother. Mrs. Swinson snorts, then laughs.

"The pair of them must think we're simple. I mean, come off it, look at them. Getting the truth out of kids like them is like trying to get blood out of a stone. They'd steal the milk right out of your coffee. Somebody's parents will have saved like billy-o to buy that watch as a birthday present or a Christmas gift." She glares directly at Tommy. "You can't just take it and not expect consequences."

Mr. Hedges looks at the woman and tries to work out why she's so angry. She's not exactly acting like a guardian, but he generally does everything possible to avoid extracurricular situations, which is why he was so taken aback that this woman thought it perfectly fine to come hammering on the staff room door with her loud demands that he listen to what she had to say about one of "his boys." She points at Tommy. "Honestly, Mr. Hedges, I think that one's a bit funny in the head, and if you ask me, they both want a good clout to brighten up their ideas." Mr. Hedges considers the red-faced woman, then looks at the two resolute boys, who sit quietly behind the small desks, and then at the watch in his hand.

"You know, perhaps you two boys should step out into the playground." He addresses Tommy. "Is it alright if I hold on to this watch for now?"

Tommy nods and stands.

"I'll have a word with you both, in here, at dinnertime, al right?"

They look at Mr. Hedges, whose stony face flashes them a quick smile as they file past him and out of the classroom.

✦

Ben and Tommy stand together in the playground. They watch Mrs. Swinson pass slowly through the school gates and then turn left. It has started to rain again, but she walks with the umbrella still rolled up as though she has forgotten she has it with her. More pupils seem to be milling about now, for there are only ten minutes to go before the bell that will signal the start of the school day. As Mrs. Swinson finally disappears from view, Tommy recognizes Simon Longbottom loping towards them with a huge grin on his face, but Ben speaks before his new friend can say anything.

"I'm talking to my brother. I'll see you inside."

Simon Longbottom looks thrown, so Ben repeats himself.

"I'll see you inside. I won't be long."

They both watch as Simon Longbottom uses his forefinger to push the wire frames of his rain-spattered glasses a little farther up his nose. Then Ben's new best friend reluctantly moves off, all the while casting disconcerted glances over his shoulder. Ben turns to face his brother.

"Is Mam coming this Saturday?"

"I think so." Tommy coughs and then offers further clarification. "She said she was if she can get time off from the library. But I suppose it all depends on her nerves."

"I know." His brother pauses. "I'll see you at dinnertime. And tonight I'll meet you over by the gates." Ben quickly gestures with his head. "Four o'clock sharp."

Tommy hears the bell for registration. However, he waits until the last boy has dashed out of the toilets and in the direction of his classroom. He bends over and puts his mouth to the tap and starts to drink the icy water, and when he's finished, he draws the arm of his blazer across his mouth. Alone in the toilets, the only noise he can hear is the sound of a broken lavatory constantly flushing and the squeak of his rubber-soled shoes as he moves anxiously from one foot to the next. Today is his second day at this school, but he's hopeful that it will be better than the first. And it could be that this Mr. Hedges is alright. Not as bad as he thought.

VI

CHILDHOOD

"Leaning on a Lamp-post"—George Formby

1st person

Ben?

It's years since I've seen one of those tellys. They look like a brown ice cube, and all the edges are rounded, and the screen's a bit like a goldfish bowl. These days you never see them in people's houses, and I bet they don't even have them in museums. The old-fashioned tellys are so strange that most people coming across one might well be inclined to think, bloody hell, what's that? That said, were I ever to clap my eyes on one of them, I'd be fascinated because of the memories it would bring up. I remember watching our set with Mam. Just the two of us on a Sunday afternoon, sitting in the living room of the new flat in Leeds and our Tommy asleep in the bedroom. I don't know why, but I like to imagine a scene where I'm standing up tall in a cot and clinging to the top rail and peering in fascination at the flickering black-and-white images, but I know that, being six years old, I was sitting bolt upright next to her on the settee, my little legs sticking out, and I had both hands threaded neatly together in my lap as though I was trying to please her.

I remember the Arnhem Croft flat really well, but it sometimes makes me sad that I can't remember that much about where we used to live in London. I know that it was small, and I'm sure that it had an inside toilet because in those days having a toilet in the house was still something of a big deal. Mind you, I can't see

Mam ever putting up with sharing a privy with other people. She seemed to take a lot of pride in insisting that we might not have had much, but at least we had standards, repeating it like it was a piece of scripture. What I do remember is that in the London living room there was a cupboard with a wooden train set that was stashed away, and I had to reach up and open a door and grab it from a shelf if I wanted to play with it. I wasn't supposed to do this, but if nobody was looking, I knew that I could just about reach it. I don't remember ever playing with the train set in Leeds, for after all, we had a telly now. Come Sunday afternoons it was just me and Mam, and sleeping Tommy, and the telly and the sharp smell of the gas fire if it was really cold out. I remember us once laughing together at a film that starred George Formby, who was gormlessly dashing about all over the place on a motorbike. He was funny, and we both loved the fact that he was behaving like a clot, but when the film was over, I've not got a clue what we did. Truth be told, I've no idea what we'd have done before the film, although I do know that, despite the evidence of a nice new bathroom in the flat, at some point every Sunday Mam stood me on a chair in the kitchen and gave me a strip wash, reminding me all the while that cleanliness was next to godliness.

What I do remember about London is that life was better outside the flat than in it. Our London street was quite wide, with tall houses on both sides and a café opposite us that we looked down on. There was a wall at the far end of the street, and if you got on your tiptoes and pulled yourself up, no doubt chafing the tips of your shoes as you did so, then behind the wall you could see slack water. I thought it was a river, or maybe a canal, but it was probably just the filthy runoff from some factory. However, as a child, I thought it looked splendid. After all, there was this mysterious body of water, and it was right at the end of my street. Of course, I'm pretty sure that I wasn't allowed to go to the far end of the street by myself, so it must have been Mam who took me. I also remember going with her to a park that was under a bridge at the end of a main road. The park was little more than a steep, grassy hill that you walked up, and when you got to the top, you could look down and see right into a football ground. If it was a Saturday afternoon, then you could hear the noise and see the little spindly men running crazily around like clockwork toys, and I loved this and used to try and follow the match. Mam would smile and ruffle my hair. You've got lovely hair, Ben, but you'll have to be careful that you don't catch nits when you start up at school. If you do, they'll shave it all off, and you'll feel a right charlie. I looked up at Mam, who would usually be staring off into the distance, and then the sudden roar would tell me that somebody had scored a goal. You like your football, don't you? And you know the names of all the players, don't you? I'd nod confidently, but she'd just smile and say, give over with your fibbing.

On the way back to the flat she'd take it upon herself to remind me of the players' names. Morrison, Chapman, Harvey, Connolley, Adamson, Connor, Firth, Young, Lewis, Appleton, and Smith. She'd laugh and then tickle me. Come on, you big soft lump, I know you can remember them, although come to think of it, I've no idea how *she* knew them. I suppose she must have memorized them from the papers, and she probably thought it was the sort of thing that boys ought to know. She'd make me practise the names till I got them right, and then she'd give me a gobstopper or an aniseed ball as a reward as we made our way back home. Come on, we'd better get a move on. Mam would reach down and take my hand, and with her other hand she'd push Tommy in the pram, and together we'd head off in the direction of the main road, where, during the week, the lollipop man patrolled the crossing when the children started to come out from school. This was the same school I was slated to attend come September. Once, when we were crossing the road right by the school, I noticed that one of my shoelaces had come undone, and so I stopped, and Mam bent down to tie it for me. Of course, in the end, I hardly spent any time at that school because we moved north to Leeds and left Dad behind.

I have a really clear picture in my head of the day a red

double-decker bus got stuck under the bridge near the park, and how everyone came out and stood in the street and gloated. I don't think anybody was hurt, but you'd have thought that the circus had come to town, for people were standing on the pavement and just gawping. I also have a good picture in my head of the rag-and-bone man trundling by our London flat with his horse and cart. Any old iron? I'd rush to the window and hop from foot to foot and beg Mam to take me downstairs and let me see the horse, and the few times that she did I could see that the horse looked even sadder and more clapped out than the rag-and-bone man. The man would slowly take his cart up the end of the street by the wall that held back the water and then do a clumsy U-turn and come rattling back with the same sad clip-clop sound. Any old iron? We never had anything to give him—nobody had—which makes me wonder why he bothered. At night Mam sometimes gave me an extra-big hug as she tucked me and Tommy into bed, and I liked that. I remember the train set, and the park and the slack water, and the rag-and-bone man, and the names of the footballers, and our Tommy in his pram, and the occasional extra-big hug. I also remember Dad. However, when we moved to Leeds, it was just me and Mam and Tommy and the telly, and George Formby behaving like a clot, and me and Mam used to laugh together on a Sunday afternoon while Tommy slept, and George Formby seemed to make her happy.

"My Boy Lollipop"—Millie Small

1st person

Ben?

We soon got used to the fact that we didn't have a dad, but it's not like we saw that much of him when we lived in London. Me and Tommy used to go outside and kick our football on the grass that was beneath the balcony, before the council gravelled it over to make a play zone. When we finished, we'd go over to the side of the lifts where a rusty tap poked out of the wall, and we'd take it in turns to cup our hands and drink water until we couldn't swallow anymore. One night we were asleep in our bedroom, and the next thing I knew I could feel Tommy shoving me, and when I opened my eyes, I could hear Mam crying, but I didn't know what to do. I was the eldest, but I didn't have any answers for this situation. Eventually I whispered to Tommy, let's just go back to sleep. I was nearly seven and trying to be responsible. She'll be alright, I said. Try not to fret. Things will be better in the morning. Tommy rolled over in his bed and closed his eyes, but I got my tiny transistor out from under the pillow and turned it on. I remember the song that was playing was "My Boy Lollipop," but it's a happy song and Mam wasn't happy, so I quickly shut it off. I lay in bed with my eyes open, and I didn't sleep that night as I was really worried about Mam.

"The Time Has Come"—Adam Faith

Every Sunday afternoon, me and Tommy used to sit cross-legged on the bright orange wall-to-wall carpet and watch the three o'clock film on the telly. Actually, first we'd watch the programme that showed the highlights of the best of Saturday's football matches, and then we'd watch the three o'clock film. Mam would be lying on the settee resting. I'm tired, so you two please behave yourselves. After the film we'd go out and play football, as we had no interest in *Songs of Praise*, or any religious programmes. Because it was just the two of us, we'd play shots-in with jumpers for goalposts, and if the ball went anywhere near a jumper, we'd always claim it was a goal, arguing that if it had been a real goalpost, it would have gone "in-off."

The film I remember the most was called *What a Whopper*, and it starred somebody I'd never heard of called Adam Faith. Mam slept through it, but me and Tommy both liked it, and I loved one of the songs even more than I liked the film. I was about nine, and I decided that I wanted the record, but this was going to be tricky as me and Tommy didn't get pocket money or anything like that, and so nicking it was most likely going to be the only option. On Saturday mornings I played football for an Under-10 side that met up in the city centre. I'd become accustomed to getting off the bus a stop early and then making a detour through the open market. Not the covered market, for that was always just setting up, and it was like Aladdin's cave in there with a game row, a fish row, a butcher's row, and even a pets row, which was actually my favourite. If, for some reason, I wanted to explore the covered market, I'd do that on the way home, but the open market was always set up before the covered one, and so I fell into the habit of pottering around there, and soon made myself familiar with nearly every stall, particularly the record shop that sold 45s with the centre bits missing. Thinking back, I reckon they must have been rejects from a jukebox or something, but they seemed okay to me, and I learned to idly flick through a few racks, and then, when the bloke wasn't looking, I'd slip one or two 45s inside my jacket and trap them against my side by tucking in my elbow, but not so that it looked like I'd broken my arm or anything. I'd carry on looking for a while, and then casually lean down and pick up my kit bag and saunter off out of the market and in the direction of the team bus. I must have been quite good at this thieving because I never got caught. One morning I was looking through the records, and in amongst all the stuff by Blue Mink and Herman's Hermits and The Small Faces, I saw "The Time Has Come" by Adam Faith, and I remembered it from the film.

That afternoon our Tommy was late back from his own Saturday game even though it was only around the corner, but by the time he walked into the flat and slung his bag down on the floor, I'd played the record a thousand times. Here, Tommy, you'll never guess what I've got. The zip on his jacket was broken, and he tended to hold it together with one hand as he walked. He let go of his jacket and slumped himself down on the settee and gave me that slack-jawed, come on, impress me look, so I played it again. His face didn't change a bit. Well, I said, don't you know what it is? He stood and picked up his bag. It's from that film, isn't it? The truth is, our Tommy must have been only seven, but he was pretty much obsessed with football. Pop music meant nothing to him. *What a Whopper.* I told him the title of the film, but he shrugged and said he was starving and asked what we were having for tea.

It seemed like he was always starving, which didn't make any sense as Mam always wrapped us both some dinner money in pieces of paper and left it for us on the kitchen table. I'd asked him a few times if he was being bullied, but he just shook his head and clammed up, so I didn't push it. Well, what's for tea? He knew full well that we were having either beans on toast or spaghetti hoops on toast, depending on what was in the cupboard. I let the song finish and then went into the kitchen and started to make our tea, which was my job when Mam had to work Saturdays at the library.

When Mam eventually came back, I put the song on again. And then a second time. By now Tommy was downstairs and kicking a ball up against the garages, so it was only me and Mam in the flat. I started to play the record a third time, and she shouted from her bedroom. Wasn't there anything on the telly? I took the 45 off the turntable before it finished, and then I turned on the telly. The science teacher at school, Mr. Thompson, had just got a colour set, and he was always going on about how great it was to watch football in colour. I knew we wouldn't be getting a colour telly anytime soon, so there was no point in dreaming. About anything.

"Those Were the Days"—Mary Hopkin

Mam started to get into the habit of coming back from her job at the library and then going straight into her bedroom and taking off her work clothes. When she came out again, we'd still be sitting in front of the telly, watching whatever was on, and she always made the same joke about us getting square eyes. Sometimes she'd be done up if she was going out for a drink with that smug prat Derek Evans, but if she was stopping in, she'd just pour herself a drink and work on her stories at the kitchen table, and when she finished, she'd join us in front of the goggle box. We all liked Hughie Green and *Opportunity Knocks*. I remember Mary Hopkin with her long blond hair and that squeaky voice that she had. Me and Tommy were taken with her, probably because she seemed to win every week, but eventually we were desperate for somebody else to win. Anybody.

Our Tommy didn't have homework, but I was swotting for my Eleven plus and hoping to pass it and then be accepted at the grammar school in town, so I always had plenty to be getting on with. Tommy, on the other hand, wasn't the slightest bit interested in school as everyone knew that by the time they got to his year they were going to scrap the Eleven plus, so he wasn't even going to have to bother trying. He'd be going to John Wardle's Second-ary Modern, which was the nearest school to our estate, and the hellhole I was dead keen to avoid. At John Wardle's there was no such thing as a fair fight, and if you turned your back on the wrong kid, you were likely to get bricked. Apparently there was a small chance that if I got in, Tommy might join me at the grammar school in town because if you had a brother that was already going there, then they could put you on a waiting list. But our Tommy didn't seem too fussed about where he might end up. I was a bit torn. A part of me liked the idea of us both going to the grammar school in town, but another part of me was ready for a bit of separation.

At night, after Mam had told us that it was time to go to bed, we'd lay in the dark and talk for a while before falling asleep. Usually about things like whether we'd be able to go to the feast when it came to the moor this year, or I'd tell him what it was like at the new Olympic-size baths where our school had started to take us older boys for swimming, or I'd ask him if he thought we'd ever live in a bought house—either a bungalow or a semi—without us having to win the pools or something. I'd nearly always finish by asking Tommy if he could imagine what it might be like to freewheel down a steep slope on a bike, but I'd never give him a chance to answer. I bet it's champion, I'd say. Owning a bike was my new obsession, but Tommy always wanted to talk about the same thing. How come our dad never came to see us? Didn't he care for us anymore? Sometimes I'd get angry and ask him how the chuff was I supposed to know? It's not like I can read minds, you know. Tommy would go quiet and say that he needed new football boots with screw-in studs, not the moulded plastic Gola boots that he'd been playing in for ages now. They were too small, and they pinched his feet, and people laughed at him for not having screw-ins as he was the best player in the school and if anybody should have them, he should. Last Christmas he wrote a letter to Dad and he gave it to Mam, who said she'd post it to him. In the letter he asked for a pair of new boots, but he never heard back from Dad, and Mam didn't say anything. I'd given up believing in him ages ago, but his disappearance really seemed to get to our Tommy. There was a boy in my house at school who liked to tell everyone that his dad had left them and gone to Australia. I was a bit jealous as he seemed to me to be really lucky, for unlike us, there was a definite end to the story of his dad. According to Steve Pamphlet, his dad had gone down under to Australia, where there was sunshine all the time and everyone had loads of money and big houses. He said that his dad had told him that Australians didn't allow Jimmy Jamaicas into the country to steal your jobs, and Aussies didn't take cheek from anybody, including the bosses, and in Australia things were so good that there was no need to even think about buying anything on the never-never. Steve Pamphlet always started off talking about himself by confidently bringing up Australia and his dad, and it occurred to me that maybe I should try something like this. I could tell people that my dad's in America, or even in jail. That would be different.

Once, after Steve Pamphlet had been bragging again about his dad and Australia, I came home and waited until Mam got back from the library, and then I came straight out with it and asked her if she knew where Dad had gone off to. She just looked at me and then went into her bedroom and shut the door. When she came back out, she told me to turn off the telly as she wanted to say something to me. You're nearly eleven now, and so I can talk straight to you. Your dad's gone off back to where he came from. Maybe he'll turn up one day, but if he does, he's not coming in this flat. She made me promise that if on the off chance he ever showed up when she wasn't around, then I'd not let him in the flat. I nodded. I'll not let him in. Ben, she said, this is important. She pushed my shoulder back. I know, I whispered. I could feel tears welling up behind my eyes. I promise. But what was I supposed to do, leave him on the doorstep? Anyhow, nobody ever knocked at our door, except gypsies selling clothes pegs and bits of lavender, or fat blokes in tight suits trying to sell you junk to clean your kitchen with, or creepy-looking Avon ladies. Your father's left me to cope with the both of you by myself, and we're doing alright. We don't need him, do we? I shook my head, but realized that

Mam probably wasn't telling me the whole truth. Ben, she said, we don't need him, do we? We're better off without your father. I nodded. That's right, and have you looked into that paper round yet? This time I shook my head. Well, see if you can't get it, love. We need all the help we can, and you're the man of the house now. She paused. Where's your brother?

"Hey Jude"—The Beatles

While Mam was around, badgering us to unpack our suitcases and get settled in our new bedroom with its nice comfy twin beds and flannelette matching sheets and pillowcases, the woman was really nice. She even brought us a tray with three cups of tea on it, and a big plate of custard creams and digestives. Mam smiled and thanked the woman, and then Mrs. Swinson backed out of the bedroom and said she'd give us some time to ourselves and told us that there was no rush. She said this twice, about there being no rush. Tommy and I began to cram the biscuits into our mouths, but Mam got mad and said we had to behave properly. She insisted that Mrs. Swinson was a kind lady, so we had to be careful not to do anything to annoy her. Mam looked around the room. She has a beautiful home, she said. Me and Tommy nodded and promised that we would behave, but neither of us took our eyes off the biscuits.

Eventually we stood up and followed Mam down the stairs and into the hallway, where we watched the two women talking for a minute or so until Mrs. Swinson opened the front door. Mam looked back at us both, then wiped her eyes with the back of her hand. Mrs. Swinson closed in the door quickly and didn't even give us time to listen to Mam's footsteps finally fade away before she started up on us about our clothes and about Mam. Upstairs, she said, and get yourselves in the bathroom. Once you've had a good wash you can come down, and then we'll have to go out and try and get you kitted out with something respectable to wear. And dry yourself properly in your small areas or you'll get chapped. She didn't smile, but then again we'd already noticed that she never smiled. Later, after tea, we had to do the washing-up, and she shouted at us to be careful with the dishes as they were antique. We were to take it in turns. One day I'd wash and Tommy would wipe, then the following day we'd change around, did we understand? We nodded but tried not to look at Mrs. Swinson, for she'd now plonked herself on a chair and was slowly rolling a stocking down the full length of her veined leg.

That first night we lay in our beds and wondered what our new school would be like. Tommy was ten now, two years younger than me, and Mam had told us that in this town we'd both be going to the same school, as juniors and seniors weren't split up. Mrs. Swinson had already taken us out and bought us our new school uniforms, but everything was too big on us. I didn't say anything to Tommy, but it occurred to me that we might have to fight at this new school, and I worried that it might well be the type of school where there was no point in reporting anything to the prefects as they might be the ones doing most of the beating up. That's how it was at my grammar school, and I reckoned that it was no doubt even rougher at John Wardle's. On our estate it was always me who had to scrap and stick up for our Tommy, as kids obviously saw something that made them want to pick on him, but Tommy couldn't fight to save his life. However, with me it was different, and although I was never going to be cock of the school or the estate, I also wasn't ever going to back down. I knew I was clever, as I was already top of the class at the grammar school, and I *did* like to show off a bit, so hardly a day went by when I didn't hear the words "Do you wanna make something of it?" coming out of my mouth. However, on Monday morning, I soon discovered that things at this new school seemed to be a bit easier.

After we'd got through the first couple of days, I started to keep an eye on Tommy, and we began to hang out together. We seemed to always get chosen on the same side for football, but these kids didn't have a proper ball, only a dirty grey tennis ball. Everyone quickly worked out that our Tommy was the best player by a mile, but being a new boy, he inevitably took a bit of a kicking, and so even when we were supposed to be having fun, I still had to stand up for him and occasionally belt a few people. Back at Mrs. Swinson's, we soon discovered that we were a disappointment to her and she was only interested in her three husky dogs and not much else. The drill was we were to come home, get changed, then come down for our tea and afterwards wash and wipe the dishes and pile them up neatly next to the draining board. Mrs. Swinson soon gave up asking us about our school or if we had any homework to do, and she just made it clear that after we'd finished our chores, we were allowed to go down to the basement and watch telly for one hour, and one hour only, and then we had to go to bed. She never came down there with us; she'd just sit upstairs and play with her dogs, particularly the young one, Simla, who she talked to more than the other two.

She once got mad when she caught us watching television when we should have been in bed, but it wasn't our fault. The Beatles had just split up, and there was a programme about them, and at the end of it they played "Hey Jude" and it just kept going on and on and on. It was great because it looked like the song would never stop, but then Mrs. Swinson burst in and turned off the telly and started to shout. When you two reach the age of majority and live under your own roof, then, and only then, can you do as you please. We could hear the dogs barking at the top of the stairs, and that was frightening. She wanted to know just who the hell did we think we were, disobeying her? Did we want to feel the flat of her hand? She said one hour, and she meant one hour. Then she started talking about God, and she said that back in the old days they had built a ship and people said that even God couldn't sink it, but he did and everyone drowned. Didn't we believe her? Well? She suddenly moved towards us like she was going to slap us across our heads, and we both flinched back into the settee. Your mother's a fast one, isn't she, fobbing you off on me so she can carry on like a minx? Like it's not manifest. And you, she pointed at me, you want to be careful looking at folks like that. One day somebody's going to give you a good leathering, and it might well be me. I can be mother, father, and magistrate all rolled into one if needs be, so if it gives the two of you a thrill to disobey me, you'd better think again and modify your ideas. Do you know what I do with dumb, insolent tykes like you two? And then she threatened to put us down in the cellar with the rats and throw away the key, and our Tommy started to cry, and I watched her face change shape as she began to laugh. There was some spit at the edges of her mouth. I've got your flaming number. Both of you. After all, you don't even know how to wipe around the toilet after you've used it, do you? But I'm not surprised. I mean, look at your mother's coat. Red's a common colour; everyone knows that. Frock, coat, or hat, it doesn't matter: it's common.

Later that night, in the quiet of our bedroom, Tommy whispered that he wanted to go home. He said he didn't like being fostered. I agreed with him, but I reminded him that Mam wasn't well and the doctor said she needed a break. She was having a hard time pleasing her boss at the library, and I had a feeling that if she lost her job, she wouldn't be able to afford to look after us anymore. We just had to be patient. I said all of this, but inside I was angry at her. Although I enjoyed being a popular boy, the smallest thing would set me off. I don't know where I got the idea from, but I used to imagine it was my fault that Dad had left us both. I couldn't think of anything I'd done wrong, but somehow I just got the sense that I was the problem, and this just made me even more frustrated. That night our Tommy wet the bed for the first time.

"In the Summertime"—Mungo Jerry

I t was Terry Neat's party, and his parents had completely abandoned the house to us. There were six of us boys and five girls, and to start with, I was a bit disappointed that there were more of us than them. His parents had put out bowls of crisps and peanuts and some bottles of pop and a sleeve of plastic cups. We had a choice: either Tizer or ginger beer. And, of course, we had use of their record player. Everybody's favourite song was Mungo Jerry's "In the Summertime," and I remember it really well because it was the first time I'd ever been tempted to sing along. Not dance, of course. At twelve years old, dancing was out of the question. We just sat around and filled our faces and then made slightly muffled efforts to sing along to the chorus. At some point Mr. and Mrs. Neat came back, and it was clear that it was time for us to leave. The other kids' parents started to turn up to fetch them. They came in and said hello to Mr. and Mrs. Neat, and thanked them before leaving with their son or daughter. Nobody came to pick me up.

We were back living with Mam now. One Saturday morning she'd just turned up at the foster home. She barged in past Mrs. Swinson and stood in the hallway and told us to pack up our things as we were leaving. Mrs. Swinson went to sit in the kitchen with the three dogs and slammed the door in behind her. Mam came up to the bedroom and stood over us and said we had to hurry, so we just chucked our things into the one big suitcase. She had come to visit us the previous weekend, and she'd waited until the three of us were alone in the sitting room before asking me what I thought of things by Mrs. Swinson, and I said everything was alright as I didn't want to upset her. She just nodded but said nothing. Then, when I went to the toilet, I had a suspicion that she talked to our Tommy by himself. When Mam left, I asked Tommy what she'd said to him, but he just shrugged his shoulders.

Once we were packed, me and Tommy lugged the suitcase down the stairs and into the hallway. Mam had already made her way back downstairs, and she was waiting for us. You two got everything? We nodded, and that's when Mrs. Swinson burst out of the kitchen and started on about how she'd tried to make allowances, but we were dirty, and we bolted our food, and we had no manners, and she went on about how she had no time for kids like us who'd been dragged up. Borstal material, she said, if not worse, but she was adamant that she couldn't lay all the blame at our doorstep. She leered at Mam: I can't abide women who are all over the shop when it comes to their responsibilities. On behalf of the blessed council, I seem to spend half my life mopping up the mess people like you make. I mean, look at how you're all tarted up, and a mother too. Conceited bugger. Why don't you just buzz off, she said, which seemed a bit soft after everything she'd blurted out. Go on, sling your hook and go elsewhere. Mam could have just walked away at this point and decided that there was nothing to be gained by getting into a fight, but that's not how Mam worked. She started to yell at the woman and she gave as good as she was getting and the two of them went at it hammer and tongs while me and Tommy just stood there next to the suitcase, wondering when we were going to be able to go.

On the Monday morning I started up at the grammar school again as though nothing had happened. Our Tommy found out that he hadn't made it off the waiting list, and so he'd soon be going to John Wardle's, but he didn't seem concerned. Steve

Pamphlet was also in my house at the gramma school, and he interrogated me as to where I'd been for the past month, and I was tempted to tell him America, to see my dad, but I just said, "Around." There was a new music teacher, Mr. Hall, who asked me if I could play the descant recorder, and when I said I could, he called me out to the side of the piano and put some sheet music on a stand and made me play "Greensleeves" in front of the whole class. He seemed a bit peeved that I did alright, and when I finished, he told me to sit back down, and he didn't look in my direction for the rest of the double music period. By dinnertime there were no more questions from anybody, just the odd glance from one or two of the teachers who probably hoped they'd seen the back of me. And then Terry Neat invited me to a party on Saturday afternoon at his house and so I went and I found myself half listening, half singing along to Mungo Jerry.

That night, back at the flat, I lay in bed across the room from our Tommy, and I told him about the song and how I wanted to nick the record out of Terry Neat's house but I dared not in case somebody caught me. He propped himself up on one elbow, and he seemed a little put out. I could tell by how he was looking at me, but he knew full well that I nicked records, so what was his problem? We didn't get pocket money because Mam couldn't afford it. This also meant that we didn't have Levi's or Ben Sherman shirts or anything decent to wear. We had nothing. Nicking odds and sods seemed alright to me so long as you didn't get caught. I told this to our Tommy, but he just kept looking at me and saying nothing, and so I changed the subject. I tried to get Tommy talking about football, but he still said nothing, and that's when I began to feel sad and a little bit ashamed. I watched as my brother lay back down and pulled the blanket up to his chin. Good night, he said. See you in the morning. I listened to Tommy's breathing becoming deeper as he fell asleep, and then I realized that I was actually angry with the bed wetter. If I wanted to nick stuff, I'd nick it. Who cared what he thought?

"Maggie May"—Rod Stewart

Beverley Armitage was the name of the first girl I ever kissed. She lived in the same block of flats as us and she went to John Wardle's. She used to come and knock on the door and wait for our Tommy so they could go to school together, but he started to leave early so that he didn't have to be seen with her, and I started to miss my bus into town so that I could be there when she came knocking. After the third time that it was me who opened the door, I could see that Beverley Armitage was getting the idea that our Tommy was doing his best to avoid her. She was twelve, a year younger than me, but I'd noticed that the age gap didn't make much difference with girls. With a lad a year could be a massive gap, but lasses always seemed a bit older than what they really were. I'd also noticed that Beverley Armitage had started to develop a chest that I couldn't take my eyes off, and I reckoned I'd better ask her out before she stopped coming around. So after failed attempt number three, and just as she was turning away to go back to the lifts, I blurted it out and asked her if she'd seen *Diamonds Are Forever*. She looked at me as if she hadn't heard properly, and so I had to go on. It's showing at the Clock Cinema, I said. We could go on Friday. She still didn't say anything, so I thought I'd better finish. If you're not doing anything, that is. Like most thirteen-year-olds, I was the bashful sort when it came to girls, and a smug, grinning Steve Pamphlet had summed me up in front of the whole class: too slow to catch a cold, let alone a lass. Of course, I had to pretend that I was in on the joke, so I laughed, but inside of myself I knew he was right. However, that morning on the doorstep, I surprised myself. In the afternoon, during the boring chemistry double period, I wrote "Beverley Armitage" on my exercise book in big swirling letters and coloured her name in with red, green, and blue felt-tipped pens. Inevitably, I missed everything that the teacher was going on about. Something to do with potassium and copper, or something like that, but having finished my doodling, I was busily now trying to work out how to pay for Friday night without it coming over like I was Mr. Moneybags.

It turned out that I needn't have worried so much, for when we got to the head of the queue, she stepped in front of me and said that her grandma had given her half a crown and told her that she had to go dutch and pay her own way. I didn't argue, but I was a bit surprised. I'd managed to save up about two pounds over the past year, mainly by nicking money out of kids' pockets when we got changed for games. I'd go to a lot of trouble to make sure that I was the last out of the changing rooms, or first back in, or both, and I soon learned whose pockets were worth going through. To start with, I'd use the money to buy comics, usually *Hotspur* or *Victor*, but sometimes *The Dandy* too. But then I decided I wanted a red Chopper bike, and so I stopped buying comics or going out anywhere, and I started to save up, but I quickly cottoned on that it was going to take me forever to save up enough money for a Chopper, or a bike of any kind, and that's when it became clear that stopping in and saving every penny for a bike I'd probably never own was a waste of time. I'd be better off buying a bag of chips and hanging out by the off-licence and watching the older estate boys smoking Woodies and doing their impressions of Rod Stewart singing "Maggie May." Getting together two pounds hadn't been easy, but every time I saw Beverly Armitage's chest, I knew that I'd be prepared to spend whatever it took to impress her.

However, it didn't take long before I began to get the message that she wasn't interested. I steered Beverley Armitage towards a double seat at the back of the front circle, but I didn't lay a finger on her during the film. I just sat ramrod still and stared at the screen. I didn't even offer her a spice, even though I had a packet of fruit pastilles in my pocket. The couple beside us seemed intent on getting thrown out as they were all over each other, and it was pretty distracting, as you could actually hear them kissing and their tongues were involved. I didn't want to look, and it was sending me spare just thinking about it, but I realized that Beverley Armitage didn't seem to be put out by their snogging, and I even caught her sneaking a peek at the courting couple. We both stood up for the national anthem at the end, and then I walked her home and started to make small talk about the film, and she tried to look interested in whatever it was that I was going on about.

It was still light when we got to her flat. I stood by the door, but I didn't know if I should ask her out again, because it's not like she'd been acting completely offhand or anything. However, she didn't give me much of a chance to properly weigh things up in my head. She leaned forward and pecked me on the cheek and said good-night in a kind of cheerful voice as though the whole evening had been okay, and then she disappeared inside. And so that was it, but there was something about the way she kissed me that let me know that she didn't want to go out with me a second time. Once was enough, and I knew I wasn't going to embarrass myself, or her, by asking again. It was only later that night, as I looked over at our Tommy, that I began to accept what was going on. I may have been a bit older, but I was a crap substitute. From her point of view, it was all a big mistake. It was our Tommy she was smitten with, and maybe she thought she could get his attention if she was nice to his brother. The Beverley Armitages of this world were not interested in boys like me, but I decided that when Steve Pamphlet asked me if I'd got anything from her, I was going to tell him, yes, a quick feel, and then shrug my shoulders and say she wasn't my type of lass, and try and leave it at that.

"Band of Gold"—Freda Payne

Things began to deteriorate after the fostering with Mrs. Swinson didn't take. At the end of the day Mam was always tired, and sometimes she didn't even have the energy to talk to us, so to my way of thinking, she needn't have bothered making the effort. Most nights Tommy was at football practise, and so I was left by myself with her as she poured a drink, then scribbled a bit at her stories, then poured another drink. It was painful to watch, and I was always happy when she gave up and just went to bed. I worried a bit about Tommy, for he didn't seem to have any time for Mam, and he even told me that he wished he was an orphan. Apparently there was a lad in his class at John Wardle's who lived in a children's home, and according to Tommy, he had more fun than we did. In fact, some of the grown-ups from the children's home even came to watch Tommy's mate play football. The one bright spot in all of this was that I managed to get a job delivering the *Evening Post*, but not before I had to practically beg the newsagent to give me the round, and even then I got myself a lecture. You just shut your gob and listen to me. I'll not tolerate any slacking. You're an estate lad, and it's a scab of a place. There's well-brought-up lads from farther out who'd kill for this job, and I always have to keep an extra bloody eye open with you lot. Always on the cadge, aren't you? I mean, face facts, nothing good will ever come of you kids. They should build a trunk road between that estate and the local lockup because that's where most of you are heading. And just because your lordship's at the grammar school, don't be thinking that you're any better than the rest of them, because you're not. I've got your bleeding number.

After school, I'd get off the bus and then chase home to the flat and drop off my briefcase and get changed out of my blazer and shirt and tie. Then I'd run back up the hill to a fence by the side of the church where the newsagent's van would have left the bag of papers. I soon got to know the round like the back of my hand, and I'd jump over fences, cut through alleyways, all the time working out even quicker ways to get the papers delivered. Some people got fed up with me because they used to be early in the round, but now, because I changed things to make the round go faster, some of them were getting their *Evening Post* up to half an hour later than usual. The only bit that really slowed the round down was when I had to go into the new sixteen-storey block of flats. If a flat was below the fifth floor, then I'd forget the lifts and just race up the stairs. Above the fifth floor it wasn't worth it; it was better to just wait for a lift, but they were really unpredictable, and usually at least one of them was out of order. If I had to use them, I'd start at the top and leave my bag blocking the lift door and work my way down. Once in a while I'd get caught by a resident who wanted to know what the hell I thought I was playing at messing around with the lifts. I'd have to use the stairs after that, but sometimes, maybe once a week, I'd get all the way down to the ground floor without being interrupted by anybody, and that sped things up a lot. I gave Mam most of the money from the paper round, but I don't remember her ever saying thank you. Twelve and six, and then when the new money came in, I got a pay rise to thirteen bob because it was easier to give me sixty-five pence as opposed to sixty-two and a half pence. Six nights a week I did the round, and I got it down to just under an hour. However, after I'd given Mam her fifty pence, I was left with pretty much sod all, and so I began to think about getting another job, and then I got lucky.

One day, when I was picking up the bag of papers from beside the church, Father Hanson asked me if I wanted to be an altar boy on a Sunday, which not only meant dressing up in a white surplice and following him around with a goblet of wine and some wafers, but it also meant handling the collection plate. A lot of people gave money in envelopes, and after the service was over, it was my job to take the collection plate into the vestry. I thought, well, God helps those who help themselves. Mam was pleased that I was going to church because it got me out of the flat on a Sunday morning, and it gave her some time for herself. Occasionally her friend Derek Evans would come to visit, and the two of them would be off out to the moors for lunch. He'd often knock on the door and then use his own key to let himself in and wait in the kitchen until Mam was ready. He usually dressed well, in a jacket and shirt and tie, but for some reason he shoved too many things in his pockets so he always looked as if he'd slept in his clothes. He didn't have much to say to me because he could see the way I looked at him, but he liked football, and he always had a word for our Tommy about United's latest game or some such thing. Even though he was only eleven, Tommy had been recruited by Farsley Celtic, and he was doing really well and playing with kids two years older than him. I was proud of him, and on Sunday mornings I liked to stand on the balcony and watch when the minibus came by to pick him up, and then I'd be off out to my collection plate caper. Whenever I left the flat for church, Mam had real peace and quiet and the place all to herself unless, of course, her podgy-faced friend had come around.

I remember it was a Monday night when the two scouts from Pudsey Juniors turned up and knocked at the door. Mam was in her bedroom, and Tommy and me were watching telly, although I was also trying to do my homework at the same time. Tommy had a feeling some scouts might be around as he told me that two men had spoken to him after Sunday's game and asked him where he lived. He'd scored twice and made the third goal, and according to him, he'd played a blinder. I called Mam and went back into the living room while she stood at the door and spoke to them both. Me and Tommy sat on the settee and looked at each other, and then we heard the door slam shut. Mam had a tube of lipstick in her hand as she came through into the living room. I told them no, you're concentrating on your schoolwork, alright? Our Tommy nodded his head. And besides, we've already spoken about you playing for Uncle Derek's team, haven't we? She puckered up without waiting for an answer, and then lobbed the lipstick onto the sideboard. For heaven's sake, be good. And don't be up when I get back. She snatched up her coat and closed in the door behind her, and it was then that our Tommy began to cry. A single tear ran down the full length of his cheek, and eventually he pulled himself together enough to speak to me. She says Uncle Derek's involved with Scott Hall Juniors, and he wants me to play for them. But they're crap, I said. There was no need for me to say that, but I couldn't help myself, and it just slipped out. What I really wanted to say was I could tell the beady-eyed bastard wasn't treating Mam right, for she always made an effort to look nice for him, but he still had a wife. He was just using her to get at Tommy, for he liked nothing more than to impress kids, and football was his way of doing so. Without football he was nothing but a sad, desperate balding fucker who liked rambling on the moors with an anorak and compass, and he knew it. Our Tommy said nothing, and he just got up and went out. I heard the front door click shut, and I knew that he'd be off down the garages with his football until it got too dark to see.

I began to think about what exactly Steve Pamphlet might have meant when, earlier in that week, he'd asked me, How many uncles have you got? I was going to smack him, but I didn't want him to think that I was bothered because I knew he thought he was better than me. If United were at home on a Saturday, he usually went to watch the match, and he always bragged about this. So, on the following Saturday, I decided to spend some of my church money and take myself off to watch United for the first time. At halftime they played "Band of Gold" really loudly out of the speakers. I'd never heard music played that loud, and I loved it. Not just the loudness, but the fact that the song was telling a story. But now I had a dilemma. I had enough money so that I could actually buy the record if I wanted to, instead of nicking it from the open market. I was a bit torn as to what to do.

"Ride a White Swan"—T. Rex

We stood together outside of the Civic Hall with the other kids and their parents and waited for the coach to come and pick us up. Mam never asked Tommy and me if we wanted to go to the seaside; it was just announced. We were going, and that was that, and we'd be spending two weeks at Silverdale Holiday Camp near Morecambe. I could tell by the type of kids who were waiting for the bus that this was a trip for poor people. They were the type of lads and lasses who were plagued with boils and spots, and who queued for free dinners at school, and who knew all about dodging the rent man or going down to the post office to pick up the family allowance money. And we were no better. I was nearly fourteen, and the emotion I was most familiar with—besides anger, that is—was shame. Mam tried to act all upbeat while we waited for the coach, but there was no getting around the fact that she was letting us go again. However, at least this time it wasn't to a foster home. It was obvious that her nerves were not getting any better, and we could tell that she needed a rest. These days, she seemed really thin, and she'd begun to act even more weird than normal. We knew that we weren't allowed in her bedroom, but now she was always asking us straight out, Have you been going in that bedroom when I'm not here? Of course we hadn't. Why would we? But it felt wrong that she should be shouting at us and accusing us of something we hadn't done. And then there were the nights that we had to spend by ourselves in the flat. In the morning we'd be having our Weetabix in the kitchen, and in she'd come, wearing the same clothes that we'd last seen her in, and she'd rush by us, stinking of cigarette smoke, and we'd carry on spooning the Weetabix into our mouths as we listened to her clumping about in her bedroom. We both assumed she'd been out with Derek Evans, but it wasn't for us to ask.

Every morning I'd make sure that Tommy's school uniform had been ironed, and that he'd had some breakfast, and then I'd check that he'd got his school bag and make sure that he set off on time. Clearly he was old enough that he should have been able to look out for himself, but I'd noticed that after Mam told the football scouts where to go, something in him changed, and it was like he'd kind of given up. He was still wetting the bed, but he'd learned to take the sheet off by himself and rinse it through in the bathtub. Then he'd hang it on the wooden clotheshorse so that it would be dry by the time he got back from school, which was always later than me because he had football practise every night of the week: twice for school and three times for Scott Hall Juniors, as Derek Evans had got him to agree to play for them. Mam told Tommy that it was nearer and more convenient, but we both knew that our Tommy was the best player on their team, and they were lucky to get him, and if it wasn't for Mam, he'd be playing for Pudsey Juniors. But Tommy didn't really want to talk about this, any more than he wanted to talk about Derek Evans, who, when he wasn't hanging around in the kitchen waiting for Mam, had taken to chauffeuring our Tommy around like he was some kind of footballing god. Apparently so-called Uncle Derek was a birdwatcher, and he kept a huge pair of binoculars in his car, and if he spotted a bird that he liked, he'd pull over and spend ages just looking up in the trees. I could tell that the dickhead was trying to impress our Tommy, for my brother nearly always came back home with a small bottle of Lucozade, which Derek Evans claimed would give Tommy energy, but the biggest upshot of all this attention was our Tommy got a brand-new pair of Adidas boots with screw-in studs and a black Adidas holdall for his kit.

As we waited for the coach, Mam lit a cigarette, then put on her helpless face. I know they're no good for me, and I'm going to give them up, but I just need a bit of help right now. Neither me nor Tommy said anything. Anyhow, this will give you both a chance to see the sea for the first time, and it'll give me a chance to get my strength back. As she spoke to us, her eyes jumped this way and that, as though she was afraid that somebody was looking at her. And then I realized what it was. She felt abashed standing up in the street with the pair of us. I could tell that she couldn't wait for the coach to arrive, but I didn't say anything. I just hoped that Tommy could keep it together until she'd gone. Don't cry, our Tommy. I was the one who'd have to look after him for the next two weeks, and looking at these lads, I could tell that there might be some rowdy stuff. Some of them looked like they were fourth formers, fifteen-year-olds, so I'd be giving up over a year if it came to a fight. I tried not to think too much about this, as it was too worrying, and then I saw the coach coming around the corner, and Mam threw her fag down on the ground and started to mash the stub into the pavement. Come on, smarten yourselves up a bit. You two be good, she said as she hugged us both together. You'll be fine as these are fully qualified people, but just make sure you write and let me know how it is, and don't you be getting into any trouble. I'd arranged for somebody to take over the paper round, and Father Hanson had got his alternative altar boy lined up, so nobody would miss me. That's what I was thinking as the coach pulled away and I looked out of the window and waved at Mam. Nobody will miss me.

It took forever to get to Silverdale; that's about all I remember of the journey. I kept nodding off, but every time I opened my eyes we were still driving and my bladder was full to bursting as I was dying to go to the toilet. I was sitting on both of my hands, but eventually we stopped at a big garage that had a café attached to it, and we were told to form a single line and wait our turn to use their facilities. Our Tommy said he didn't want to go, but it was obvious that they wanted everyone off the coach, and so he just got to his feet and didn't say anything else. As we were climbing back on board, Derek Evans was at the front, handing everyone a crab apple and a cheese sandwich wrapped in greaseproof paper. Alright, Ben. Alright, Tommy. Your mam says I'm to keep an eye on you two, so don't you be worrying yourselves; there'll be no problems. You'll have a nice time. As the coach pulled out and into the traffic, I asked our Tommy if he knew that Derek Evans would be coming along too in his own car. He shrugged his shoulders. What's that supposed to mean? It means that Uncle Derek said he goes every year, and he says that you can bank on everybody having an ace time. An ace time? I think he might be having you on. Well, do you believe him? Our Tommy never answered me.

They bullied Tommy at the camp, and I didn't do anything about it. Neither, as far as I could see, did Derek Evans, who always managed to make himself scarce every time he saw me coming. Good job too because I was already dreaming about chinning him and knocking that cocky little smile off his face, even though I knew Mam would go spare if I started anything. But if Mr. Bleeding Bird-watcher cared so much, why didn't he do something for our kid when he got called names? It didn't matter how good Tommy was at football: they laid into him and gave him the treatment, which usually meant rubbing chewing gum into his hair, or spitting in his glass of water and making him drink it, or just smacking him around. On the other hand, I suddenly found myself being quite popular. I had a bit of money in my pocket, I knew about music, I wasn't that bad at football, and I had a pair of Levi's that I took off only at night, when I went to sleep on the top deck of a bunk bed from where I could look down and see everything that was going on. They put Tommy in a different dormitory, so it was hard for me to keep an eye on him, so I suppose I shouldn't blame myself too much. However, even though I could sense that he was having a difficult time, Tommy chose to say nothing to me about the bullying, and it was only later that he let on to me what had been going on, but by then it was too late to do anything about it.

Whenever I ran into him at the camp, he looked like some little lost boy you wanted to hug. There was nothing in his eyes. No light, no nothing, but what was I meant to do, give him a pat on the head and a cuddly toy? He should have said something. One day he did tell me that he'd like it if I could buy a postcard so we could send it to Mam, and I said I'd get one, but I never did. I just hoped that he wouldn't mention it again, and sure enough, he didn't.

In the mornings they left us alone to run around in the boggy fields that were surrounded by crumbling stone walls. In the afternoons we were taken down to the beach, where some of the younger kids started digging to Australia, which was a really popular game, but I used to wander off and stare at the worn-out donkeys giving rides on the beach, or gawp at the big dipper at the funfair or the tubby ladies sitting in deck chairs in their baggy bathing costumes. My favourite thing of all was to listen to the military band that would strike up in the bandstand at exactly three-thirty every afternoon, although I could never work out why they always finished off with a sing-along of "O Come All Ye Faithful" given that there was still five months to go until Christmas. After that I'd go back to the beach and take off my plimsolls and socks and stand right where the water stopped rushing, so that the sea licked my toes and I could pretend that it was a dog that I owned who would never leave my side. And then it would be time to go back to Silverdale.

There was an older boy and a girl in charge of our dormitory. Peter and Rachel. They said they were eighteen, and it was clear they fancied each other as they were always smiling when they were around one another. Peter liked T. Rex, and he used to whistle their songs. I could tell that he thought he looked like Marc Bolan, but his hair was too short, and he wore glasses. However, he did put glitter on his face, and I liked that. I can't speak for the others, but I had a soft spot for Rachel, who had beautiful hair and a pink woollen bobble hat that set it off nicely. I used to like to be around her whenever she was in the dormitory talking to us, but if I looked too long at her, I could feel myself colouring up.

She'd tell us to make our beds, but mine was always made. When it rained and we had to sit inside and play board games, I'd always try and sit near her, but it was no use. It was obvious that if it wasn't Peter, it would be some other older lad that was going to come along and snatch her up before I had a chance, but I tried not to feel too cheesed off. Rachel looked at me a lot. Well, at everybody really, but she was the first person that I can remember who smiled at me and maybe meant it.

"All the Young Dudes"—Mott the Hoople

The thing I remember most about the summer after we went to Silverdale was Mam descending into a kind of madness. I'm not sure if I can explain it any better than that. "All the Young Dudes," was always playing on the radio. It was a pop song that sounded like something you'd play at a funeral. I liked it a lot and became a bit obsessed with it. The song was always snaking through my head, rolling around from one ear to the other, and it made me think of a woman dancing and slowly turning her hips. I suppose that's the sort of thing that fourteen-year-old boys think about, or at least this fourteen-year-old used to think like that. Our Tommy never cared much for pop music, and so he probably never even heard the song. The Munich Olympics would come later, but the summer started out the same way that every summer started out, with Tommy spending every waking hour kicking a ball up against the garages. There were only six of them to serve all the flats, but then again the council was not stupid. They knew that most people on the estate wouldn't have a car, and those that did would be happy to just park it on the road. The names of the cars back then sounded so glamorous. They still do. Cortinas, Capris, Avengers, Zodiacs, Zephyrs. However, the cars on our estate were never new, but if you had a car, it meant that you were doing alright. That said, most people who had a car had more sense than to pay the council fifty pence a week to rent a poxy garage, especially when the rent for a two-bedroom flat was just under four pounds. I knew this because it was my job to take the rent book and an envelope of money down to the council office every Saturday morning. No bloke in his right mind was going to pay an extra ten bob a week for a garage when he could take that cash and get blathered down The Squinting Cat and still have change.

After the two weeks we spent at Silverdale, Tommy came back, and after he'd eventually told me some of what went on there, he just clammed up, and he wouldn't talk anymore. For the whole year he always looked like he was about to bawl, and I could tell that he wasn't his true self. Twelve months later, and not much had changed with our Tommy, who would get up in the morning and take his football and go and boot it up against the garage doors until it got too dark, or until one of the neighbours got riled and shouted at him and told him to fucking stop it or he'd have him. Oi, cut it out. The noise is fucking killing me. Which is pretty much what Mam would say to me as she got ready to go out. Except she wouldn't swear, of course. Ben, can you turn off that radio now? It's doing my head in. We *have* got a telly, you know. That summer I remember she started to wear a kind of garish pink lipstick, but I don't remember her ever doing her fingernails. Go on, turn it off, for heaven's sake. I'd usually just turn it down, and that would put an end to her complaining. We were good at making truces and not letting things get out of control, but there were times when she'd just get on my tits. However, more often than not, I'd say nothing and just pick up the transistor and go and sit with it in the kitchen and wait for my song to come on again. Derek Evans had broken Mam's heart when he gave her back the key to the flat. These days I didn't have any idea who she was going out with. I did, however, know that our Tommy would be down the road kicking his football up against the doors of the empty garages and keeping his own counsel.

"School's Out"—Alice Cooper

Our Tommy disappeared the same summer that they had the Olympics in Munich, West Germany. I used to watch every day, mainly the athletics and the swimming, and I remember all the excitement over Mark Spitz and Dave Wottle and Lasse Virén, and then the sudden confusion when the athletes were killed. I was confused too. Towards the end of the summer our Tommy eventually stopped kicking his ball up against the garages, and he started up training again at Scott Hall Juniors. Then one stormy night he was away at football practise, and he never came back. I didn't know what to do, as Mam was out, so I lay in bed listening to the wind and rain and tried to get my head around who our Tommy might have gone to stay with. He had his football mates, and I thought maybe he'd gone off with one of them, but I didn't know them, and I didn't much care to either. Brian, Luke, Graham: I just knew their names, but we didn't have a phone in the flat, so he couldn't call us up to let us know where he was, and anyhow, I doubt if his football mates had phones in their houses. Derek Evans usually ran him back home from training in his car, but I had no idea how to get in touch with that prat, so I just lay on top of the blanket and stared at the wall.

Eventually it started to get light out, and I looked across at the empty bed, where his pillows were standing to attention in that odd way that our Tommy liked to leave them. I heard Mam outside on the balcony, and then I listened to the noise of the key in the lock and the banging of her coming in and kicking off her shoes. I got out of bed and opened the bedroom door, and she looked at me as though it was somehow wrong of me to be seeing her like this. I just blurted it out, and she stood there for a minute, trying to take it in. Well, where is he then? She was asking me, as though I knew, but that was the whole point of telling her: I had no idea where he was. Wasn't she supposed to be the mother? Get ready for school, she said, and then she went into her bedroom and closed in the door behind her.

When I came back that afternoon, Mam was sitting on the settee and two uniformed coppers were in the house. The woman one was sitting next to Mam and comforting her, and the bloke was standing up like he owned the place. Mam looked up at me and said that the bloke copper wanted to have a word, and then she started to cry again. The copper took me into the kitchen, and we sat at the table. He asked me if I was yearning for anything to eat, and I wanted to tell him that all we had was spaghetti hoops and toast, but I didn't say anything, and I just shook my head. Then he started to ask me about Tommy's friends, and if I'd noticed anything different about him in the past few days, and all sorts of stuff. No, I said. He seemed just the same, although he was a bit upset about having to play for Scott Hall Juniors, but who could blame him? I suppose he had kind of stopped talking, but I told the copper that this not talking lark went all the way back to Silverdale, where he'd had a particularly tough time. Did he make friends there? I shrugged my shoulders. How should I know, we were in different dormitories. But I didn't say this. And these days, was he the kind of boy who liked to comb his hair differently once he'd left the flat? He got me with that one. Why would our Tommy want to do that? Then the woman copper came into the kitchen and said that I'd have to stay with social services for a day or two, as my mother had to go into hospital for a checkup. Then there was a knock on the front door, and the woman copper opened it and let in two ambulance men carrying a stretcher. She showed the pair of them into the living room, and then she closed in the door to the kitchen. I knew that Mam would be mad if I barged my way in to see what was going on, so I just kept sitting where I was, and I tried hard not to cry. I used my tongue to wet my lips and stared down at the chequerboard pattern on the lino. The bloke copper put his hand on my shoulder. You'd best go and pack a bag, he said. They'll soon be here for you.

In the end it was a charmless, bearded man in a social services van who picked me up. The ambulance had long gone, and they'd waited until I was in my room before slipping Mam out of the front door, so I wouldn't see her leaving. The woman copper went with her, and that left just me and the bloke copper waiting for social services. When the bearded man arrived and I stepped outside and looked over the balcony and saw "Social Services" scrawled in big letters on the side of his van, I was embarrassed, for I knew that everyone on the estate would know that I was going into care. I sat in the front of the van and didn't even bother asking the man where he was taking me. When he pulled up outside of the big detached house on the corner of Manston Drive, I thought to myself: I pass this place every day on the bus, and I can see right into the garden from the top deck. It's about halfway to town, so if I end up having to stay here, then my journey to school will take only fifteen minutes, plus the ten minutes walking through the market and the arcades. After he'd yanked up the hand brake, the social services man turned to face me and spoke for the first time. I'm not sure if this is an appropriate use of public resources, but it's not up to me. But I can tell you, the Gilpins are a nice family, so do us all a favour and try to behave yourself. I didn't say anything to him, but I'm sure he could tell what I was thinking by the way I was glowering at him. So he changed his tune. Well, come on then, let's be having you. We don't want to keep them waiting.

The Gilpins had two girls, Helen and Louise, who were a bit younger than me, and they both were kind of chunky and giggled too much for my liking. Their mother put on an educated voice and made some halfhearted effort to introduce me to her daughters, but I could see straight off that her whole life revolved around pleasing the two girls. Her husband, on the other hand, wanted to make friends, which was the wrong way to go about things. Maybe he'd been dying for a son or something, but I sensed that he was trying too hard. The social worker bloke said so long then, and shook hands with Mr. Gilpin, and then Mrs. Gilpin showed him to the door. The moron pretty much just dropped me off there like he was some kind of taxi driver and then he left, and that was it.

The two girls were going off to bed, so Mr. Gilpin took me into the kitchen and made us both a ham sandwich, and then he offered me a cup of stewed tea, which, after one sip, I had to leave as I knew I couldn't stomach it. He asked me if I liked the Olympics, and I said I did. We took our sandwiches and sat in front of the telly on this really large, comfy settee, and we watched Kip Keino win the steeplechase. David Coleman was commentating and talking really fast, and I looked across at Mr. Gilpin, who kept nodding, and then smiling at me, and then looking back at the telly and nodding some more. I could tell that he also liked the Olympics, but I was now wondering about his clothes, for he had on fur-lined slippers, suit trousers with a crease, and a ratty-looking cardigan over a shirt with a grubby collar, all of which made him look about ten years older than he probably was. When his wife came in, he quickly got up and turned the volume down a bit. Mrs. Gilpin didn't say anything, she just pulled the curtains, and then sat down and watched for a while, but you could tell that she wasn't really following what was going on. Eventually she smiled at me and said, chop-chop, isn't it about time for bed now? I didn't stand up. Well, come on. Let's not be having a falling-out about it. I wanted to remind her that we'd only just started back after the summer holidays. Hadn't she ever heard of Alice Cooper? "School's Out," missus. It's on the radio every day, and it still feels like the holidays, so why was this woman being so stroppy?

I rolled from one side of the bed to the other side, then back again, and realized that it was the sheets that were making me feel funny, for they were clingy and made an odd scratching noise when I moved about, like somebody needed to oil them. And then I remembered: the bag of newspapers would still be sitting next to the fence by the church. Tomorrow I'd have to go and tell the newsagent that he'd have to get somebody else. I wondered if I'd ever see the inside of our flat again, but I had a feeling that I might not. Of course, nobody explained anything to me: not the copper, not the social worker, not even Mr. Gilpin, although it's possible that he was in the dark like me. I stared out of the window at the stars and wondered again about our Tommy. Where was he? Why wasn't anybody telling me what was up with him? I wasn't some kid, I was fourteen, and whichever way you looked at it, I had a right to know.

"Rock and Roll" (Parts 1 and 2)—Gary Glitter

After nearly a week at the Gilpins', I went to see Mam in hospital, and I found her sitting by herself in a big room full of plastic chairs. She was staring out of the window like she was in her own world, and she didn't even shift herself to turn around when I walked in, even though I know she must have heard me as my trainers made this horrible high-pitched squeal whenever they rubbed against a wooden floor. Mr. Gilpin pointed at her as though he reckoned he was helping me out, and then he whispered that he'd wait outside for me in the car. By now I knew that he'd have happily moved lock, stock, and barrel into his Austin Maxi if it meant he'd be able to get away from his wife and two roly-poly kids. After all, I was pretty sure that he cared more for the car than he did for them, and maybe fostering me was his way of finding somebody to talk to, for the three of them pretty much ignored him. I walked over to Mam and sat in the chair opposite her and said hello, all the while trying to hide the fact that the place was making me feel all queasy inside. She looked directly at me, and as she recognized me, a kind of tired smile spread over her face. I'm sorry, she said. I suppose I should have kept a closer watch on both of you. Will you forgive me? She looked like all the life had been knocked out of her, and I wanted to say that it wasn't her fault, but I just couldn't get the words out. When I think about it now, I'm convinced that they must have had her drugged up on all sorts of medicine, but to me she just seemed like she was half asleep and not really making much of an effort to stay awake, and I wondered how long it was going to be before I could get back to Mr. Gilpin's car. However, I knew I had to make the visit last a bit longer or it would be rude, but I didn't have a clue what to say, and I knew that she wasn't going to ask me anything about what I was up to. And so we sat together for nearly an hour, me itching to get up and leave and Mam with that vacant look on her face, and neither one of us able to talk about what had happened to my brother.

At school I decided to try harder because that's all there was now. There was no Tommy, and I didn't feel like talking to anybody, and so inevitably I soon discovered that I had no mates. I'd always been a bit of a clever clogs when it came to schoolwork, and the teachers often said if I continued to make an effort, I could do very well. I decided to swot up and try and come top in everything, except the science subjects, of course. It was my way of keeping my mind off the depressing reality that I'd been fostered out again, and this time it looked like Mam wasn't coming to rescue me. Mr. Gilpin obviously felt a bit sorry for me, so he started to give me fifty pence pocket money every Saturday, and I could double it if I helped Mrs. Gilpin with some jobs around the house. The two girls didn't have to do anything, and they still got more than me, but I wasn't complaining, for the money gave me a reason to stop nicking things. Mr. Gilpin told me I could use the record player whenever I wanted, but Mrs. Gilpin let me know that she didn't much care for my Gary Glitter single. Too much shouting, she said, which made me play it even louder in the hope that she might ask me to take it off. But she never did ask me to take it off, and eventually I realized that she never would, and so I started to play it quietly. I'd already worked out that Nancy Gilpin thought she was better than other folks, and she was deluded enough to think that her two girls were at the front of the line when they were handing out brains. I was shocked when, pointing out of the window, she told me that the next-door neighbour's dog was allowed to do his business in the house, like I'd be interested in hearing this. When it became clear that I wasn't—despite the additional information that they were proper Asians, for the wife had a big red spot on her forehead—I could tell that she immediately wrote me off and lumped me together with her scruffy husband. However, the sad fact was I now had no choice but to live with these people, and perhaps try and forget Mam.

After she gave me the silent treatment at the hospital, I didn't hear from Mam for a while, and Mr. Gilpin must have sensed that things hadn't gone that well, for he didn't ask me anything, or suggest a return trip to see her. The truth is, Mam's silence made me feel as though I'd done something wrong, as though it was me who had to explain myself, and the only way I could forget this whole hurtful nightmare was by concentrating on my schoolwork. At night I used to tell myself that maybe one day she'd be better and we could work everything out, but sometimes the feelings got so upsetting that I seriously thought about changing my name. And then Mam started with the phone calls and letters and post-cards, and it must have been Mrs. Gilpin who said something to social services, for a posh woman in a fancy twinset came to see me and told me that Mam was disrupting the Gilpins' household. I didn't say anything, but the social worker woman gave me a fake smile and said that she'd be bringing Mam on Christmas Day, but Mam never showed up, and I spent most of the day by myself feeling dismal in my bedroom. Things got worse when Mam turned up outside of school, and the teachers wouldn't let me out until she'd gone, and I just wanted the whole thing to end. Why couldn't she just go somewhere and get better instead of all this? Why was she embarrassing me?

"Life on Mars?"—David Bowie

After a while I decided that Helen, the older one, wasn't so bad. She was thirteen, and her little sister, Louise, was nearly eleven, but of late I'd noticed that Helen had lost a lot of weight and started to fill out upstairs. She'd also started to buy the *New Musical Express*, and every week she'd Sellotape the double-page posters up on her bedroom wall. It was mainly David Cassidy, and the Osmonds, and even the Bay City Rollers, but she also liked some okay music. After school she'd sometimes ask if she could borrow my records, and I told her that was alright as long as she didn't scratch them. She'd started to write the names of her favourite singers on the covers of her exercise books in all sorts of psychedelic patterns, and it was Helen who brought up the idea that we go to the Rollarena, where David Bowie was doing his final tour as Ziggy Stardust. If you agree to come with me, then Dad will let me go; otherwise you know he's just going to say that it's crackers to waste your spending money on a bloke dressed up in aluminum foil, with a bog brush hairdo, and who looks like he's good to his mam. Do you remember? That's what Dad said when he saw him on *Top of the Pops*. He wanted to know if this David Bowie fellar was doing it for a dare. Although I was two years older than her, Helen talked to me like we were the same age.

We'll have to queue for tickets, I said. She shrugged her shoulders as though this was obvious, and so I agreed. Okay then, let's go.

The concert was on a Thursday night, and I came back early from school to get changed, not that I had any glam gear to get into. Since I'd started studying really hard, I'd kind of lost all interest in clothes, which was just as well since even the hard cases and suedeheads were now starting to wear tie-dyed scoop-neck tee-shirts and glitter, and I didn't want to be associated with them in any way. However, I knew that Helen would be going in for something flashy, and I was more than a bit curious about what she'd be wearing. She wasn't back from school yet, so I nipped across the landing and snuck into her room. She had a smart dressing table mirror with three panels so you could adjust them and see what you looked like from the sides as well as the front. Before I knew what I was doing, I was fingering her cuddly toys, and then I started pulling open the drawers and touching her clothes. Steve Pamphlet was always boasting about going all the way with slags late at night in the shop doorways in town, but I'd never even touched a bra. Her underwear felt so soft and comfortable, and so I picked some up and smelled them and rubbed them against me a little, and then I could sense somebody standing behind me. I put the pile of panties back into the drawer and turned around and saw Mrs. Gilpin staring at me. She had on a headscarf, but I could see that her hair was in rollers, and I guessed that she must have been out in the back garden for she'd never be seen in the street with her hair in such a state. I'll never forget that look on her face. She was glaring at me like she'd finally sized me up and found out who I really was and there was no hiding it now. I knew that we'd never recover from this moment, and I just wanted it to end, but Mrs. Gilpin seemed to glare at me forever. Then, as though nothing had ever happened, she slowly turned and walked out of the room, but she left the door wide open so I'd know that I was expected to follow. Immediately.

"Dat"—Pluto Shervington

I don't take a good photograph, and as if to prove it, there's a picture of me that was taken at one of those photo booths not long before I left the Gilpins' house for university. After Mam died, it was my history teacher who kept chucking compliments in my direction, and I liked the attention, so I started to do extra lessons after school. That's when he put me on the list for Oxford and Cambridge, but I could tell that he didn't have much faith that I would do the work necessary to give myself a chance, although I was determined to prove him wrong. In the photograph I'm seventeen and staring into the camera, with my big, unshapely hair and my bulky black-rimmed specs, and I'm not smiling at all. I'm focused, and there's not even a little hint of a smile. I've also got on the worst jumper in the world: a blue, round-necked polyester number, with two white hooped stripes. The truth is I look downcast, which is pretty much how I remember my time as a foster child in the Gilpins' house. In my own mind, I reckoned that once Mam died the social services people must have told the Gilpins that the decent thing to do would be to see it through until I went off to university. It must have been agony for them because it was undeniable that Mrs. Gilpin hated me, and I didn't exactly think much of her either. Right from the off, whenever she spoke to me, she'd always been a little abrupt, and then after the thing with

Helen's clothes she never stopped looking at me as though I'd somehow interfered with her precious daughter.

In the end I was there for nearly four years, during which time I continued to be interested in pop music, but I also began to watch a lot of films. Once I'd done enough work to pretty much guarantee high grades in my exams, I started to skive off school and go to the so-called independent cinema near the polytechnic, where I'd watch themed seasons of films by mainly American and French directors. I even bought a paperback book called *The Film Director as Artist* and decided that this is what I wanted to be—a film director—but only after I'd finished university. However, first of all, I had to get out of the Gilpins' house, and the sooner the better, for the whole family more or less ignored me. Helen never asked to borrow any more records, and Louise made sure that she was never alone with me. Even Mr. Gilpin stopped trying to be friendly; he occasionally smiled in a kind of pitiful way, but his wife must have told him that I was some kind of deviant because, aside from the driving lessons that he got me as a seventeenth birthday present, he went out of his way to avoid me.

When I wasn't watching films I went to concerts by myself. Elton John, the Faces, Supertramp, Emerson Lake & Palmer: I saw loads of gigs. Even Joan Armatrading, which felt odd. A kid at school called Patrick wanted to see her, and I suppose she was okay, but there wasn't much in the way of a drum solo. It just wasn't my type of music, and I had a feeling that I shouldn't have gone with somebody as I much preferred going by myself, so the next time Patrick asked me to go with him to a gig I just made up some pathetic excuse. Patrick wanted to do law at university because his dad was a solicitor and his grandfather had been a barrister. He said he didn't have any choice in the matter. I applied to university to do history, and was soon asked to attend two interviews. The first one was a joke. I took the bus to Durham and walked around a bit until I found the university history department, only to be told that the interview was the following week. I'd got the date wrong.

I was surprised when Mr. Gilpin said he'd drive me to the

second interview, but I said I didn't mind taking the bus or the train to Oxford. Which? he asked. I said the train, and he opened his wallet and handed me a fiver. He did so in a way that made me realize that we were to keep quiet about this. The night before the interview I was watching telly and Helen and her boyfriend came in from the pictures and told me to budge up on the settee as they plonked themselves down next to me. Lester Nisbett had on tragically unpolished brown platform shoes that were even bigger than hers, and a whisper of hair where he hoped a moustache might one day grow. He also had that "some bird's gonna get lucky tonight" kind of cockiness about him, and judging by the fresh love bites on Helen's neck, he had every reason to be confident. He asked me if could I tell him what the lyrics of that Pluto Shervington song meant. No, I said, I couldn't. I hadn't got a clue. Come on, Benny boy, of course you do. He winked at Helen and started to laugh, and suddenly it was clear that they'd both been on the lager and limes. He's not telling the truth, you know. You know that, don't you? Helen tried to suppress her giggles, but she wouldn't meet my eyes. Tell me something, why are your lips so fat? And it's like you've got wool on your head instead of hair. And what's that white stuff on your skin? By your elbows. It's all ashylike. Jesus, you look like a fucking burned sausage. Helen burst out laughing, but she still wouldn't meet my eyes.

"Bohemian Rhapsody"—Queen

I had to stay overnight at the college as they did two interviews for candidates, one in the afternoon and then another one the next morning. I was told that dinner would be served in the dining hall at seven precisely. The first interview had gone badly. In fact, I was sure that the three lecturers could see that I was out of my depth, and I decided they were basically taking the piss out of me and couldn't wait for me to leave the room so they could collapse into heaps of laughter. The main one of them had on a cravat, and everything about him suggested swellhead, especially the way he was twirling his propelling pencil in between his fingers like it was the simplest thing in the world. Why shouldn't one walk naked in the streets on a hot day? Any thoughts on that, young man? What kind of question was that? You shouldn't walk naked in the streets because you'll look like an arsehole and offend people. I didn't say that, but whatever it was that I said in response obviously didn't impress them. All of them did that thing where you nod and make some notes and kind of hum like you're really thinking about what was said, but it's transparent that you're not. And then I got the next question. To whom does a member of Parliament owe his loyalty: his party, his constituents, or his conscience? Depends, I said. Depends on what the issue is. I waited, but their silence let me know that I was supposed to expand on my answer, which was when I started to waffle and get all confused.

There was no way I was going into the dining hall, so although it had changed from spitting rain to a downpour, I went wandering up the High Street until I found a fish-and-chips shop. The wind was brutal, and the cold was cutting right through me as all I had was a thin jacket and my old United scarf. Fish and chips once, please. With scraps. But I didn't say the part about scraps because I knew they wouldn't get it. By the time I got back to the room I was drenched to the skin, and so I turned on the two-bar electric fire and sat and ate the fish and chips right out of the paper and listened to the tranny I'd brought with me. The song went on for ages and sounded more like a piece of classical music than a pop song. When it was over, I screwed up the fish-and-chips paper and rammed it into the bin and then thought of our Tommy, which I did pretty much every day.

I also thought about Mam and the business of her not showing up that Christmas and then waiting outside the school for me. The posh social worker woman had come around a second time in order to explain about Mam's behaviour and she said that in time she thought that things would probably be alright between the two of us, but she reckoned it best if Mam just gave me some space. I remember I didn't say anything, so she went on and told me that Mam had been going through a rough patch, but she was getting better and onto the right track. And then later, the same woman came to the Gilpin's a third time, and told me that apparently Mam was planning on leaving the library and going down to London to try and start to put her life back together, whatever that meant. I listened to the woman but there was only one thing I wanted to ask Mam and that was, What about our Tommy? But I knew Mam wouldn't want to deal with this, and so I looked blankly at this posh woman perched on the Gilpins' settee in her familiar fancy twinset and decided that until Mam did want to deal with this, then there really wasn't anything to say as far as I was concerned. I'd be concentrating on my school work, and hopefully one day getting a place at university, and then clearing off out of the Gilpins' house.

"Dancing Queen"—Abba

The summer before I went to university was the hottest on record, and Abba were at number one for nearly two months. Even now when I hear the song, I start to sweat. Every morning was a scorcher, and there was no need to check the weather or wonder when it was going to break. It wasn't going to change. It was like Spain. Or what I imagined Spain to be like. I was still living with the Gilpins as I didn't have anywhere else to go until university started. I had no money for a flat, and so I just tried to stay out of their way. I'd sneak in from the pictures long after everyone had gone to bed, and I'd hide out in my room until they'd all gone out in the morning. Eventually I got a job in a dingy backstreet garage, pumping petrol and checking water and oil levels. It wasn't a summer job, so I had to tell the bloke who interviewed me that I had ambitions in the auto trade and one day I hoped to own a petrol station; otherwise he'd have never given me the time of day. He made a steeple of his hands and asked me if I had a driving licence, and I said yes, I did, for I'd passed my test first time. My would-be boss nodded approvingly and made a cat's cradle of his fingers as he stood up from behind his desk. I looked at him, then back down at the desk, where I couldn't credit the state of his blackened ashtray; it was a dirty metal contraption with a button on top that you plunged and two little trapdoors that flapped open and prompted the ash to drop inside. How could anybody run a business with something that filthy on his desk?

I soon discovered that he was a retired copper, and he was trying to be liberal and all nice, but I could tell that he was as thick as two short planks. Half his clients were Pakistanis and Indians dressed up in all the gear, but he tried too hard when they came in, and he was always putting it on. They smiled sweetly, but I could tell that, like me, they didn't think much of him. His other clients were corporate accounts types, ill-mannered buggers who just signed for their petrol and wanted to be treated as though the sun shone out of their arses. They were the ones who got short-changed, because I soon learned how to fix one particular pump so that the meter wouldn't clear. If the smarmy bastards asked for five gallons and the pump already had on two, I'd give them three gallons, and they'd have to pay for five. Naturally I'd keep the cash for the two gallons, and nobody was the wiser. I was skimming off at least a tenner a week, and then towards the end of September I quit with nearly a hundred quid in the bank. I packed up my things at the Gilpins' and rented a van so I could drive south to university, but I decided to wait until Helen and Louise were at school before taking my leave.

That morning I could see it on Mrs. Gilpin's jaundiced face that she was hoping that my going to university would be the end of everything. Good riddance to bad rubbish. Both she and her husband stood by the door and watched me lift the last box into the van, and then I came back into the front hallway, where Nancy Gilpin leaned in and gave me a pretend hug like she didn't want to catch anything. Her husband offered me a firm handshake, and he wished me good luck, and I said thanks, and that was it, they were rid of me. I could tell that Mr. Gilpin wanted to say something more to me, but he could never come straight out with anything, he always had to go all around the houses, and now, with his wife gaping at him like a pit bull, there was no time. As usual, he'd missed the moment. I drove away from the Gilpins' house on Manston Drive, and I took care not to look into the rearview mirror. Once I was sure that I was out of sight, I sped up and turned the van towards the moors, which was the opposite direction to where I should have been going.

I stopped by the side of the road and stared at the depressing landscape. Bloody hell, I thought, even with a full moon it must be pitch black up here at night. And cold, and our Tommy didn't have his duffel coat with him. I shouted. Tommy! I walked a few paces away from the van and looked out into the distance. Tommy! Tommy! But it was no use. I should have done more for Tommy, and that's what had been keeping me awake for years now: the feeling that it was my fault. As a family we had nothing, so of course it was straightforward enough for somebody to turn our Tommy's head. It's easy to turn a kiddie's head when he has nothing. I'm sorry, our Tommy. Sorry for laughing at you at Silverdale when you wet the bed. Everyone laughed at you, but I shouldn't have. However, I had no idea what was going on. Honest, not a clue. I took a few steps onto the actual moorland. There was nobody around, which was just as well, but I really wasn't ready to climb back into the driver's seat and point the van south. Not just yet. I wasn't ready to abandon our Tommy again, so I made up my mind to stay put on the moors. Hours passed as I walked for mile after mile, and as the daylight eventually started to fade in the sky, I could feel the moors closing in on me, and for the first time in ages I began to feel close to my brother.

VII

FAMILY

Ronald Johnson carefully put the cup of tea back into the circle of the saucer and placed the unfolded newspaper on the tabletop. That was his grandson; he was sure of it. The boy was taller than he had imagined, and although he moved quickly past the window, he could see his daughter's face in the upper lip and the eyes. There was a girl with him who was small and blond, with a kind and smiling face, and it looked as though they were holding hands, but everything had happened so fast. One second they were passing the huge glass window, so close that he could have reached through and touched them, and the next they were swallowed up by a crowd of jabbering, nervously excited students, who, once the traffic lights had turned red, streamed across the road towards the imposing nineteenth-century building where they would be taking their final examinations.

He took a deep breath and then picked up his cup and finished his tea before pouring himself a refill from the faux Wedgwood pot. The waitress arrived with his order of crumpets, and having put down the plate, she fished into her apron pocket and produced three miniature jars and gave him a choice of raspberry or apricot jam or marmalade. He was stumped and looked inanely at the poor young woman, who eventually took pity on him and left all three. Retired now, and in his late sixties, he often found himself worrying about the possibility of losing dignity, and these days he tried doubly hard to keep up standards. He always made an effort to dress properly in a jacket and white shirt and one of his wide selection of ties, none of which had stripes. In the past, he had tried blue shirts, and even pink, but anything but white made him feel like a dandy. He was a stickler for sturdy black shoes with a nice high polish, but since he'd lost his wife, he'd begun to experiment a little with his trousers, and he'd become fond of both turnups and flannels, so one or the other, or a combination of both, might appear, depending on his mood.

A new batch of kids were jostling around and waiting for their chance to cross the road. As he took them in, it suddenly occurred to him how light, almost weightless young people are, innocently floating along, unburdened by any experience of life's sudden twists or turns. These students have joy, without fully understanding the prized nature of such a commodity, but soon enough they will be packing up their things and leaving the safety of their university years and setting out on their journeys. As he butters his first crumpet, he reminds himself of how important it is that he make contact with his grandson while he knows where he is, and before he loses sight of him completely. Once he graduates he'll no doubt be off, and heaven only knows if he'll ever be able to track him down again. Yesterday evening, after he'd found a place to park the car and checked in at the hotel, he took the pleasant walk across the centre of the town and presented himself at the porter's lodge and asked if it might be possible to see Benjamin Wilson. The man ceased his form filling and peered up at him over the top of his reading glasses. In a sympathetic voice, he let him know that the college was closed to visitors, but told him that he was free to leave a message. He could see that the porter wanted to press him, and would most likely have flouted the rules and ushered him in and in the direction of the boy's room had he shared more information, but he thanked the man and turned to leave. "Hang on a minute." The porter opened the door to his small room and stepped out in front of him. "They're all doing exams in the morning, over there." He pointed across the street. "If you don't want to leave a message, you can always see him either before he goes in or after he comes out."

Once he arrived back at the hotel, he asked at the desk if there were any messages for him, half expecting Mrs. Barrett to have phoned, but the waistcoated receptionist shook his head and smiled, and then wondered if Mr. Johnson might be dining with them this evening. It had been a long drive, and he had completely forgotten about food, but he realized now that he should probably eat something despite feeling in no mood to sit alone in a dining room full of people. "Perhaps you might prefer to see the room service menu?" Indeed, he did prefer this, and an hour later he finished his platter of trout, new potatoes, and peas and stacked everything neatly back onto the tray, which he set down on the spare bed beside the large envelope of letters, and an assortment of her other writing, that represented all that he had left of Monica. For a moment he couldn't work out whether to call downstairs and ask them to come for the tray or if he should just leave it be for the night. Either way, he knew that he needed a bit of peace and quiet so that he could peruse the contents one final time before giving the large buff envelope to his grandson, believing, as he did, that at this stage of the game that's where the material rightfully belonged.

✦

Ben looked across the examination hall and saw Mandy scribbling away at her paper, and he was once again conscious of the fact that he had nothing to offer her in exchange for the ongoing gift of her family's warmth and generosity. Since they had started going out with each other at the beginning of their second year, he had spent every vacation with her folks in Wiltshire. Her older brother was away in the army in Northern Ireland, and her father always reminded him that while Michael was fighting the good fight, they had plenty of room in the house. Ben had explained to Mandy about having been brought up in a foster home, and presumably she must have said something to her parents, for they had never asked any questions. If they were nonplussed by anything, he knew they would be respectful enough to ask Mandy and not him, but he wasn't sure how much she would be able to help them out. She seemed to understand that talking about his mother and father, or his brother, was difficult for him to deal with, so she never raised the subject. When Mandy's granny died, and she had to go back home for the funeral, he did, however, tell her that he had just the one memory of his own grandparents on his mother's side. He must have been about six, and both he and his brother were tired out when they got to Wakefield, and so, even though it was still light outside, they both were bundled upstairs and into bed. Then, before either of them knew what was happening, they were soon back on a train again. Tommy fell fast asleep, but Ben remembered looking up into his mother's face.

"Doesn't your mam and dad want us to stay with them?"

His mother pulled him closer to her side.

"No, love, we were only visiting. We just popped in to say hello, and now we're off to our own flat."

Having announced this, his mother slammed the door shut on any further discussion of his grandparents, and as both he and Tommy eventually discovered, the idea of talking about family in general was completely off the agenda as far as their mother was concerned.

✦

The waiter asks him if the food is to his liking, and he simply nods, for his mouth is full of pasta and meatballs. The fellow couldn't have chosen a more inopportune moment to start quizzing him, but he doesn't seem to notice and offers a quick, self-satisfied grin and then moves on to the next table, where he presumably asks the same question. Having walked around the town for the best part of two hours, during which time he kept himself mentally spry by browsing the displays in bookshop windows, he hurried back to the main street and took up his watch across the road from the examination building. He positioned himself halfway between the college and the teashop where he had ordered breakfast, but it soon dawned on him that either his timing was off and the students had already finished for the morning, or perhaps they were exiting out of some back entrance that he was unaware of. When a bus pulled up beside him, and an excitable driver shouted, "Well, you getting on or what, mate?" he registered that he should move. He mumbled an apology and took a step back from the bus stop, and then watched as the elaborate doors concertinaed shut with a cushioned thud. There was no point to his dilly-dallying in the street, so he decided to go and find the rather unpretentious-looking Italian restaurant overlooking the river that he had walked past this morning. He hadn't troubled himself to inspect the menu, but the presence of a blackboard on the pavement in front of the establishment convinced him that the food would be fresh as it looked as if the chalked-up offerings changed from day to day.

This morning, before he left the hotel, the lady on the front desk had handed him a folded piece of paper that contained a message from his next-door neighbour Mrs. Barrett. Would he please, when he had a spare moment, telephone her? But, the message reassured him, there was "Nothing urgent." Last year he had finally come to the conclusion that rattling around in a big semi-detached house by himself was more aggravation than it was worth. It was the postman who, having witnessed him struggling down the driveway towards the rosebushes with his secateurs at the ready, pointed out to him that the pain in his knees might be alleviated by considering the advantages of a bungalow. His home had barely been on the market for a week before he found himself at the centre of a bidding war, which eventually concluded with his being offered well above his asking price. For a man now living on the combined efforts of his state and his teacher's pensions, the added sum of money was a great bonus and enabled him to buy into a new development that was in a small village to the west of the town, where he soon discovered that most of the newcomers were either retirees like him or first-time buyers looking to get a foot on the bottom rung of the housing ladder. The bungalow next to his was occupied by a Mrs. Barrett, who had moved in a week prior to his arrival. Recently widowed with no children, and never having had to work a day in her life, she seemed a little lost, but she was very nicely mannered and had obviously been accustomed to having access to the resources necessary to keep herself looking in tiptop condition.

To begin with, she asked him if he'd be interested in joining her at church on Sunday morning, but he had to tell her straight that this wasn't his thing. He did, however, suggest that he'd enjoy her company for an evening stroll to The Bulldog, where they might enjoy a half-pint, or whatever took her fancy. A month or so later, when his chest problems began to flare up again, a hangover from his childhood pneumonia, she began to regularly bring him soup and sandwiches with the crusts cut off, and she insisted on faffing about and doing the occasional bit of tidying up around the bungalow. He was soon back on his feet, but he now found himself taking her for a twice-weekly run out in his Ford Escort, usually to the supermarket in the town centre, where the prices were better, and as a result, he was forced to listen to her going on about her Alfred as if he had been the thirteenth disciple. Some part of him knew that he should be grateful that he had such a caring neighbour who clearly enjoyed his company, but this woman had bullied her way into his life, and he simply wasn't ready to deal with another person and all her needs and foibles. While he was wrestling with his concern over how best to bring this up with her, he noticed that certain items were starting to disappear from his place and were suddenly making an appearance over at Mrs. Barrett's bungalow. First, a carriage clock, and then the silver tankard that the school had presented him with on the occasion of his retirement, but because, during his illness, he'd given Mrs. Barrett the spare key to his bungalow, it was no mystery to him how his things were getting over there.

He'd bought a bottle of sweet wine from Asda with the express purpose of using it to help lubricate what he imagined might be a taxing conversation. It was a sunny afternoon, and they sat opposite each other on the garden chairs he'd brought with him from the old house, and they listened to the birds trilling and twittering in what he considered to be an annoying fashion. "To your good health," he said. They clinked glasses, and he had to admit he'd never seen Mrs. Barrett looking so happy and contented. As a result, instead of admonishing her for her petty pilfering, or asking for the spare key back, he unexpectedly found himself telling her the story of how, not that long after he'd lost Ruth, he received the phone call from the secure hospital in London during which the woman told him that his daughter had taken an overdose of pills and he'd have to come down and identify the body. He asked the woman, "What, come down now? It's after seven, and even if I leave right at this moment, I don't think I can get down there before midnight." The woman reassured him that there was no rush and tomorrow would be fine, but after he put down the phone, he sat in the gloom for nearly an hour, and then, worried that he was about to be overwhelmed by grief, he suddenly rose to his feet and grabbed his jacket. He went out to the car and drove down through the night to London, and once there he sat outside the hospital, with his driver's seat reclined, until the gates opened at seven. It was a coloured nurse who greeted him at reception, and she ushered him into the hospital proper and steered him to a room where he had to make the identification.

The whole thing was depressingly straightforward. They simply pulled back a sheet, and he nodded and quickly turned his head. They'd closed Monica's eyes, but they'd not done anything else for her, so her makeup was all streaked, and he could see that she was as thin as a rake. She looked emaciated. Bloody hell, Monica, it's not right. The processing was swift; he signed two forms, and they told him that cremation was usual, unless he had other instructions, and they could send him the ashes if he so wished. After everything that had gone on, it just didn't seem fitting to have her lying with Ruth. I'm sorry, Monica, but I can't warrant it. And what was he going to do with ashes? What bloody use were ashes? They let him know that social services would be informing her son, and so at least he was spared that awkwardness, and then the nurse handed him a large envelope containing some letters and papers and said this was all Monica had. He wanted to ask about his wife's gold watch, but he imagined that his daughter must have lost it or had it stolen from her possession, and so he said nothing, and that was it: his Monica was gone.

Mrs. Barrett leaned over and touched his arm. "Ronald, are you alright? Let me go in and make you a nice cup of strong coffee." By the time he came back to himself, he realized that his neighbour was inside his bungalow by herself, and that's when it occurred to him that he ought to get Monica's envelope out of there and put it where it belonged. Really, he couldn't risk his daughter's effects going walkabout, for these days it was all he had left of her.

✦

It was Mr. Gilpin who told Ben that a social worker would be coming around to see him in an hour or so. He'd scarcely stepped in the door from school, but Ben had a good idea of what was going on, and he'd been bracing himself for the visit. The week before, he had been to see David Bowie on his own, for at the last minute Mrs. Gilpin had banned Helen from going with him. When he came back from the concert, only Mr. Gilpin was up, sitting in a darkened living room, and the man looked as if he had been given the task of telling him something, but it was obvious that Mr. Gilpin couldn't find it in himself to do so. When he got back from school and Mr. Gilpin told him that a social worker wanted to speak with him, he reckoned that this was it: this person would be telling him to pack his bags and get ready to move either to new foster parents or to a children's home.

He heard Mr. Gilpin shout upstairs to him. When he came down, he could see that the young man had on big horn-rimmed glasses, behind which there was a sad look painted on his smooth, oval face. "Sit down, Ben." Having spoken, Mr. Gilpin was quick to excuse himself, and he left them alone in the living room. As soon as he'd gone, the social worker cleared his throat and told him that there was no easy way to say this. "I'm sorry, Ben, but your mother's passed away in London." Ben looked at the man, but didn't say anything. "Are you alright, Ben?" He had been sure that things couldn't get any worse than they already were, with only Mr. Gilpin speaking to him. But right now Mr. Gilpin could stop talking to him if he wanted. He felt as if somebody had punched him hard, in the face, but it didn't hurt. He couldn't feel anything. The young man reached over and clumsily covered his hand. "I'm so sorry, Ben." He wanted to pull his hand away, but it wasn't this man's fault. "I just want to let you know that your grandfather might be in touch. We've given him your details."

✦

After he finishes his pasta dish and pays up at the restaurant bar, he decides to stop off at one of the better bookshops and buy some notepaper and envelopes and then make his way back to the hotel. Once there he will write a short letter to his grandson, telling him that he would like him to have what is in the envelope, and letting him know that he is very sorry to have missed him. Having done so, he will then undertake the short walk back across town and deposit everything with the helpful college porter and leave it up to the lad as to whether or not he's inclined to communicate. On returning to his hotel room, he discovers that an elderly cleaner is only now finishing off his room and emptying the wastepaper bins before readying herself to move on down the corridor, and so he stands stiffly to one side and waits. Once she closes in the door behind her, he takes off his jacket and hangs it on a wooden coat hanger in the wardrobe, and then he remembers Mrs. Barrett's message but he doesn't feel in the right humour to call. After all, he knows full well that she will simply be anxious to know if he is feeling alright, and then she will want to be reminded of not only the time but the day he is coming back so that she might have a nice meal ready for his return. As he slips off his shoes and lies back on the bed, he tries not to think unkind thoughts about his neighbour, for he now understands that the poor woman's erratic behaviour is all down to her memory's gradually failing her. These days Mrs. Barrett is living increasingly in the present, which, he imagines, might not be such an unacceptable place to dwell.

✦

After she died, Ben threw out all of her letters and postcards to him. He also got rid of the newspaper clippings about finding Tommy, and the articles to do with the trial of Derek Evans. He'd kept everything in a grey rucksack that he stashed under his bed, but a week or so after the visit from the young social worker he took the whole lot down to the skips behind the supermarket and hurled the bag in. The only thing he saved was a small black-and-white photograph of him and Tommy that was taken on the day they arrived at Silverdale by either Peter or Rachel, he couldn't remember which one. He put the snapshot in his pocket and then went to the newsagents to buy ten Benson and Hedges and a box of matches. He sat on a bench on the Green where everyone could see him, and he smoked one fag after another until he'd finished half the pack, but nobody said anything to him, and if he was honest, he didn't even like the taste of the cigarettes. More than anything, he wanted to believe that she'd done the best she could, but he just couldn't get his head around the fact that she'd given him away, which meant that there was probably something the matter with him. Why didn't she try harder and put him first? Why didn't she want him? When he got back to the foster home, he found Mr. Gilpin sitting in the kitchen by himself, and he could see by the look on the man's face that he could smell the smoke, but Mr. Gilpin didn't say anything. Instead he just asked Ben if he wanted to talk about his mother, and he reminded the foster child that he was happy to listen. Ben shook his head. After a painfully uncomfortable silence, it was Mr. Gilpin who eventually got up from his stool and left his own kitchen without saying anything further.

✦

When he opens his eyes, he can see shadows in the room, and the noises emanating from the street have a different, more subdued tone. It is immediately apparent that he must have fallen asleep, and so he turns his head. Sitting on top of the coverlet on the spare bed, he sees the envelope containing his daughter's writing, and he notices on the desk the unopened pack of notepaper, with matching envelopes. Yesterday's drive must have knocked the wind out of him, and last night he hadn't got much sleep as he tossed and turned and worried about how to handle the upcoming day. He now knows that he should act decisively, and so, having opted to forget about writing a short letter, he stands and begins quickly to smarten himself up. He scurries across town, careful to dodge the platoons of swerving bicycles, and when he reaches the college, he sees that it is a different porter. He is a younger man with slicked-back hair, and he might even be the son of the fellow with whom he spoke earlier, for they appear to share a family face. He asks if Benjamin Wilson is in his room as he wishes to leave something for him. This seems to amuse the junior porter, who begins to chuckle.

"Well, sir, if you want to go to his room, that's one thing. However, if you want to leave something for him, then that's another thing altogether, isn't it?"

He understands that if he is going to leave the envelope, then he will have to ask this man for a sheet of paper and a pen so that he might at least let his grandson know that he has visited and give the lad some contact details.

"But the truth is, you won't find him in his room. They've set up a tent outside of the college bar, and all the third-years are enjoying themselves, shall we say. You're free to go through and give him your package yourself, if that's what you'd prefer."

There is a girl leaning against him, the same blond girl that he saw him with this morning. Her glass of Pimm's is choked with bits of fruit, and it's discernible that there is nothing under her flimsy sweater to restrain any part of her in the event of a sudden movement. The lad is holding court with a pint of beer in his hand, and he appears to be laughing at a joke that one of his friends has just told.

"Excuse me, Benjamin."

He hears his name and turns and sees a well-dressed old man, in a navy blazer and what look like cricket trousers, standing before him. For a moment he wonders if he's somebody from the university. Maybe he has made some brainless mistake on his papers, for the bloke has a large envelope in his hand, and he looks really serious.

"I'm sorry to disturb you, but there's no reason that you should know who I am. Do you have a minute?"

His friends are staring now, and Mandy has grabbed his arm as though determined that he shouldn't go anywhere.

"A minute? Yeah, alright."

"Thank you. I'm sorry to interrupt your evening."

✦

The lad said that he had no objection to a short walk, so Ronald Johnson decided to take the young man to the bar of his hotel as opposed to some noisy town centre pub. As they walked, he asked him how his exams had gone, and once again he apologized for the intrusion and for dragging him away, albeit temporarily, from his friends. They soon reached the hotel and edged their way across the bar and took possession of two black leather chairs in the far corner underneath a life-size oil portrait of a founder of the university. The busy facility appeared to be full of parents and their children celebrating the end of term, but the waiter was surprisingly quick, and he placed the gin and tonic and pint of lager on the table in front of them and then confirmed that the drinks were to be charged to a room. Ronald Johnson touches glasses with his grandson, before nudging the slice of lemon over the edge and into the fizzing concoction and then lifting the vessel to his mouth. "Cheers." He looks at the boy over the rim, and can see that he does indeed have an aspect of his mother, particularly around the unblinking almond-shaped eyes. However, not wishing to be caught gazing, he resolves to come straight to the point and not waste any more time.

"I have some of your mother's writing, and a few letters to you that she never sent." He gestures towards the large envelope that he has placed on the table before them, but he can see the boy looking quizzically at him as though wanting to ask, How come you have this stuff? "They gave the material to me at the hospital in London."

Memory blunders towards Ben as he suddenly feels undone by the very sound of this man's voice. He has spent six long years attempting to empty his mind of his mother's treatment of them both, and now here he is, in this hotel bar, suddenly remembering the dumb stories that Derek Evans encouraged her to write that he said he'd pass on to the arts editor of the *Post*. Tommy insisted he was alright, but Ben was always trying to tell his brother that Mam's friend was a liar, and there was no way he could get any stories published or the autographs of any footballers or pop stars like he promised. He hated this man, and he knew that he sometimes stopped over, but he didn't tell this to Tommy. Bloody hell, Mam must have been desperate for a friend if she lowered herself to that. In fact, thinking about it like this was the only way that he'd ever been able to square anything in his mind. I mean, really desperate.

"Excuse me, sir."

They both look up and can see that the waiter is standing over them, but he is addressing the younger of his two guests. In his hands he holds a maroon-coloured tie, which he offers to Ben, who reluctantly takes it from the man.

"Dress code, I'm afraid. I hope you don't mind wearing it while you're with us here in the lounge."

Ben fastens the tie around his neck and tucks it under the collar of his tee-shirt, and then he thinks of Mandy. He said he'd only an hour, so he ought to be getting back soon. After all, if this man has driven all this way just to give him some of his mother's belongings, then that's fine, he's done it now. If there's something else, then he should say it and stop beating around the bush. He is already dreading having to explain the visit to Mandy and his friends, and he wants to get out of this place before the bloke suggests having more drinks. All this small talk about what his post-university plans might be is just a waste of everyone's time, and they both know it.

✦

Why can't the boy see that they are all each other has now? He isn't asking for anything except communication and perhaps some understanding. Obviously the lad has no idea how upset he was when he read in the newspapers what had happened to his brother. But he simply couldn't get in touch because Monica would never have entertained any sympathy from him. And then later he'd once turned on the television set and seen a fellow called Wilson speaking at one of those commonwealth meetings where the queen is in attendance, and he couldn't help wondering if this was the scoundrel that Monica ran off with. He stares at his grandson. Maybe the boy knows the chap, and he has found some way to reestablish a connection with his father. So many questions that only this young man can answer, but he can now feel himself running out of options and beginning to panic.

"Would you care for another lager, Ben? Or perhaps a meal? You could always invite your pals, you know. My treat."

"Well, thanks very much, but we've got plans. It might be a bit hard to change things now."

Yes, of course. Plans. And more plans. On the walk over to the hotel the boy let him know that he was hoping to go around Europe by train for a month or so with his friend Mandy. Their intention was to come back and get jobs over the summer that would enable them to save up and then take off again for the Far East and Australia and avoid the English winter. He wanted to ask the boy why, but he instinctively knew this would be a foolish question, and so he kept walking and tried not to think of his aching knees. And now he sees his grandson looking at his watch for a second time, and so he signals to the waiter to bring him the bill so he can sign it to his room. It's clear that this meeting has now arrived at its natural terminus. The boy begins to strip off the tie, while he in turn reaches into the inside pocket of his jacket and takes out his chequebook.

"I'd very much like to give you some money, Ben. To help you with your travels. Would that be alright?"

✦

He lies squashed up in his single bed with Mandy, but it is he who has volunteered to be jammed up against the wall. He stares at the ceiling. When they first started going out with each other, he shared with her the photograph of him and Tommy, and he let her know that his brother had gone off to a place where he couldn't follow, and that was about all that he could bring himself to say. However, it was evident that Mandy understood, and she never pushed it. With regard to his mother, he said very little beyond the obvious. Mandy turns slightly towards him and lets her finger ride the bumpy topography of his lips.

After he came back from the hotel bar, they said a clumsy goodbye to the others, and he and Mandy hurried off to sit together in the corner of a quiet pub, where she listened carefully to everything that he told her (my mother couldn't cope, with anything really). He told Mandy that after his grandfather had handed him the cheque for one hundred pounds, the man smiled and then started to tell him all about his new bungalow. It was only then that he understood that his grandmother must have died.

"I do a spot of gardening these days. And I've got plenty of space if you'd like to stay."

Mandy looked momentarily baffled. "He actually said that?" Almost imperceptibly, Ben began to shake his head. "Look, Ben, if you really want to go up there, you know I'll come with you."

He finished his drink and then turned to look at her.

"I wanted to tell him, I don't need to read her old letters to know that in her own screwy way she cared." He paused. "I'm tired. Let's go back to my room tonight."

Mandy takes her finger from his lips and then shuffles over a little to give him a bit more space. Ben continues to look at the ceiling in his bed-study room, and he remains isolated in worries as murky as fog.

"Do you feel like you've got something else to say to him, Ben?"

"I don't think so, Mand. I feel badly about it, but I don't really have anything to say to him. Nothing."

✦

He knew that a midmorning departure would enable him to avoid any kind of traffic issues. The motorway is practically empty, aside from the huge articulated lorries charging their way south towards London and the Channel Ports. Again he reminds himself that the ability to forgive is a virtue worth cultivating, but this is something that his daughter never understood, especially after the business with Dr. Greenwell and his accusations. (Let me put it to you simply, Mr. Johnson. My daughter doesn't much care for the way you leer at her.) Why Hester would say something like this made no sense, but Ruth forgave him, not that he'd done anything wrong. She stood by him. The buff envelope is on the passenger seat. He wanted to see if the lad would remember to take it with him when he left the hotel bar. It soon became clear, however, that in his rush to get back to his friends he was going to leave it behind, so he decided not to remind the boy in the hope that its absence might serve as a spur for him to seek out his grandfather. He remembered to put his address and phone number on the back of the cheque so there couldn't be any excuse. His mind is racing now. As he passes the Leicester Forest East service station, he realizes that he is going to have to say something. Sadly, the Mrs. Barretts of the world just won't do, not while he still has something to offer his own flesh and blood. The woman means well, but she's not Ruth, and she never will be. He is going to have to ask for his spare key back as it's been promised to another. He deliberately didn't say anything to his grandson, but he hopes it's understood. He'll just have to be patient and wait for the lad to contact him.

VIII

ALONE

I had a feeling it was coming, but I'm still shocked by the way they're carrying on. After all, I paid my rent on time for the first two months, and we seemed to be getting on fine, but now that I've lost my job up the road, and just need a bit of patience, they've suddenly changed their tune. The American one is the problem, but if I'm honest, I never much cared for him. He knocks on my door and starts to jabber away like he's my friend, but I'm not dense, for I know that he ran away from fighting in Vietnam and he probably reckoned that nobody would find him in London. I've got his number. While the other one goes off to work, this one stays at home and plays the part of the wife, cleaning the house and singing along to the wireless and drinking vodka, because he thinks nobody can smell it on him. Really, Monica, we don't want any unpleasantness. But I tell him, look, I can't give you what I don't have, can I? Those buggers at the community centre they liked me when the Jobcentre people sent me for the interview, and they gave me the position without a second thought and said that having been to university, I had a different kind of background, which would be good for everyone. However, as soon as I began to do the actual job, running the youth workshops and taking charge of the nursery and organizing the domino evenings, they began to turn on me and tease me, particularly the younger ones, who started telling me that my face didn't fit and calling me all the names under the sun. I asked them straight out, If this is supposed to be a centre for everyone, why doesn't my face fit? Of course, nobody wanted to say anything about that. The American man looks at me and listens to me going on, and he shrugs his shoulders and tells me that it will be best if I can produce the rent money before his friend comes back from his solicitor's job at six o'clock.

Last Friday, after all the kiddies had left the nursery and I'd locked and bolted the door, the people at the community centre told me they were letting me go, and since then I haven't had anything to do in the daytime. This being the case, for the whole week I've just stayed in the tiny attic room that I rent in these people's house, and I've tried to keep myself to myself. At the dead of night when they're both sleeping, I come out and creep around the place and get myself a cup of tea or some toast, but even though I've been making a real effort not to make any noise, I suppose they could tell that something was the matter and that I didn't have a job to go to anymore. It must have been obvious to them.

When six o'clock arrives, I hear him coming up the stairs, and then he begins hammering on the door. He's a rude so-and-so, and he doesn't even wait for me to open it up before he starts his lambasting. I tell him that I don't have the rent money, and that I've already said this to his American friend, and this is his cue to get nasty, and he points his finger and says no wonder they got rid of me. According to him, I'm not right. We've tried, Monica. I mean, come on, you're thirty-six now, aren't you? What's my age got to do with it, and what does he mean they've tried? It was me who saw the postcard in the newsagent's window saying they had a top-floor room for rent, and it was me who went to a phone box and called their number and then came around and saw the room and paid a month's rent up front. It's not like *they* made any effort. I came to them. Listen, we both think you need a more structured environment. We're not equipped. He looks behind me, and he can see that I've already packed up a few things in my holdall. I'm not daft, I could see what was coming, so I've got myself ready. I'm sorry, Monica, but we need the rent. I want to tell him that he should send his American friend out to get a job instead of letting him waste the whole day just swanning about the house to no particular purpose. However, I don't say anything. It's June, and in four months' time I'll be going back to university, so until then I'll just have to get another job and find somewhere else to live. These two smarty-pants think they know everything, and they act like they're the only ones in the world with a room to let, but they're not.

The first time I lived in London I frittered away most of my time watching the city like I was looking at a programme on the television set. I could see the people, but they couldn't see me, and I can't say it was a happy time. This time I've tried to take part, but look where it's landed me. I pick up my bag and start down the two flights of stairs, and when I get to the door, the American one flits into the hallway like a little mouse and pushes a pound note into my hand and whispers, "Good luck," before running off back to the kitchen. I walk slowly up the road in the direction of the community centre, but I know I'm not welcome there, so I cross over and go into the Sutherland Arms and order a half of lager and lime and take the drink outside and sit and watch the kids playing in the mews. Then it occurs to me that I know the man who's sitting at the next table with a pint of Guinness, for he sometimes comes into the centre and talks to people in the bar. He's an actor who, when he's not working, drives a minicab. He smiles and asks me what's on my mind, so I tell him my troubles, and he listens. Then, without asking, he picks up my glass and his own, and he goes into the pub and brings us both another drink. This time he sits down at my table. I have a room, he says. The previous tenant moved out last week, and you can take it till you set yourself up. He asks me if I know Shepherd's Bush, and I say I know where it is, and apparently this is good enough for him.

The man is not like most people, for he has a matter-of-fact casualness about him, and it looks like nothing could ever cause him to fret. When he laughs, I can see all of his teeth, and I feel as though there's no bullying gene in him. So I tell him about the time I spent in hospital last summer, and how after the detective came and spoke to me I counted out the pills and took them, and how they decided to take away my eldest and give him to another family until my nerves were better. When my son came to the hospital to visit me, I didn't know what to say to him, and the poor thing was too shocked to know what to say to me, and so he had no idea what to do with himself. I tell the man this bit of the story, but then I make up my mind to say nothing else, and I just sit with him outside of the pub and we both enjoy the evening sun going down, but I can see him sneaking the odd look and smiling like he's pleased with me.

He tells me that it's only three stops on the tube and then it will be my station. When I get out, I should turn right onto the main road. You'll know it, he says. The station has only the one exit, and it gives out onto a busy, busy road. I'm to walk for ten minutes, then make a left turn at the third traffic light. The house is about a hundred yards down the side street, and he takes a key off a big ring that is attached to his belt, and he writes down a telephone number on the back of a betting slip and passes both the key and the slip to me. Call if you need anything, but it may be a few days before I can get over there to see how you're doing. But please, you must make yourself at home.

I sit on the tube and it strikes me that if I hadn't run into this man, I'd probably be on my way to Hyde Park in search of a park bench that I could use as a bed for the night. Instead of this I have a key in one coat pocket, and a pound note in the other one, and I have a place to stay until I get myself up on my feet again. It's nearly dark by the time I find myself standing outside the three-storey house, which has a huge tree in the front garden, so it's difficult to see the windows. Even before I put the key in the door, I know that it will be gloomy inside, for how can any light get in? The bare floorboards of the entrance hall are littered with pools coupons and unclaimed letters that nobody has shaped to pick up. It looks like they've been kicked to one side, although there's a small shelf that runs the full length of the wall, and presumably it was put there so people could set things on it. In front of me is a staircase that I imagine leads up to the other flats, but I use the same key and open the door to the right, which leads into what the man called the garden flat.

The bathroom is straight in front of me; I can see a small bathtub and a sink and a toilet all crammed together, but no windows. There's a cord hanging from the ceiling, but I don't give it a pull because I'm not ready for any sudden brightness. An open door leads to a small living room with a kitchenette in one corner, a settee that is too big for the cramped space, and a battered wooden chair. I decide that the closed door to the left must be the bedroom. I put down my bag in the tiny hallway and listen, but I can't hear anything. No voices, no traffic, no noise of any kind, and so I go into the bedroom as I'm tired. However, it's disgusting and smells like dirty feet, and I know that I won't be able to sleep in such a room, so I close in the door and pick up the bag and carry it into the living room. I take off my coat and put it over the settee and tell myself that I'll lie down for a minute, but the next thing I know it's the morning and I can see light outside.

It occurs to me that I should probably leave this place and find somewhere more suitable, but my whole body feels tired and I can't even lift up my arm. The last time I felt so jiggered was when the woman came and said I'd be leaving the hospital and I told her that I wasn't ready. I know, love, she said, but we're sending you off to Bridlington for a few weeks of convalescing. Nice gardens and fresh air and walks by the sea, it will do you the world of good. I closed my eyes. The woman had already asked me if there was anybody I could spend time with, and I told her that last year my father had written me a letter in which he informed me that my mother's cancer had come back and she'd died. What cancer? She hadn't told me anything. She went quickly, was all he said, as if that justified his not getting in touch, so no, there wasn't anybody I could spend time with. When I opened my eyes, the woman was still talking and reassuring me that I'd probably be able to get my job back at the library, and that I shouldn't worry, for Ben was being looked after by a lovely family, but it might be a bit of time before I'd have everything back to normal. I looked up at her, and I remember thinking, you bloody well better get my eldest back to me. As the light outside begins to fade, I turn over on the settee and realize that I've gone through the whole day in one place. Tomorrow is Sunday, and this is the worst day of the week, for nothing is open. Even here in London most shops are closed, but I can still go and look at the cards in the windows of the newsagents along the main road to see if anybody has any rooms to rent, and then have a quick glance at the "situations vacant" in the window at the Jobcentre. I have to get another job. That's the way it has to be: first a job, and then I can see about paying for another room.

I've not been well, so Sunday also went by without me doing much, but it's Monday now, and I'm feeling a bit better. I've even done a bit of exploring. I discovered that the top-floor flat is empty and two planks of wood have been nailed across the door as though somebody is trying to keep people out, or trying to keep people locked up inside. An old lady lives in the first-floor flat, and she seems to like to keep herself to herself. I met her this morning when I heard the front door open, and I rushed out thinking that my actor friend had finally come to see me, but it was the old lady, and she was coming in, carrying a paper shopping bag from the supermarket. Good morning, she said, in her crisp, well-pressed voice, and then she asked me if I needed anything. I told her that I'd found some crackers in a kitchen cupboard and some jam and margarine in the fridge, so I was alright, thank you very much. She said that it was a shame about the state of the house, but she'd been living in the first-floor flat for over twenty years and she'd watched the place start to fall to pieces. She said she hoped the new owner was going to put some money into the house to bring it back, but so far he hadn't done anything. I mean, she insisted, the bones of the house are solid; it's just that the place needs a little helping hand, that's all. I agreed with her, mainly because I wanted somebody to talk to and she wasn't judging me. In fact, she was looking at me nicely, and I liked that about her. You know, she said, he might have plans for the place because he's quite famous. Apparently he's on the television sometimes. She thought for a moment. You know, he should just invest a little bit of money in our house before it tumbles down all around us, that's what I think. It could go at any minute.

Last night I couldn't sleep, so I decided to try and get into the top flat. One of the pieces of wood came loose, but I could tell that it would take some real effort to move the other one. I went back downstairs and poured myself a cup of red wine. In the cupboard under the sink I'd found nearly a dozen bottles of red and white wine and some whisky and vodka, along with three packets of chocolate biscuits and some boxes of white paper napkins that remained tightly sealed in see-through wrapping. This morning I have a headache. I lie on the settee and it occurs to me that I really should go out and set about getting a job, but I can't help wondering if this is the day that my actor friend is going to come and see me like he said he would. There's no telephone in the flat, so I can't call him, and if I go off down the road to try and find a phone box, I might miss him. I reckon I should try and have a bath, but the water comes out brown, and when it eventually starts to run clear, it's cold like ice, and so I forget that idea and decide that when he comes around, I'll tell him about the problem with the water. I open the bedroom door to see if it stills stinks in there, and it's only now that I notice that in the corner there's a French door to the garden. I stop up my mouth and nose with my hand and pass into the bedroom, and then out through the door, where I discover that everything in the garden is overgrown with weeds and bushes. Next door is lovely, and well maintained, but the garden to this house has been let go, although the brick path suggests that somebody once laid out the place with care. I don't know the name of the brightly coloured flowers, with orange and yellow petals, that I can see over the broken-down fence, but the truth is I don't know the names of any flowers besides the ones that everyone knows, like roses and daffodils. But just being outside in a garden lifts my spirits, and suddenly everything seems alright.

The man from next door comes out and starts snipping away at some plants with a pair of big shears. I say hello, but he turns his back and continues cutting up the foliage. I get it. He wants me to know that he's seen me, but he's also letting me know that I'm not worth his time. He has on a reasonably smart jacket, and a polo-neck jumper, but the trousers don't match. They look like something you'd wear on a building site, with stains on the front, and I can see that the back pocket is half torn off. To make things worse, he has on boots that look like they've never had a brush over them. My guess is that he's some kind of foreigner, for he's trying to say something about who he is with the jacket—or more like who he was—but I can tell that he's no better than I am, although his behaviour suggests that he thinks he is.

In the evening I hear a knock on the door to the flat, and it's my friend, standing there with a big bag of groceries and another bag cradled under his arm that is full of bottles that are clanking. He asks me if he can come in like it's my place, and I just step to one side and watch him drop everything in the kitchenette. He's wearing his coat around his shoulders like it's a cloak, and I'm surprised to see that it looks like he's combed his hair with water, because this can make even the most intelligent bloke look dim-witted. Eventually he rests himself down on the unsteady wooden chair and takes a good gander around until he turns back to me. You've not been looking after yourself, have you? I can see it in your eyes, for they've got dark circles under them. He stares at the settee and tries to understand what's going on. He points: You're sleeping there? I nod, and he shakes his head. He apologizes and tells me that the girl who was here before was a filthy hussy and he should have come and cleaned out the bedroom and made every-thing decent, but he didn't have the time. I'm looking at him now because he's right, he should have made everything decent, for I'm not used to filth, and coming over here with food and drink isn't going to get him anywhere with me.

He passes me a sandwich and a can of beer. Then he takes the same for himself and comes and sits next to me on the settee like we're at the pictures, and we both stare out in front of us while we eat and drink. He asks me if I like it here, but my mouth is full, so once again I just nod, and this seems to make him happy. However, he won't stop going on about the state of the place, and he keeps looking left and right as though it's all a big surprise to him, but we both know that this can't be the case. I bought this place as an investment, but it came with a sitting tenant. Have you met the crazy woman yet? I tell him that she's been very nice to me and I've been thinking that maybe she and I can get to be friends. He seems surprised to hear this, but he says nothing and just stands up and goes to get himself another beer. When he comes back, he leans over and kisses me on the mouth, but when I don't return the kiss, he looks at me like I've failed some kind of a test, and then he sits back down next to me. You should get out more, he says.

Last year, when I was in the convalescence home in Bridlington, there was a man who used to try and trick me into going out for a walk with him in the gardens. When he thought that nobody could see us, he would grab my hand and beg me to put it on him, but I reported the man, and somebody must have had a word, for after I told on him, he started to ignore me. Two weeks later my social worker said I could go back to Arnhem Croft, and the following week I went back to work at the library, but Denise told me that I had to be careful because my eyes were saying something that was going to get me into bother with men. I asked her whatever did she mean, but she just laughed and said that we both knew that men liked that big-eyed "help me" look, but I should watch myself. That night, as I was waiting for the lift, I saw Lucy on the playground swings. She was messing about with two boys, and all three of them were passing around a bottle of cider and smoking cigarettes. I looked at her, but I didn't wave because I'd long ago stopped talking to her mother, who these days seemed to spend most of her time in Harrogate with some bloke who owned his own garage. I was sure that the mother would have poisoned the girl's mind against me, and I was right because I heard Lucy shout, Oi, what are you looking at, you mad bitch? Then the lift came, and when I got out, I hurried along the walkway to the flat without bothering to sneak a look over the edge because I was pretty sure that Lucy would be staring up and waiting for my face to appear so she could chuck some more abuse in my direction.

My friend stands up and looks at his watch as though he has an appointment to keep, but we both know that it's all for show. I'll see you later this week, Monica, but please try and eat something to build up your strength. I've left the shopping for you on the counter. I stand up now and tell him that I might not be here as I really need to get a job. This place doesn't have a telephone, so how can anybody get in touch with me? He looks at me with a hurt expression on his face. Do you want me to put in a telephone? I'm not asking him to do anything; I'm just telling him the facts. I'm grateful that he's letting me stay in the flat, but I need some kind of permanent address, that's all. My friend is already standing by the door, and I can see that he's dying to leave, and it's obvious that he won't give me the time to either properly explain myself or thank him for the groceries. Look after yourself, Monica. I hear the front door slam shut, and I hope that the noise hasn't disturbed the old lady on the first floor.

It's still light outside, so I rummage around for another can of beer in the bag that has the drinks in it, and then I go out into the back garden and find a spot on the overgrown path where I can sit cross-legged and bathe my face in some sunshine and think again about how to get a job without having to deal with the people at the Jobcentre. I remember now: I forgot to tell him about the bathwater being cold, but it doesn't really matter as I've got used to just splashing some water onto my face and making the best of it. After he kissed me, he told me that I should venture out more, but to where? I've not spent anything from the pound note, and it makes no sense to go wasting it when I don't have another job. When I think about it, the last time I went out by myself was on Christmas Eve, when I put on my coat and left the flat and went to the Mecca Ballroom, although I'd told myself that I'd never again go back to that place.

I sat at a table on the balcony and wondered how a woman like me could have got herself mixed up with a man like that. I knew right enough how it began, but I thought it was my fault that he soon got bored with any intimacy. I was just grateful that he still took an interest in the kids, but when he started asking for photos of them, I should have known, shouldn't I? I'd had ages now with it all turning over in my head: the four weeks in the hospital, then convalescing in Bridlington, and now back at the flat and working again at the library, and even though people kept telling me it wasn't my fault (his own sister took her kids off to Canada to get them away from him), I knew that I was to blame, for after he gave me the key back, I got so wrapped up in just thinking about myself and trying to get other blokes to fancy me. I could see people down below on the dance floor, acting stupidly and getting increasingly drunk, and I felt sick in my stomach and wished I'd stayed at home. Tomorrow would be Christmas Day, and just because I'd made a few phone calls to the so-called foster parents in an effort to try and speak to my own son, it turns out I now wasn't allowed to see him unless my visits were supervised. On Christmas morning I didn't answer the door because I knew that it would be the social worker come to take me to see Ben. I pulled the blanket up over my head and waited until she'd finished shouting through the letter box before I got up. Then I turned on the television set, and I didn't move from in front of it for the rest of the day. I thought, he'll understand why I haven't come to see him even though it's Christmas Day. After all, it's a matter of dignity. Nobody's going to watch over me while I talk to my son. I'm not a bloody criminal.

After nearly a week locked away in the flat, I decide to take a trip out and present myself at the Jobcentre. However, the mousy woman, with one arm of her spectacles held together with Sello-tape, insists that they have nothing for me, and although we manage to keep everything civil and polite, it's clear that I don't like her and she doesn't like me. As I'm walking back to the house, I can see that the man from next door is standing by his gate and looking up at his house, as though he's making sure that it hasn't caught some kind of disease as a result of its close proximity to my actor friend's house. As I pass him by, he speaks without looking at me. Isn't it about time you moved on? I stop and turn and face him and tell him that I'm a grown woman and where I stay and what I do are none of his bloody business, but I can see from the look on his face that this isn't going to shut him up. The others didn't stay this long. Don't you have a home to go to? I take a step towards him. No, I say, I don't have a home to go to. Are you happy now? I go inside and hurry up to the first floor and bang on the door of the old lady, but there's no response. I worry that maybe she's dead and lying in there all alone, so I sit down outside of her door in the hope that maybe I'll hear her moving about. But after a few hours it's still quiet, and so I stand up and make my way back down to the garden flat.

I can't sleep, so I just sit on the settee and listen to the noises of the night and finally decide that I can't possibly spend another moment in a house with a dead person, so I put on my coat. When I get to the phone box, I dial my friend's number and wait, but nobody picks up, so I put down the receiver and try again, but again nobody picks up, so now I don't know what to do except walk the streets. It's soon lunchtime, and there's hardly anybody in the pub, so I buy a half of lager and take it to the table in the corner and drink it slowly, and then fetch a few more, and nobody bothers me. When I've finished, I go and call yet again, and this time he answers the phone, and I can hear it in his voice that he's surprised to hear from me. He tells me that he's positive that the old lady is fine—she sure as hell understands what is meant by a sitting tenant—then he says that maybe I should think about finding another place, for it's clear that his flat doesn't suit me. I don't know what to say, for I was only trying to be helpful, and I certainly wasn't expecting this. Look, I'll come by on Saturday or Sunday and we can talk about it. Maybe go for a drive, he says, and this makes me feel better, although I can tell that he's just rushing me off the phone.

The weekend is finished, and he didn't come. I go and knock at the old lady's door again, and this time I can hear her moving about, and so I definitely know now that she's not dead and she's just avoiding me. Of course, the sensible thing to do would be to ignore her, but I stand outside of her door, for I know that at some point the woman has to come out. So, I'm outside of her door waiting, like the time in January that I stood up outside of Ben's school and waited for him to come out, and all the other boys came out, but not my son. And then a red-faced teacher marched across the playground and told me that I had to go now or they would call the authorities, whoever they might be, and he folded his arms, and I didn't really see any point in causing a scandal and making life uncomfortable for anybody, including Ben. The next day I could see that Denise was annoyed when the social worker turned up at the library and whispered to me that we had to talk. We went into the staff room, and she read me the riot act and tried to get me to agree that what I did was out of line. Apparently, I can't wait for my own son after school, it's not allowed. After my social worker left, Denise gave me my final warning.

A few days pass, and I decide to go back to the phone box down the road. I dial, but nobody picks up the phone, so worried that maybe I called the wrong number, I dial again, but again it just rings out, and so I stand there listening and wondering what I should do now. I don't have enough money to go to the pub, but I need something to help me sleep, for it takes me ages to nod off, and no sooner have I nodded off than I find myself suddenly awake again, for any little noise or movement seems to disturb me. The day before yesterday I went to the small library opposite the tube station and asked the man behind the returns desk if he would give me a job as I had experience in library work. I told him, I like the smell of books, but he looked at me as if he hadn't the foggiest idea what I was on about. He was a young bloke, definitely younger than me, and he asked me about my previous employment, but I just stared at him because it got me remembering. About a month after the social worker came to the library, Denise called me into her office and asked me to close the door. Then she just asked me straight out if I'd been around to a Mrs. Gilpin's house this morning, because she'd just had her on the phone. That's when I understood what was going on. I didn't deny it, and I told her that I'd gone around there and knocked on the door and told this Mrs. Gilpin that I wished to see my son, but she just looked me up and down like my label had fallen off and told me that I had to go, but I let her know that I'd go only once I'd seen my son, and that's when she started to get nasty and said she'd be calling the police if I didn't leave. Not wanting to provoke a full-scale row, I gave her a piece of my mind and left, but apparently she thought better of calling the police and chose instead to phone my job, and that was all the excuse Denise needed to tell me that I couldn't work there anymore. Despite our friendship, she said, which made me bite my tongue. What friendship? Ever since I came back from convalescing, she'd kept her distance and treated me like a leper. Monica, despite our friendship, I can't overlook the fact that you're habitually late and you just don't seem to be able to keep your mind on the task at hand. I had to calm this Mrs. Glipin down, as she was ready to send the police around to have a word with you. Now you know that I can't have police officers coming into the library, you know this, don't you? I started to tell her that this wasn't fair, but she told me that she'd already spoken with the council head office, and with my social worker, and everyone was in agreement. They were going to pay me till the end of the month, but as it turned out, they did have a part-time position in another library, if I was willing to think about that, but as of now I was free to leave. And so that was that, and although I didn't tell the nice young man at the library the whole story, I did tell him that since moving to London, I'd worked at a community centre, but my heart was really in the library profession. Well, he said, but I could see that he was talking and thinking at the same time, we don't have anything at the present, but if I wanted to try again in the autumn, he happened to know that one of the part-time staff would be on maternity leave. He lowered his voice as he said this, and I thanked him but it didn't seem right to let on that I'd be back at university in the autumn, so this wasn't going to work.

I tried the other branch library, but I lasted only a week. It was located on a side street behind an out-of-date shopping centre. Today nobody would think of building a shopping complex that didn't have a roof, and piped music and warm air, and places to sit down, but this concrete monstrosity was arranged in a big L shape around a huge car park. At one end of the place was a post office, a newsagent's, a shoe mender's, a bookie's, and a dry cleaner's; at the other end was a supermarket, and hugging the right angle in between was a secondhand charity shop, a maternity boutique, and a council office where you could pay your rent. On the far side of the car park, where the main road was at the farthest point from the shopping centre, there was a row of bus stops with identical plexiglass shelters, and a few seats on which the shoppers could sit themselves down while waiting for their buses to appear.

Around three o'clock in the afternoon was when the first of the men liked to wander into the library. By four o'clock all three of them had arranged themselves around the central reading table, and they busily flicked through the daily newspapers whose spines were wooden sticks. It took me only a day or so to realize that their preferred seating matched exactly where the large clunky radiators were located. It was February now, and the weather was chilly, and these three men liked to spend their afternoons idling in the warmth before I imagined they took themselves back to the pub for the evening. I was pretty sure that their mornings would most likely have been wasted in the bookie's, before a lunchtime packet of crisps and a pint of beer and then a slow trundle around to the branch library, where they would make themselves at home for a few afternoon hours. Not that I cared, but my new boss clearly did, for I caught the woman glaring at the men and making little attempt to disguise her contempt for them.

By the time the large clock above the door—with roman numerals decorating its face as opposed to numbers—showed five o'clock, I'd have already finished my reshelving, collected my handbag from its peg in the seedy staff room, and be heading out, having nodded a sociable good-night to my boss. But the woman never said a dicky bird in reply, nor did she raise her head up from the checkout desk to look me in the eyes. Resentment, I assumed, at the fact that the local council had placed me in her library as though I were some kind of dodgy gift, and she'd therefore not been given the opportunity to do a conventional interview. Besides me there was only Miss Williamson, who had officially retired five years earlier but who had agreed to help out from time to time, for she was both familiar with the place and had little else to do. However, my sour-faced boss need not have worried herself, for I'd already decided that I wasn't staying. I'd made up my mind on the very first day that this depressing branch library wasn't going to be in my future, and on the Friday afternoon I handed in my cards.

I pour the whisky into a cup, but I know that it's not going to agree with me. However, I need something to help me sleep. When I wake up, it's bright in the room, and once again I've no idea where I am or how I got here. I remember losing Tommy, and the hospital, and then Bridlington, and Christmas Eve at the Mecca, and then trying to see Ben, and Denise getting rid of me, and the useless branch library, and catching the train to London. I remember the room at the top of the house, and the American man in his pinny who'd run away from fighting in the war. I dash into the bathroom, and I'm sick all over the place. I'm feeling too ill to do anything but a little wiping off with some toilet paper and then a quick flush. I drag myself back to the settee and lie down and close my eyes, but my head's still pounding, so I sit up and try and steady my nerves. I suspect that it's warm outside, for the daylight bleeding around the corners of the curtains is getting in my eyes. I don't have a bathing costume, but I reckon if I take off my shoes and strip down to my bra and pants, then I'll still be respectable. I stand up and hide the bottle of whisky back in the cupboard, and I open the last can of beer and drink it quickly and leave the empty tin on the kitchen counter.

Don't you have any shame? When I open my eyes, I can see the man from next door staring at me, but I'm not interfering with him. I'm sitting on the small step by the French door minding my own business, and I ask him why he's looking at me. Now he's really got his mad up, and he's shouting and calling me indecent, and why don't I take a hint and clear off like the other slags? That's what the man at the Mecca Ballroom called me on Christmas Eve when I wouldn't let him take me home. You're just a sorry old slag, he said, and I threw a glass of beer at him, and he said, You've bloody gone and done it now. I laughed at him, and then the manager came and asked me to leave. But I'm not going to give this man the satisfaction, so I just stare at him as though he's talking a foreign language, and when he's finished ranting, I tell him, all nice and quiet, Don't talk to me. I can see it on his face that he's still angry, but he gives me a dirty look, then turns and leaves, and I hear him slam his back door as he goes inside. I'm enjoying the sunshine, and I have a right to be here because my friend said I could stay as long as I wanted and he gave me a key.

I look at myself in the small bathroom mirror and set about putting on some makeup. I place the cup of whisky on the edge of the sink and make a mental note to be careful that I don't knock it off and onto the floor. My mother gave me my first lesson in how to apply makeup when my father was away on a school trip to the Lake District. However, she warned me that I must never let him see me with mascara or lipstick on, for he'd take a wet flannel to me. It still makes me livid that in his letter he didn't even tell me where she was buried, which would have been the caring thing to do, so at least I could go there and say a proper goodbye. In the morning I'll make my way to Hyde Park, and at least I'll look presentable, so long as I don't smudge this mascara when I finally drop off to sleep. Tomorrow I'll find an empty bench to sit on, and then I'll devise a plan of action that will take me through the summer until it's time to go back to university. I can admit it to myself now: waiting around in this flat for my actor friend to help me out has been a waste of time. I've made a mistake, but when I wake up, I'm going to clear off out of here and start to put things right.

In the morning the front doorbell wakes me up, but I decide not to get up and see who it is, for I have an ominous feeling. However, the person won't stop pushing the bell, and then I hear loud knocking on the door to my flat, and I wonder if there's a fire or something because the walloping won't stop. When I open up, I see a policeman in front of me with his hat under his arm like it's a rugby ball, and out of the corner of my eye, I catch a glimpse of the old lady as she tries to disappear up the stairs before I can see her. The policeman tells me that I have to come with him to the station, for they want to talk to me about something. I tell the man that I have to get dressed, so he says he'll come inside and wait for me while I do so. And then I see him lift his hand to his face as though he'd suddenly smelt something rank. I'll wait out here, he says, but leave the door open a little. So he's standing outside of the flat, and it doesn't take me long to put on my slacks and jumper and smooth out my hair, but before I even have time to brush my teeth, he's at it again, banging on the door and telling me to hurry up as he doesn't have all day. I'm hoping that the officer has a car outside to take us to the station, for I really don't want to walk down the street with a policeman so everyone can stare at me.

I seem to have been waiting forever in this big wood-panelled room with people sitting, then standing up, then sitting back down again. Everybody's taking turns to speak, but even though their mouths are moving, I can't hear any sound, and it's almost as though I'm underwater. Three wise monkeys are sitting behind a bench, and they keep nodding and looking over at me, then listening to whoever is talking, and suddenly my ears pop and I can now hear the policeman who was knocking on my door talking about how I wouldn't come out straightaway, and how I put up a bit of a struggle and tried to lock myself in the bathroom. I want to laugh because it seems funny that he should be making all of this up and fooling them, but I can see by the way they are looking at me that this is serious and his lies are making me look bad.

The man from next door has on his smart jacket, and he starts to talk now, and he says that I dance about naked in the garden, which is also a lie. I'm thinking to myself that this man must be sad and lonely to have to make up stories like this about a woman who hasn't done him any wrong, but I know that I'm not supposed to say anything, so I just stay quiet and listen to one lie after another and I try and work out for myself just what is happening. Then things get really out of control. The old lady stands up and says that she tried to be courteous to me, but apparently I don't have any decorum. One of the magistrates speaks to her directly now, and he asks the woman if I've ever harmed her in any way, and she shakes her head. He asks her if she has seen me wandering about naked, and again the old lady shakes her head, but she seems confused. Then she repeats herself, this time very slowly, and insists that I don't have any decorum, as if this was some kind of crime.

I feel the hand of a policewoman squeezing my elbow, and she tells me to get up in a sweet voice like she's my friend or something, and one of the magistrates asks me if I understand the gravity of the situation, and so I nod and say yes, but I'm not sure what all the fuss is about. I haven't mistreated anybody or damaged any property, so why can't they just mind their own business? The same magistrate starts to ask me about my actor friend, calling him Mr. Francis, and he wants to know how we know each other, and so I tell him that we met in a pub by the community centre, and I leave it at that. Has he ever troubled you? What business is it of his? But I tell him no, and he asks me if any other men have touched me since I've been in the flat, but before I have a chance to tell him what for, he wants to know where I get money, and if any men have ever given me any money, and I say no, then no again, then no in a louder voice, and now the sound has gone again, and I can't hear what they are saying, but I'm talking and my arms are flying about in front of my face and I'm still talking, and I'm trying to get my arms to stay still, but I can see from how these people are looking at me that I'm not making any sense.

The policewoman is in the back seat of the car with me, while an older woman in a blue jacket and white frilly blouse is twisted around in the front passenger seat so she's facing me. She keeps asking about my family, and if I have anybody that I would like her to get in touch with, but all I want to know is where is this car taking us. Again she starts up tormenting me with the family talk, almost begging me to tell her if the man who owns the house is my boyfriend or just somebody I see from time to time, and she asks me this as though whatever I say will be alright by her and won't cause any problems for anybody, but I can tell by just look-ing at her that this ignorant woman has never read a book in her life, and so I don't say anything and I close my eyes.

After I stopped turning up at the library by the shopping centre, there was nothing to keep me in the city anymore. I was banned from both my son's school and the house he was living in, and the social worker had told me that I had to give him some space. So I thought, I'll give him some space and I'll move to London for a few months and let everything settle down. But be-fore I took off for London, I had to sort something out. As I walked down the cul-de-sac, I saw him bent double over his car, merci-lessly polishing the bonnet with a yellow duster, and behind him the sprinkler was taking care of the front lawn with its absurd, robotic rhythm. I came right up next to him, and when he looked up, I could see it in his eyes that he wasn't sure. I'd weathered a bit since he'd last seen me, and I'd also chopped my hair really short. Jesus, I'd been through a lot, so what did he expect? He seemed lost for words, but I had no intention of standing there playing silly buggers with him, so I just asked him straight out to give me something of my mother's, a brooch or a necklace, as I was going to London and I wanted to take a part of her with me. Monica, he said. Please, Monica. But I cut him off and told him that it was wrong of him to do what he'd done and not tell me that she was ill, or even let me know where she'd been laid to rest, but he didn't say anything; he just held on to his cloth with both hands and stared. And then he told me to wait where I was, and he disappeared inside the house. When he came out, he handed me her slender gold watch and three five-pound notes and told me that this was all he had in the house, but it was to help set myself up in London. I looked at him but said nothing, for he was a small man now. I hope, he said, then he stopped. I thought, God, he's not going to bawl, is he? I hope that you find what you're looking for in London, he said, and I hope that you know you've always got a home here, but then he dried up. He just kept staring at me until I couldn't take it anymore, and so I turned and walked away. And this woman in her ridiculous frilly white blouse wants to know about family?

I sit at the back of a room with a group of women, and we're all watching the BBC news on a colour television set that's stuck high up on the wall. The place is like a prison, but it's not a prison. It's also cold, even though it's summer outside, and the room is lit with ugly fluorescent tube lighting. When I got here, they took away my clothes and then told me to take a shower. When I finished, they gave me this nightdress to wear. It makes me look undignified, and I have a feeling that this is the idea, but at least it's clean. I asked for a belt as the thing is hanging off me like a tent, but they let me know that no belts are allowed. I then had to open my mouth and stick out my tongue, and they gave me a tablet that started me going all fuzzy, then tired, and then the coloured nurse said that I would soon be asleep, but I'm still sitting here watching television although I'm not sure what the man on the news is going on about.

The nurse has a deep cleavage, and she should cover herself up more. She asks me whatever did I eat to make myself so sick, but before I can reply, she pushes my head down into the plastic bucket and tells me to let it go—you've got to get it all out—but I haven't eaten anything all day, so there's nothing to come out. I'm trying to tell her that it's the bloody tablet that's made me sick, but I know she doesn't believe me. She gives up and slowly gets to her feet. I watch her wipe her hands on the backside of her uniform, and then we look at each other for a moment before she starts to talk. They put you in this isolation room because you're a top risk, Monica, but it's up to you. If you want to do something irresponsible, then go right ahead, but you'll have nobody to blame but yourself. I don't say anything, and we continue to eyeball each other. Look, she says, if you want to put something on your stomach, just press the bell, love. I hate to see you like this. Really, you need to pull yourself together.

Apparently the library trolley comes around every morning. The volunteer woman stands by the door while I look at the books that are piled on top of it without any order of any kind. Everything's just random, and then I notice that the woman has put a hand on her hip. Don't you like reading then? She's smiling now, like she's got one over on me, but it's easy to tell that behind that wide forehead of hers nothing has been imprinted. You know, it helps to pass the time if you read a bit. There's one there on royal gardens, you might like that, for there's lots of pictures in it. It's quite popular actually. I look at Miss Librarian and wonder what her problem is. How dare they call this thing a library trolley? Book trolley would be better, for all it contains are scattered books that people have left behind, and I don't get the sense that this woman gives a damn whether you ever return them or not. I pick up the glossy book on royal gardens and realize that it would have helped if my actor friend had brought me a book or two to the flat. Now that would have made the time pass a little easier.

At the end of the day the coloured nurse knocks on the door, and she opens it without waiting for me to say anything. She tells me that it's six o'clock and time for me to go to the dining room and meet some of the others now that I've had a rest. But one look at the place, and it's clear that I can't stay, as it's full of people sitting at tables in neat rows like some kind of eating factory, and I ask the nurse if I can please go back to my room because I'm not feeling too good. She says I'm free to go back by myself anytime I like, and so I tell her thank you. But she doesn't stop there. She looks hard at me and then nods as though a thought has just struck her. You can also go outside to the courtyard and then come back in and eat a bit later. You don't have to run off to your room if it's a ciggie that you want. I want to laugh, but I keep a straight face and I tell her that it's alright, it's just that I'm not feeling too well.

Jesus, I shouldn't have said that, for now I've got the doctor standing over me. I'm sitting on the edge of my narrow bed, looking up at him while he shines a bright light into my face. He has a beard and moustache, and I wonder why he wears them because they make him look older than he is. He has to be about my age, but he looks about fifty-odd, and his teeth are yellowing, which isn't right for a doctor. I can give you only one pill at a time, and I'm afraid I can't leave the bottle. You're not very good with pills, are you? He looks at some papers in my file and asks me what went on at the house in Shepherd's Bush, and then he quizzes me and wants to know about any male visitors. I shake my head, and he mutters something to himself and asks me if downstairs is itching, but the coloured nurse seems annoyed and whispers in his ear, and he stops his questions. I remember when the detective came to my hospital bedside and told me that they'd found him. It was maybe a week after he'd gone. That's when I took the pills. I'd swiped a bottle when nobody was looking, and I tipped them all out on the bed. It said there were twenty-four, but it turned out there were only twenty-three in the bottle, and I wondered how many times I'd been done like this. I took them, one at a time, but it didn't work, and they soon brought me back around. Anyhow, I suppose all of this is in my file.

I wake up in what feels like the middle of the night, but the door is locked from the outside, and the room is pitch black. They didn't tell me that they lock us in at night, but I'm not surprised. I fumble my way back into bed and pull the scratchy blanket up to my chin and reckon that I'm probably in this so-called hospital because I won't tell them what they want to hear. When I was a girl at school, I was always the one asking questions. Then, when the two boys came along, I was the one always answering questions.

Now I don't ask questions, or answer them, which is probably why everybody's fed up with me. There's no mirror in this room, which I'm sure is deliberate. In fact, there's nothing in this room except me and the bed. I can't remember much else about the room, or even what I'm wearing, so I'll just have to wait until the light begins to stream in at about five o'clock, I think, but I'm not sure how long I'll have to wait.

The coloured nurse has brought me a big bowl of cereal and a plastic spoon, and she's set them out nicely on a tray. She asks me how I slept, and I say, very good, although the right answer would be, not much, but I don't want to be rude. She tells me that the doctor has said there's really no reason for me to be here and that things have obviously just overwhelmed me, haven't they? I agree and tell her that I'm going to university in October, and she gives me a crooked smile. That's marvellous, darling, but you've still got to eat. She tells me that it's another nice day, and I tell her that if I wasn't in here, I'd be in Hyde Park. Well, she says, I'm sure we'd all prefer to be in Hyde Park on a day like this, but I think you've got to try to trust people a little, and not be so defensive. Not everyone's out to get you, love. If you open up a bit, then we can assess you properly, and the sooner we do that, the sooner we can think about you leaving.

I sit in the common room next to a woman who is too thin. She asks about my book, and I decide there's no reason to ignore her. I can see the veins sticking up on her arms, and her face is all angles with a thin covering of skin pulled tightly across her skull and cheekbones. What makes it really sad is the fact that she's pretty, or rather she was pretty, but I imagine that nobody's ever told her this. I open the book and explain to her that it's all about royal gardens, and she says that my accent suggests to her that I've travelled quite a distance, and I tell her I must have because I used to have two children and heaven only knows where they are now. I laugh out loud, and so she laughs too, just to be polite. That's funny, she says. I let her know that after the pills I spent another three weeks in the hospital and they told me that Ben would have to stay with these Gilpin people. At least until I was back on my feet and capable. That was nearly a year ago now. Last summer. She mops her brow with the sleeve of her nightdress. It's hot, isn't it? Yes, I say, and then she tells me that she's sure I'll like it in the courtyard. After everything I've just told her, that's the best she can come up with? It's hot and I'll like it in the courtyard. I'm sorry, but nobody can say that I didn't try. Once I realized that I'd messed up, I did everything I could to try and get Ben back. She suggests that we go for a walk and have a little explore. What's your name? I tell her Monica, and she seems to think that's quite a pleasant name. A bit unusual, she says, then smiles. But quite pleasant.

IX

THE JOURNEY

Seeing him step gingerly from the neglected barn, where he has sheltered from the fury of a sudden storm, and pass into the weak March sunlight, an onlooker might initially mistake him for a furtive man who hides in hollows and picks berries, a sad fellow who wraps himself in nostalgia for a happier past that has been swept away by ill luck and squibs of gin. But this is unequivocally a man of quality whose loose-jointed stride is soon long and true, and whose descent to the floor of the valley is assured. He effortlessly straddles an old stile, and is alert enough to sense that the moist air is now filled with the newly liberated scent of heather. He draws deeply upon the fragrance, and notes the tint and form of every flower, the texture and density of the many varieties of moss, and he is mindful of the nests of tadpoles wriggling furiously in the streams. On the other side of a narrow beck he sees a small patch of turf surrounded by clear springs, and he discerns a makeshift pathway of large flat stones that he decides might serve as dappled steps along which he can navigate his way to the safety of the green island.

Once there he lays down his bag and strips off his cloak and shirt, revealing a stout but firm stomach that suggests that this man's appetite for good food and wine has not yet been corrupted by addiction. Wading ankle deep into the water, he scoops rivers to his face and lets the cool, sweet taste soothe the inside of his dry mouth. He stretches his arms above his head and feels the fresh breeze pass by both sides of his body. Two hours before dawn, he left his house to the sound of the dogs barking wildly, as though some unseen hand was administering a vicious beating. He instructed Joseph that he should quieten them so their unruly noise would arouse neither his sensitive wife nor the children. Joseph whistled and then released a string of unintelligible curses that soon had the beasts whimpering and then rolling on the ground with flapping tongues as though anticipating some tantilizing surprise. As he strolled away from his residence, he looked up and imagined the sky to be a black velvet glove that might, at any moment, reach down and lift him into the starlit heavens and propel him on an altogether different journey. However, he quickly averted his eyes and continued his lonely pilgrimage. Sometime later, the first light of daybreak arrested his attention, and he realized he could now see his fidgeting fingers, and the spongy soil on which he was walking was visible beneath his feet; then dawn broke with a quietly confident majesty that would have caused a less secure man to fall to his knees in supplication, but he pulled his cloak to against the morning chill and simply increased his pace.

He lowers himself down on his heels, knees jutting out on either side like awkward wings, and again he disturbs the sleeping beck by plunging his cupped hands beneath the surface and hoisting icy water across his broad shoulders. He kneads the cascading ribbons into the leathery skin on his chest and back with quick circular gestures that suggest thoroughness as opposed to haste. Tonight he will sleep at the familiar rooming house, which for many years has accommodated this gentleman's eccentricity, without demanding any explanation of why he chooses to promenade on foot across country instead of taking to the roads and riding in a carriage in a manner more becoming for one of his status. The fact is, walking affords him the gift of exercise and an opportunity to refresh his mind and achieve a clearer understanding of deeds past and tasks present, but he has never shared this intelligence with anyone. The anxious commerce of Liverpool, conducted in crowded, dusty rooms choked with tobacco smoke, will offer him scant recourse to luxuriate in reflection, and this being the case, he has discovered that time invested in the ruminative quality of his excursion generally pays dividend once his mind begins to be assaulted by the discordant cacophony of the blustering world of business.

He worries about his children, for the radiant yet desperate light in the eyes of the passionate girl suggests a troubling delicacy, while the son's wilful behaviour hints at an obstinate temperament that neither his wife's line nor his own has ever accommodated. The young man always affects to listen, but with a slither of icy dissent lodged in his bosom, and he behaves churlishly towards both parents as though life has somehow been unfair to him. His angry and despondent wife finds it increasingly arduous to cope with the most trifling details of daily survival, and last night, after she had taken to her bed, he reclined in his chair and wondered if they would ever again enjoy the pleasant tenderness of time shared as man and wife. His children squabbled noisily next to the hearth, but then his daughter broke free, and the poor girl stood trembling before him as though ill clad in a hard frost. (Please, must you go, Father? Your ship is in Antigua, isn't it? Are there problems at your sugarworks?) Old Joseph tended the roaring fire and said nothing, but neither son nor daughter could disguise their great frustration at the prospect of their father's impending absence. Of course, the children had often been told that their father had little choice but to conduct dealings in Liverpool with men whose hearts were hard like stone, and whose Christian charity went no further than the looking glass: these men of commerce were his colleagues, the gentlemen for whom the children were continually being deserted, but last night both daughter and son found it difficult to mask their disappointment. Joseph looked on, and when he recognized an appropriate moment to speak, he rescued the situation and reminded his tongue-tied

Master to be wary of petty thieves and vagabonds during the sixty-mile walk, men who, spying a gentleman, would undoubtedly demand both pocket watch and money.

He stands rooted in the water and observes the distant hills, and the newly formed bank of ashen clouds lurking dismally above them. It will rain again, of this he is sure. He remains still and vigilant; a passing native would see a stout bird silently waiting for a languid fish or a drifting insect. However, he is perplexed. A whole life built upon swift decisions, and now, marooned in this beck, he is crippled by a lack of certitude that tastes bitter in his mouth. Some years ago his acquiescent wife had accepted the notion that the distractions of Liverpool had most likely captured her husband's mind, but of late she has been unable to prevent her tolerant acceptance from curdling into peevish bitterness. And now the children are also judging him harshly; he sees it in their defiant scrutiny, and yet he can find no comforting words for them. Half naked, he carefully picks his way across slippery stones until he reaches the safety of land. The forsaken water ripples and purrs as though lamenting his absence, and midway through the day his heart beats with a dread with which he is unacquainted. He listens to the rumble of distant thunder and understands he is truly alone.

✦

The challenges of climbing up a steep ravine or scrambling down the hurried slope of a hill have provided him with welcome relief from the ubiquity of the moorland. Now, as the last streaks of daylight fade from the blackening sky, he can finally see the warm glow from the half-dozen oil lamps that decorate the windows of the rudimentary rooming house, and he is relieved to think that soon he will rest. As he approaches the shabby establishment, he is reminded that the place has long since passed its infancy, but he relishes the prospect of a plate of hot food and a freshly aired bed. Less pleasant to contemplate is the thought that this arrival marks the end of his precious solitude, for he will now have to reenter the company of his fellowman. Some ten miles ago he endured his sole encounter of the day: a savage-looking individual with both fists clapped on the head of a staff, who loitered at a crossroads and verbally accosted him, impatient to ascertain if he knew of a slab of stone that might serve a penniless wayfarer as a resting place after a hard day scampering on the moors. He answered the menacing man in the negative and, without breaking stride, increased his pace, feeling no stirrings of compassion towards the ruffian. Standing now outside of his moonlit lodgings, he is somewhat alarmed by the muted babble of human conversation that disturbs the tranquillity of the evening, but he knows he must prepare himself.

She wears a tight-fitting bodice and black frock that he is certain must surely impede the boldness of her movement. However, as she serves him, she maintains a magnificently upright yet relaxed posture, and he notices that as ever, much care has been exercised to season everything to his taste. His customary small oak table and chair have been discreetly set in place in the farthest corner by the window, presumably while he briefly repaired to his room. Once there, he washed his hands and face, and the overly solicitous servant boy praised his excellent wardrobe although it was unmistakably blotched and bog spattered. Nevertheless, he offered up a small coin to the scrawny youth, who seemed resolved to please regardless of remuneration. The servingwoman steps back from his table and he looks up at her. Despite her solemn countenance and irregular features, it would be unfair to label this statuesque woman ill favoured or without grace. He knows that later she will charm the guests and play refined melodies on the harp, but she will do so as though skating on a pond of thin ice, circling daintily, careful not to crash through to any depth. (Have you a ship come in, sir?) A furious fire roars and bellows beneath the wide brick flue; it lights up the room and casts outlandish shadows in every direction. There is a playful shyness to the woman, who bestows the merest inkling of a smile upon him before she quits the room. No ship. The recent letter said nothing about a ship.

Dear Sir,

I can no longer maintain the expense of housing your friend, its being past six months since I last received payment of rent. She fails rapidly, and appears to be making haste to leave us, for she possesses neither the strength nor the inclination to beg nature to refrain from tormenting her. I summoned, and paid for, the doctor, who informed me that she cannot sustain much more of this feverish agony, for winter has extended itself and made circumstances unfavourable for all, but especially treacherous for one in her condition. She periodically rallies and lingers, before once more resuming her difficult journey down a steep path of degradation, a descent made all the more hazardous, for she is unable to comfort herself with powders or draughts. I am fearful that the dread contagion, which is clearly visiting misery upon her, may spread rapidly among my properties and encumber me with sick and dying tenants who shall find themselves without means to pay monies owing to me. Sir, I require your assistance, for while it is evident that Providence has treated her brutally, I must insist that she meet her obligations or accept the consequences . . .

Moonlight streams through the bedroom window, but sleep refuses to soothe his weakened body, and he stares unhappily at the timepiece on the plain mahogany dresser. Outside, he hears the hooting owls as they swoop and hunt near the pile of manure to the back of the barns, and he listens to the high wind as it continues to sob and wail through the flailing trees. In the grate a childish fire sputters and makes one final attempt to snap to feeble life, and as it does so, he again rehearses the events that have propelled him to undertake this inauspicious expedition. He remembers the financial prattle of his Liverpool colleagues' being irksome to his ears, and as they continued to pontificate, he sat rigid and forlorn as though occupying a church pew. Excuse me, I shall take some air. They watched him leave, knowing that one among them would soon be appointed to counsel their partner on the dangers of a surfeit of melancholy, but at present Mr. Earnshaw's state of mind was the least of their worries. Once he was out in the street, his gloomy cohorts felt liberated, and they continued to scrutinize the carefully composed entries in the large dusty ledger that lay open before them.

She walked towards him with head held high, but it was obvious that the beguiling woman saw no one. And then, as she turned onto Rope Street, she felt his captivated glow upon her, and she began to fly down the road as if the devil himself were giving chase. Madam, please. Madam. Passersby glowered, but as she slowed to a lively walk, her haughty pout signaled that she cared little for people's opinions. Will you not simply speak with me for a moment? My God, she misunderstands. The woman suspects that I am proposing a transaction. He laughed, which triggered a spasm of disdain to blemish the woman's face. Please let me just walk with you a little way. He talked incessantly and marched by her side and attempted to create a great thaw in her defences, but she acted as though she had no perception of what it might cost a man to disclose his affection. My children mock my stubborn choice of clothes. And he talked. I come from a place where a surgeon, two grocers, a confectioner, a butcher, a cabinetmaker, and a wine merchant all ply their trades within a reasonable distance. He talked.

He is assaulted by the noise of clattering clogs that rises from the courtyard below, and then he listens to the ceaseless stamping of restless horses as, eager to step out of the cloud of their own steamy restlessness, they shudder and heave. Moonlight continues to stream in through the uncurtained windows, but he knows that he must soon depart if he is to reach his destination by sundown. Beyond the woman, his two children have populated his dreams and conspired to treat him unfairly. Despite his pleadings, the dreamworld son seems determined to emphasize that his father no longer retains his favour. Meanwhile, the girl has frightened him with her indignant outbursts, and demanded to know why he has not done his children the kindness of consigning both son and daughter to a foundling hospital. Still clad in his stockings, he rubs his eyes to wakefulness and remembers that the children have asked him to buy them gifts in Liverpool, and he hopes that the purchase of a fiddle for the boy and a riding whip for the girl might, on his return, enable him to pass future nights unperturbed by their hectoring.

✦

Suddenly the day yields to darkness, as though it no longer has the will to continue. With a wet cloak upon his back and a carpet-bag over his shoulder, he enters the seafaring town and begins to pass through the less public lanes and alleyways where the corpses of dogs and cats rot in the gutters. A shared journey in a post-chaise would have spared him the unpleasantness of proximity to people who are not overclean in either their habits or their persons, but his gruelling trudge is now reaching its conclusion, and there is no reason for him to confuse his mind by speculating on what might have been. Putrid vapours stupefy his senses, and as he proceeds deeper into this area of shameful squalor, his hand habitually hastens to his mouth to prevent his succumbing to a choking fit. All about him, in the very shadows of the port's abundant wealth, it is impossible to ignore the evidence that the greater part of this town has a face that appears to have been exhaustively bruised by misfortune. He lowers his damp head and enters a court where the dwellings sag indifferently, one supporting the next, and where he can see offal-choked, verminous rooms—doors unlatched to all—that he knows to be peopled by men and women who nurse a lifelong commitment to quenching their thirst and who will fly into a murderous rage should they feel slighted.

A dirty-fleshed, drunken fool emerges suddenly from the shade and sneers at him, and then the man's eyes flash and he laughs. (Her gentleman, if I'm not deceived. The stuck-up bitch is where she should be, but it is not this court.) The scruffy brute staggers in all directions, his head bobbing in the heavily fermented mist that he replenishes with each rasping statement. We must go next door, he insists. The dreary wretch then obliges him to drop a coin into his blackened palm in order that he might conduct his guest no more than ten faltering paces down the lane, where they both bend double and pass through the tunnel-like entrance to a closed-in court. There are six houses in the yard, each boasting two stories, all of which give out onto an unpaved central area that is littered with bodily refuse. A water pump has long ago given up service, but on the wall above it a dog has been hung for amusement, and it squeals and tumbles helplessly at the end of a piece of frayed rope. The half-witted man smiles toothlessly and points to an open door in the corner.

He carefully edges his way up the unstable staircase and enters the foul-smelling attic room, which boasts not a single stick of furniture. The air sits sluggishly in the abandoned quarters, and he steps carefully, for some seepage stains the floor and appears to be still leaking between the ill-matched boards, no doubt soiling the inhabitants below. He looks up, for he hears footsteps in the stairwell, and then a lamplit face appears and greets him with a cheerfulness so out of keeping with the environment that he wonders if this intruder is in full possession of his faculties. (Kind sir, the severity of the season has caused great distress to those already beset with ailment and pain. It is all part of this dreadful infestation that has reduced so many of my tenants to the severest condition imaginable with no prospect of relief.) The landlord advances boldly into the room, the light from his lamp pooling unsteadily on the floor, and he stands close by, which merely confirms his lack of fellowship with either soap or water. (Once she began to flounder, vitality rushed suddenly from her body and left behind an empty vessel. Thereafter the Lord ushered her out of the misery of the present world and delivered her into the everlasting glories of the world to come.)

They sit together in the quietest corner of the raucous Flying Horse Inn, and he listens to the landlord's dull sermons as the man swills his beer with a hand that trembles on the glass. It is true, he thinks; some of these people have no more civility than the swine in their pens. (But she'd neither been baptized, nor was she of this parish, so I paid a man to swaddle her in a tight sheet, but as you have discovered, the detestable odour still triumphs. Soon after, the cart raced to the burial ground on the far side of the extension of the town, and I guarantee that once there she found some rest.) With comical impatience, the man signals for another flagon of beer, and then he lowers his voice. (You do understand that the woman was given to blatant falsehoods. The artful minx affected a superior attitude, but when her stomach was empty, she would walk through the streets seeking those like yourself, with elegant shirts and silken breeches, and murmur a wistful account of having fallen on hard times.) The landlord laughs, but then his expression grows grave. (Believe me, sir, there were many men conversant with her merits, for eventually she gave free admission to her bed, but I swear I was never one of those who sent the boy out while they took advantage.) A buxom woman well past her first bloom thumps the beer down onto the table, but the landlord ignores both the woman and the beer and produces a slip of paper from his waistcoat. (I would truly like to be in better favour with the goddess Fortune, but I have a final reckoning. I take it you'll be settling her accounts.)

✦

The handsome oak room is populated with men of commerce who customarily refuse the possibility of consensus, preferring instead to become heated with their own opinions, which they proclaim with a confident swagger calculated to override both logic and consideration. Their chief topic of interest is the fluctuating prices of sugar, rum, and slaves on the Exchange Flags, but on this blustery evening, the working day having been concluded, pipes and tobacco and newspapers and punch are much in vogue at the Kingston Coffee House, and no further industry is being conducted, as the men now sprawl with books bound in soft leather and stretch out before the fire. A jaded lodger, keen to impress upon onlookers the idea that no man need greet him cordially, sits at a table towards the rear of the room. Before him a knife is embedded in a slab of meat and candlelight plays on a silver goblet, and a rush of uncertain sensations courses through his body. Earlier in the evening, the landlord had set him down for an ass. After he had paid the man his money, the drunkard furrowed his brow in mock confusion and insisted there were no personal effects and claimed that he could offer no information with respect to the child.

His child. At the conclusion of their second dinner she slipped off her dress in the backroom of the Queen's Head tavern, and his heart fell when he saw that she had been branded with the initials of another man. Suddenly he felt only tolerably well, and he became aware of tightness in his lips, and then his face began to colour and quiver uncontrollably. Once their enterprise was terminated, his conscience remained unsullied with regret, for although their union had not been sealed with missives sent by Cupid's post, he had not stooped to using her brutally, and he understood that his wife would never inquire of him regarding time expended in Liverpool. Two days later he began the return journey across the moors, but long before he reached home, his mind had already turned back to Liverpool and thoughts of again entertaining this woman, who seemed willing to establish an arrangement by which she might call upon him at the Queen's Head tavern whenever he had commerce to conduct in the town she now called home.

A year later their child was born. When she asked of him if he might arrange for her and the boy to return to the trafficking islands, he happily went in search of a captain he might trust. However, he soon divined them all to be testy, irritable creatures who tendered him no assurances that once at a distance from the laws of the land they would not use her and the boy heartlessly, and so he offered the woman money in exchange for the convenience of continuing their arrangement and sparing his soul the burden of worrying that he might have dispatched them both to a sad fate. But what hope now for the boy on the streets of this town? He knows full well that it will be only a matter of time before the child is propositioned with a tot of rum and overwhelmed and pressed to serve as a prize upon one of His Majesty's ships, or else accused of thievery and snatched up and spirited away to a workhouse.

At the first light of dawn he leaves the Kingston Coffee House and makes his weary way to the docks. He stares intently at the bold shield of the moon that is still conspicuous in the sky, and he speculates that it must be the pulse of the sea that anchors the moon to the heavens and prevents it from wandering. At this hour of the morning the slumbering town appears ready to slide grace-fully beneath the surface of the water and disappear from view. He mumbles to himself. And God's cleansing shall be visited upon all. He looks out at the miscellany of docks that are care-lessly cluttered with a jumble of masts and sails, swaying first one way, then back again. These murmuring pools are flecked with rotting debris, and the water is combed by the wind, gurgling and puckering when the breeze rises and then abruptly settling as though someone has swiftly drawn a thin oily skin across the sur-face and whispered, be still. The black-haired child is asleep but fitfully twitching, and then his eyes slowly open. Even at this ten-der age his sombre aspect suggests an abundance of pride. There is a luminosity to the boy, as though he is cognizant of something that others cannot see, and this knowledge bequeaths upon him a full awareness of his destiny. Come to me, young lad. We have no business meddling in the affairs of heaven. Come to me, son, and let's go home.

X

GOING HOME

The rain continues to beat frantically against the window, and the peals of thunder grow menacing as though the storm is now passing immediately overhead. The frightened boy sits on the edge of the chair, but he refuses to look at the man with whom he is travelling, preferring instead to stare at the space between his muddied feet. Occasionally the boy throws a glance in the direction of the fireplace, as though he expects to find an answer to his predicament hidden away in the heart of the flames, but he quickly returns his troubled gaze to the floor. The man looks hopefully in the boy's direction, and then he leans over to touch his arm, but the boy pulls away and casts him a look that is freighted with contempt.

The man had surmised that it would be possible for them to reach their destination before the storm broke. When they began their journey the first rumblings of the squall could be heard in the very far distance. The man gestured proudly to the gorse-stubbled landscape as though he owned it, pointing out birds and small animals and flowers and baptizing them with names that he was eager the boy should remember. However, before they had ascended the first gentle peak, the low, fast-moving clouds had bathed the whole moor in shadow, and it was apparent that the man had underestimated both the fierce weather and his own tired state. Once the driving rain began to lash down in earnest the man peered desperately into the gloom for any sign of a farmhouse or barn where they might find shelter. After struggling against the strengthening wind for what seemed like an eternity, he eventually made out a single light in a distant window and attempted to quicken his step, but he realized that he was in danger of leaving the boy behind. He stopped and took the distressed lad firmly by the arm, and with his free hand he brushed the rain from the child's eyes and began now to drag him through the rumpus.

The stranger opened the door to his cottage and looked at the uneven apparition of man and boy that greeted him. The flustered man's dripping clothes suggested some status in this world, but the ill-dressed child seemed adrift and lost. It occurred to the stranger that this boy might have been discovered upon the moors, a runaway of some sort, and perhaps the connection between the two had been forged in the adversity of this calamitous unrest. There was no time for speculation, however, for the wind was howling, and it took what little strength he possessed to hold open the door against the turbulence of the gale. The stranger stood to one side in order that his visitors might step clear of the gravel footpath and enter, and he watched as the nervous man gently pushed the boy ahead of him.

As the stranger closed in the door behind them, the man quickly removed his sodden jacket, but he decided not to suggest to the boy that he do the same. Instead, he surveyed their grey-bristled host, who was tall and gaunt and who looked as though nature had carved his dull features from the bark of a gnarled tree. The man noticed that there was moist life in the stranger's dancing eyes, and a firmness to his handshake that defied his accumulation of years. He assumed that he was possibly a farmer of some kind, a stubborn fellow who scratched a meagre living from a carefully demarcated piece of rutted earth. Tending to sheep, and conceivably a few cattle, with some attempt made to raise poultry and collect eggs, most likely constituted the extent of this man's lean agricultural world. No doubt the solitary rhythm of his life would be interrupted each Sunday, when the stranger would wash and change and reach for his Bible and stride across the moors to the village church, where he would be temporarily reacquainted with others in the human family. Thereafter he would probably return and quietly resume the bleak routine of his existence and simply wait for Sunday to once again announce itself.

Two high-backed chairs flanked the roaring fire, and the stranger invited both man and bedraggled boy to each take a seat and warm themselves. The sparse, low-ceilinged room contained a wooden dining table with a set of poorly matched stools, and little else. The walls had no experience of paint, the windows were deprived of the indulgence of curtains, and the stone floors were blessed by neither carpet nor a scrap of rug. In the corner stood a second door, through which the stranger soon passed, leaving his visitors alone. The man looked at the shivering boy; then he travelled back in his mind to his first encounter with the child's mother. Despite her headstrong nature, it was evident to him that the woman was ill-suited to be a mother. It wasn't her fault, but life had ushered her down a perilous course and delivered her into a place of vulnerability. At the outset, he had felt a kinship with her, although he could never be sure what her feelings were towards him, but it didn't matter now. She was woefully distracted, that much was clear, and it was his responsibility to step forward and act. It was his duty to take the scruffy lad into his care and protect him.

The boy is still unwilling to look at the wispy-haired man, and he continues to stare at the space between his soiled feet. A few hours ago, when the storm began to break all around them with volcanic anger, the man took the boy's hand and urged him to rein in his fear, but the lad wrenched his hand away. Suddenly, white scars of lightning began to run from sky to earth, but the man remained unaware of the full extent of the boy's consternation until the lad began to cry out for his mother. The agitated man looks all about the stranger's spartan room, and then he takes a log from on top of the pile to the side of the hearth, and he tosses it onto the flames, which immediately leap to new life. He resists the temptation to extend his legs in front of the blaze, and then he is momentarily overwhelmed by a sudden bellowing of thick, stifling smoke. The boy inches forward to the edge of the chair and begins to rub his eyes and then cough. Outside, beyond the asylum of this old man's cottage, dusk is falling and they both can hear the relentless malice of the storm as it continues to wail. The man waits a moment, then risks leaning over to touch the boy's arm, but the angry lad pulls away.

The stranger returns and pulls up a stool, and joins them by the fire.

"Are you lost?" The man shakes his head and assures his host that as a rambler he is very familiar with the region.

"It's just the weather that places us at your mercy. That said, we're both grateful."

The stranger looks now at the silent boy and smiles.

"Is the boy hungry? I have only a little food, some dry bread and milk, but whatever I have I'm disposed to share."

The man laughs now, as though keen to draw attention away from the boy.

"Thank you, you're too kind, but we won't intrude upon you any more than we've already done. This unpleasantness will soon be over, and we'll be on our way."

"I see."

"It's been a troublesome evening for both man and beast."

The stranger listens to his guest's cautiously expressed sentiments, but he finds it difficult to give credence to anything that falls from the lips of this anxious man. He starts to wonder if he ought to offer the child a bed for the night, but he senses that the man would be loath to allow his charge to fall under the dominion of another without some kind of struggle.

As the storm finally begins to abate, the man glances impatiently in the direction of the window, intent now to end this charade. There is a difference between shelter and hospitality, and the stranger has offered both, but the man has been content to take only the former. He stands.

"Thank you, but it sounds like it's starting to blow itself out, and so we should be on our way."

The stranger also stands, but he says nothing. The boy seems reluctant to relinquish his seat, and he looks directly at the wizened old stranger, who now finds himself trying to banish from his mind the full significance of the boy's panic-stricken demeanour.

"The child is welcome to stay."

✦

The man and boy stop to rest at the summit of a hill from whose vantage point they can discern a brick farmhouse in the valley below. A lamp burns in each one of the downstairs windows, and the man imagines a family sitting cosily by a warm fire. High on the hill, however, the surging blasts can occasionally still bear the weight of a man, but the frenzy is weakening by the minute, and so there will be no need for them to enter this valley and again seek refuge. They have survived the worst of the upheaval, and the man knows full well that their odyssey across the inhospitable moors will soon be at an end. He seizes the exhausted boy's hand in his own and focuses his attention on the ghostly blackness before them. Let's go now. As they move off, the boy feels the man squeezing his hand ever tighter. *Let go of me.* The rain has stopped, and the clouds are clearing, and above them it is now possible to see a constellation of silver stars in the night sky. We're going home. And then the man repeats himself. The boy looks into the man's face, and again he asks him to please take him to his mother. Home. Quick, come along, let's go. Between sky and earth the boy skids and loses his footing, and the man stoops and picks him up. For heaven's sake, one foot in front of the other. The boy stares now at the man in whose company he has suffered this long ordeal, and he can feel his eyes filling with tears. *Please don't hurt me.* Come along now. There's a good lad. We're nearly home.